The Secret in Their Eyes

A NOVEL

EDUARDO SACHERI

The Secret in Their Eyes

Translated by John Cullen

OTHER PRESS · NEW YORK

Production Editor: *Yvonne E. Cárdenas*
Text Designer: *Simon M. Sullivan*
This book was set in 11.75 pt Photina and 12.5 pt Filosofiá
by Alpha Design & Composition of Pittsfield, NH.

10 9 8 7 6 5 4 3 2 1

LIBRARY OF CONGRESS CATALOGING-IN-PUBLICATION DATA

Sacheri, Eduardo A. (Eduardo Alfredo), 1967-
[Pregunta de sus ojos. English]
The secret in their eyes / by Eduardo Sacheri ; translated by
John Cullen.
p. cm.
Originally published in Spanish as La pregunta de sus ojos.
ISBN 978-1-59051-450-4 (pbk.) — ISBN 978-1-59051-451-1
(e-book)
1. Detectives—Argentina—Buenos Aires—Fiction.
2. Murder—Investigation—Fiction. 3. Buenos Aires
(Argentina)—Fiction. I. Cullen, John, 1942- II. Title.
PQ7798.29.A314P7413 2011
863'.7—dc22
2011013294

To my grandmother Nelly

for teaching me
how valuable it is
to preserve and share
memories.

Translator's Note

At the time of the novel, the Argentine judiciary was divided into two jurisdictions, investigative courts and sentencing courts. Judges—examining magistrates— presided over investigative courts, and every judge's court comprised two clerk's offices. A clerk employed about eight people, of whom the second in command was the deputy clerk and chief administrator, the position held by this novel's protagonist, Benjamín Chaparro.

A period of great turbulence in Argentina culminated in the so-called *Guerra Sucia,* the Dirty War, which lasted from 1976 to 1983. During these years, the Argentine state was the chief sponsor of massive and systematic political violence, whose victims included not only members of armed guerrilla groups such as the Montoneros, but also students, activists, trade unionists, teachers, journalists, and leftists in general. In such an unstable and dangerous environment, even the basically apolitical Chaparro is at risk. State terrorism in Argentina during the Dirty War resulted in the disappearance of at least 13,000 people; some estimates run as high as 30,000.

The Secret in Their Eyes

Retirement Party

Benjamín Miguel Chaparro stops short and decides he's not going. He's not going, period. To hell with all of them. Even though he's promised to be there, and even though they've been planning the party for three weeks, and even though they've reserved a table for twenty-two at El Candil, and even though Benítez and Machado have announced their willingness to come from the ends of the earth to celebrate the dinosaur's retirement.

He halts so suddenly that the man walking behind him on Talcahuano toward Corrientes barely manages to avoid a collision, dodging past with one foot on the sidewalk and one on the street. Chaparro hates these narrow, noisy, light-deprived sidewalks. He's walked on them for forty years, but he knows he's not going to miss them after Monday. Not the sidewalks and not a great many other things in this city, where he's never felt at home.

He can't disappoint his colleagues. He must go, if only because Machado is coming all the way from Lomas de Zamora just for the occasion, despite his bad health and advanced age. And Benítez likewise. It's not a terribly

long way from the Palermo neighborhood to Tribunales, but the fact is that the poor old guy's pretty much
a wreck. Nevertheless, Chaparro doesn't want to go.
He's sure about very few things, but this is one of them.

He looks at himself in the window of a bookstore.
Sixty years old. Tall. Gray-haired. Aquiline nose, thin
face. "Shit," he feels obliged to conclude. He scrutinizes
the reflection of his eyes in the glass. A girlfriend he had
when he was young used to make fun of his compulsive
way of looking at himself in shop windows. Chaparro
never confessed the truth, neither to her nor to any of
the other women who passed through his life: his habit
of gazing at his own reflection has nothing to do with
self-love or self-admiration; it's never been anything but
another attempt to figure out who the hell he is.

Thinking about that makes him even sadder. He sets
out again, as if motion could save him from being pricked
by the barbs of this new, additional sadness. From time
to time, walking without haste on that sidewalk forever
untouched by the afternoon sun, he checks himself in
the shop windows. Now he sees the sign for El Candil,
up there on the left, across the street and thirty meters
on. He looks at his watch: 1:58. Almost all of them must
be there by now. He himself sent off the people in his
department at 1:20 so they wouldn't have to run. The
coming court session doesn't begin until next month,
and they've already closed and archived the cases from

the previous session. Chaparro is satisfied. They're
good kids. They work hard and learn quickly. The next
thought in the sequence is *I'm going to miss them*, and
as Chaparro refuses to squelch around in nostalgia, he
comes to a stop again. This time, there's no one behind
to crash into him, and the people coming his way are
able to navigate around the tall man in the blue blazer
and gray trousers who's now looking at himself in the
window of a lottery office.

He turns around. He's not going. He's definitely not
going. Maybe, if he hurries, he can catch the judge before she leaves for the restaurant, because he knows she
stayed behind to finish an order for someone's release
from preventive detention. It's not the first time the idea
has occurred to him, but it *is* the first time he's summoned the modicum of courage needed to act on the
idea. Or maybe it's just that the other prospect—the
prospect of attending his own retirement luncheon—
corresponds to his notion of hell, and he wants to avoid
infernal torments. Him, sitting at the head of the table?
With Benítez and Machado beside him, forming a trio of
venerable mummies? Listening to that pathetic de Ál-
varez pose his traditional question—"Let's do it Roman
style, all right?"—so that he can spread around the cost
of some high-end wine and knock back most of it himself? Or Laura, asking everybody in sight to split a portion of cannelloni with her so she won't stray too far

from the diet she just started last Monday? Or Varela, meticulously descending into his trademark alcoholic melancholy, which will move him to tears as he embraces friends, acquaintances, and waiters? These nightmarish images make Chaparro increase his pace. He goes up the courthouse steps from Talcahuano Street. They haven't closed the main door yet. He jumps into the first available elevator. There's no need for him to tell the operator he's going to the fifth floor; in the Palace of Justice, the very stones know him.

With resolute steps, the soles of his tan loafers resounding on the black and white floor tiles, he walks along the corridor parallel to Tucumán Street until he stands before the tall, narrow door of his court. He hesitates mentally over the possessive "his." Yes, why not? It's his, it belongs to him much more than to García, the clerk, or to any of the other clerks who preceded García, or to any of those who'll succeed him.

While he's busy with the lock, his immense bundle of keys jingles in the empty corridor. He closes the door behind him rather forcefully, letting the judge know that someone has come in. Wait a minute: Why "the judge"? Because she's a judge, sure, but why not "Irene"? Well, just because. He's got enough with asking for what he's going to ask for without the extra burden of knowing that he must address his request to Irene and not simply to Judge Hornos.

He knocks softly twice and hears her say, "Come in."
When he steps into her office, she's surprised, and she
asks him, "What are you doing here?" and "Why aren't
you at the restaurant already?" In posing these questions,
she uses the familiar *tu* form—or, to be more precise,
since they're in Buenos Aires, the familiar *vos* form—but
Chaparro wants to avoid getting bogged down in forms of
address, because those, too, can be a source of confusion,
liable to sabotage his clear intention to make the request
he decided to make outside on Talcahuano Street, not far
from Corrientes Avenue. And it's disheartening that this
woman's presence throws him into such turmoil, but in a
spasm of self-discipline, Chaparro concludes that there's
nothing for it, that he absolutely, definitely, totally, *must*
cut short the process of psyching himself up, stop screwing around, and make, once and for all, the request he's
come to make. "The typewriter," he says, blurting it out
with no preamble. Brute, wretch, oaf. No subtle lead-ups.
Nothing like You know what, Irene, I was thinking that
maybe, that in one of those, that it could be that, or what
would you say if, or any other colloquial formula that
might serve to avoid precisely the look Chaparro sees on
Irene's face, or the judge's, or Her Honor's, that perplexity, that uncomprehending speechlessness caused by surprise at his abrupt manner.

Chaparro realizes he's put his foot in it, not for the first
time. He backs up to the beginning and tries to respond

to the question madam asked him in the first place, the one about the retirement luncheon, at which, considering what time it is, they must be paying tribute to him right now. He tells her he's afraid of getting maudlin and nostalgic, afraid he'll wind up talking about the same old things with the same old people and dissolving into pathetic melancholy, and since he looks into her eyes as he tells her all that, there comes a moment when he starts to feel his stomach sinking toward his intestines and a cold sweat breaking out on his skin and his heart turning into a snare drum. Because this emotion is very deep, very old, and very useless, Chaparro dashes back into the outer office to close the window, thus peeling himself away, as best he can, from those dark brown eyes. However, the window is already closed, so he decides to open it, but then a blast of cold air makes him decide to close it again. In the end, he has no alternative but to return to Irene's office, prudently remaining on his feet in order to avoid any obligation to look at her directly as she sits at her desk with the file open in front of her. She follows his movements, his looks, and the inflections of his voice with the same very attentive attention she's always given him. Chaparro shuts up for a while, knowing that if he keeps on going down that path he'll end up saying irreparable things, and then, just in time, he returns to the subject of the typewriter.

Although he has no idea what he's going to do from now on, he tells her, he'd love to take a stab at his old project of writing a book. As he speaks the words, he feels like a fool. An old man, twice divorced, now retired, and he thinks he'll be a writer. The post-retirement Hemingway. The García Márquez of Buenos Aires's western suburbs. To make matters worse, Irene's—or, preferably, the judge's—eyes sparkle with sudden interest. But he's already gone too far to turn back, and therefore he expatiates a little on his desire to try writing, it's something he's wanted to do forever, and now he'll have more time, so maybe, why not. And this is where the typewriter comes in. Chaparro feels more comfortable, because here he's treading on firmer ground.

"As you can guess, Irene, at my age I'm not going to learn how to use a computer, you know? And I've got that Remington in my fingers like a fourth phalange." (*Fourth phalange?* Where does such idiocy come from?) "I know it looks like a tank, and it's got that minuscule ribbon, and it's olive green, and it makes a sound like artillery fire every time you hit a key, so I'm taking a chance and hoping no one will need it, and naturally it would only be a loan, absolutely, a couple of months, three at the most, because believe me, I'm not up to writing a very long book, as you may imagine" (and there he is again, doing his self-deprecation number).

"And besides, all the new kids use computers, and there are three other old typewriters stored on the top shelf, and if you need it, you can always let me know and I'll bring it back here," Chaparro declares, and he's not through.

But he stops talking when she raises a hand and says, "Don't worry about it, Benjamín. Just take it, it won't be a problem. It's the least I can do for you."

Chaparro swallows hard, because that "you" at the end, the *vos* reserved for family and friends, sounds very familiar and friendly indeed, and then there's the tone she's using, the one she uses on certain occasions, occasions that have been engraved, one by one, in his memory, bright feverish slashes in the monotonous horizon of his solitude, despite the fact that he's dedicated almost as many nights to forgetting them, or trying to forget them, as he has to remembering them, and therefore he finally gets to his feet, thanks her, gives her his hand, accepts the fragrant cheek she offers him, closes his eyes while he grazes her skin with his lips, as he always does when he has a chance to kiss her—with his eyes closed, he can concentrate better on the innocent, guilty contact—practically runs into the small adjacent office, picks up the typewriter with two rapid movements, and escapes through the tall, narrow door without looking back.

He retraces his steps along the corridor, which is even emptier now than it was twenty minutes ago, takes elevator number eight to the main floor, goes down the hall toward Talcahuano, exits by the side door with a nod to the guards, walks up to Tucumán Street, crosses it, waits five minutes, and climbs, as best he can, onto the 115 bus.

When the bus turns the corner at Lavalle, Chaparro twists his head around to the left, but of course at this distance he can't see the sign for El Candil. By now, Irene—or rather, the judge—must be walking to the restaurant, where she'll explain to the others that the guest of honor has skipped out. It won't be so bad—they're all gathered together, and they're hungry.

He pats his rear trouser pocket, pulls out his wallet, and puts it in the inside pocket of his jacket. He's never had his pocket picked in his entire forty-year career, and he has no intention of being ripped off for the first time on his last day in Tribunales. Walking as fast as he can, he reaches the Once railroad station. The next train is leaving on Track 3, bound for Moreno and making all stops in between. In the train's last three cars, the ones closest to the platform entrance, all the seats are occupied, but from the fourth car on, Chaparro finds many available places. He wonders, as he always does, if the passengers standing in the crowded rear cars choose those spots because they're getting off soon, because they've been sitting all day and want to stretch their legs, or because they're stupid. Whatever their reasons, he's grateful. He wants to sit in a window seat on the left-hand side, where the afternoon sun won't bother him, and think about what the *hell* he's going to do with the rest of his life.

1

I'm not sure about my reasons for recounting the story of Ricardo Morales after so many years. I can say that what happened to him has always aroused an obscure fascination in me; perhaps the man's fate, a life destroyed by tragedy and grief, provided me with a chance to reflect on my own worst fears. I've often caught myself feeling a certain guilty joy at the disasters of others, as if the fact that horrible things happened to other people meant that my own life would be exempt from such tragedies, as if I'd get a kind of safe-conduct based on some obtuse law of probability: If such and such a catastrophe befalls Joe Blow, then it's unlikely that it will also strike Joe's acquaintances, among whom I count myself. It's not as though I can boast of a life filled with success, but when I compare my misfortunes with what Morales suffered, I come out well ahead. In any case, it's not my story I want to tell, it's Morales's story, or Isidoro Gómez's, which is the same story but seen from the other side, or seen upside down, or something like that.

Although the morbid interest my subject arouses in me isn't the only reason why I'm writing these pages, it carries some weight and plays some part. But mostly, I suppose, I'm telling the story because I have time to tell it. A lot of time, too much time, so much time that the daily trifles whose sum is my life quickly dissolve into the monotonous nothingness that surrounds me. Being retired is worse than I'd imagined. I should have known it would be. Not because of anything I knew about retirement, but because things we fear generally turn out worse when they happen than when we imagined them. For years, I saw my older colleagues in the court bid farewell to their working days in the naive expectation of enjoying their newfound leisure. I saw them depart in triumph, each of them convinced that retirement would be the closest thing to paradise on earth. But disappointment would make quick work of them, and it wasn't long before I saw them return in defeat. In two weeks, in three at the most, they had exhausted all the supposed pleasures they thought they'd been postponing during their years of routine and work. And for what? To drop by the court of an afternoon, as if by accident, just to chat or drink some coffee or even lend a hand with some moderately complicated case.

Because of that, because of the many, many times I'd found myself face to face with one of those guys whose retirement years were empty and therefore wretched, because of the many, many occasions when I'd looked into eyes imploring an impossible rescue, I swore a vow never to fall so low when my turn came. There would be no useless time-wasting for me, no nostalgic visits to see how the kids in the office are doing, no pathetic spectacles put on to extract a few seconds' worth of compassion from fortunate people still able to function.

So now I've been retired for two weeks, and I've already got time on my hands. It's not that I can't think of anything to do. I can think of a lot of things, but they all seem useless. Maybe the least useless is this one. For a few months, I can pretend to be a writer, as Silvia used to say when she still loved me. Actually, I'm mixing up two different periods and two distinct modes of address. When she still loved me, she'd talk confidently of my future as a writer, most probably a famous one. Later, when her love had wilted and died in the tedium of our marriage, she would say I just pretended to be a writer, and she'd say it with scathing contempt, speaking from the tower of irony she'd chosen to occupy, a fortification from which she liked to fire missiles at me. I can't complain, because I'm sure I said equally evil things to her. How terrible that after ten years of marriage, what chiefly remains is the shameful inventory of the harm we did to each other. But at least it was possible to quarrel with Silvia. My first wife Marcela and I couldn't even talk about my writing ambitions, or—come to think of it—about anything else. It hardly seems possible that I shared such large chunks of my life with two women of whom I retain, not without difficulty, a handful of hazy memories. Then again, my blurry recollection is yet more proof (as if more were needed) that I'm getting old. I've survived two marriages just to find myself facing a good stretch of time alone, roaming the arid plateau of bachelorhood. Life is long, all things considered.

Anyway, I was never that serious about being a writer. Not when Silvia spoke the word admiringly, and not later, when she spat it at me sarcastically. I did have dreams (some dreams impose themselves on even the most skeptical hearts) that featured idyllic scenes of the writer at work in his study, preferably in front of a large window with a view of the sea, preferably in a dwelling built high on a rocky outcrop buffeted by wind and rain.

Evidently, the habit doesn't make the monk, because even though I've transformed my living room into a prototypical working writer's sanctuary—I'm sure there's a better way of saying that—it hasn't yet done the trick. I can affirm, however, that I've made things quite pleasant in here. Of course, I don't have the sea and the storms, but I've got a well-ordered desk: on one side, a ream of typing paper, blank, almost new; on the other side, a notebook that contains no notes; in the center, the typewriter, an imposing olive-green Remington barely smaller than a tank and made of equally thick steel, or so my colleagues in the court used to joke, years ago.

I step over to the window. It overlooks, as I've said, no stormy sea, but rather a tidy little yard, twelve by fifteen feet. I gaze out at the street. As usual, there's not a soul in sight. Thirty years ago, these empty streets were full of people, young and old, but now the young people have gone away, and the old ones have gone inside. Like me. It may sound funny, but maybe there are several of us; our desks are thoroughly prepared, and we're going to write a novel.

Deep down inside, I suspect that this page, which I'm resolutely filling with words, is going to wind up like its nineteen predecessors, crumpled into a ball and thrown into the opposite corner of the room, where there's a wicker umbrella stand I inherited from I no longer know whom. After every false start, I yield to a lingering athletic impulse and try to toss my wadded rejections into that stand, with an elegant flick of the wrist and indifferent success. I get so excited when I score, and the small frustrations of my missed attempts increase my determination to such a degree, that I'm almost more interested in my next shot than in the remote possibility that this will be the page on which the story I allegedly intend to tell will at last begin. Sixty years old, and I'm clearly as far from being a writer as I am from playing basketball again.

For the past several days, I've sought to resolve certain questions crucial to my project. My plan was to start the actual writing only after I found the answers, because I dreaded the exact situation I now find myself in: sitting in front of the typewriter and chasing my tail while the last vestiges of my resolve evaporate. Early on, I realized that I don't have enough imagination to write a novel. My solution was to write without inventing anything, that is, to narrate a true story, to give an account of events to which I had been, although indirectly, a witness. And so I decided to tell the story of Ricardo Morales. I made this decision because of the reasons I gave at the beginning, because it's a story that needs no additions from me, and because, since I know it's true, I may dare to recount it all the way to the end. I won't have to incur the shame of telling lies in order to fill in gaps or enhance the plot or persuade the reader not to chuck the book away after fifteen pages.

Having decided on a subject, I consider the first practical difficulty: What grammatical person am I going to write this thing in? When speaking of myself, should I say "I," or should I say "Chaparro"? It makes me gloomy to think that this single obstacle suffices to dampen all my literary enthusiasm. What if I choose to tell my story in the third person? Maybe that would be the best choice, as I wouldn't be tempted to make use of excessively personal impressions and experiences. I'm quite clear about that. I'm not trying to reach or provoke any kind of catharsis with this book, or (to be more exact) with this embryo of a book; nevertheless, the first person feels more comfortable. That's because I'm inexperienced, I suppose, but in any case, it feels more comfortable. And what do I do about the parts of the story I didn't witness directly, those parts I can intuit, even though I have no certain knowledge of them? Do I include them in the story, just like the parts I know about for sure? Do I make them up from A to Z? Do I ignore them?

Let's simplify things and go step by step. I'll begin in the first person. That's hard enough; I don't need to go looking for more difficulties. And it will be better to tell what I know or presume to be true; otherwise, no one's going to understand a fucking thing, including me. Another problem is my vocabulary; the word "fucking" jumps out of that last sentence like a neon light surrounded by darkness. Should I use everyday coarseness and crudeness? Should I eliminate such expressions from my written language? Ah, fuck it, too many questions—and there I go again. The only logical conclusion I can reach is that I've got a foul mouth.

And here's something even worse: I'm going to write Morales's story, that's clear, but it means I have to begin at the beginning. And which beginning would that be? Although I think my narrative skills are pretty pedestrian, I've got enough discernment to see that the old "Once upon a time" formula isn't going to work here. So what am I to do? Where's the beginning? It's not that this story doesn't have a beginning. The problem is that it has four or five possible beginnings, all of them distinct from one another. A young man kisses his wife good-bye at the door of their apartment, walks with her down the hall, kisses her again, and steps out into the street, on his way to work. Or two guys, dozing at a desk, jump at the sudden, strident ringing of a telephone. Or a young woman who's just been awarded her school teaching degree poses for a group photo with other graduates. Or a judicial employee, namely me, thirty years after all those possible beginnings, receives a handwritten letter from an unlikely correspondent.

Which of these scenes am I going to use? All of them, probably; I'll pick one to start with and insert the rest in the order that seems least risky, or maybe just as I go along. I've already dedicated several afternoons to this endeavor, but the prospect of failure no longer seems so devastating. After all, the more pages I reject, the more my long-range shot will improve.

2

May 30, 1968, was the last time Ricardo Agustín Morales had breakfast with Liliana Colotto, and for the rest of his life he'd remember not only what their talk was about but also what they drank, what they ate, the color of her nightgown, and the lovely effect produced by a ray of sunlight that lit up her left cheek as she sat there in the kitchen. The first time Morales told me this, I assumed he was exaggerating, because I didn't think he could really remember so many details. But I was wrong; I didn't know him well enough yet, and I misjudged him. I didn't yet know that Morales, who had the face of a confirmed idiot, was a man endowed with intelligence, memory, and a power of observation the likes of which I'd never encountered in my life before and would not encounter again. Morales's faithful memory had a single focus: the guy remembered with an equal abundance of detail anything and everything that had to do with his wife.

Later, when Morales consented to talk to me about himself, I listened as he described what he once was: a bland, colorless fellow destined for a bland, colorless life. He showed no compassion for that fellow, identifying his former self as the kind of guy who passes through family, schools, and jobs without leaving any trace in the consciousnesses of those around him. He'd never had anything special, nor anything good, and he'd always found that perfectly fair. And then he'd met Liliana, who was, to an enormous degree, both special and good. That was the reason why he remembered that morning so well, not because it was their last. He kept it in his memory just as he'd kept all the other mornings in the little over a year that had passed since their wedding. Afterward, when Morales described to me, in meticulous detail, everything that had happened at that last breakfast with Liliana, he didn't go about it the way an ordinary person would. In general, people cobble together memories of their experiences from the hazy vestiges that have remained in their minds, or from fragments recalled from other, similar experiences, and with those vestiges and fragments they try to reconstruct circumstances or feelings they've lost forever. Not Morales. Because he felt that Liliana gave him happiness he wasn't entitled to, happiness that had nothing to do with his life before he met her, and because the cosmos tends toward equilibrium, he knew he'd have to lose her sooner or later so that things could return to their proper order. All his memories of her were tinged with that sense of imminent disaster, of a catastrophe lying in wait around the corner.

He'd never stood out for any reason whatsoever. At school, in sports, and even within his family, he'd earned nothing but occasional words of praise for qualities that were basically trivial. But on November 16, 1966, he'd met Liliana, and that meeting had sufficed to change him and his life. With her, through her, thanks to her, he'd become different. When he first saw her coming through the bank's revolving door, while he watched her ask the guard which window to use to make a deposit, and as she approached Number Four with short, firm steps, Morales had known that life would never be the same again. Clinging to the desperate certainty that his fate was in this woman's hands, he'd dared to suppress his shyness, drawing her into conversation as he counted her money, smiling at her with his entire face, looking into her eyes and withstanding her gaze, and hoping aloud that she'd come back soon. After she left, he'd quickly checked the records to verify the name of the company whose account she'd deposited money into, and he'd even gone so far as to phone the company with some invented excuse in order to obtain a few details about the young woman.

Some time later, after they were officially engaged, Liliana had confessed to him that she'd liked his boldness, the methodical audacity of his pursuit, his refusal to take no for an answer, and that those were the reasons she'd finally decided to accept his invitations. When she got to know him better, she said, when she'd come to know his essential shyness, his lack of confidence, his eternal shame, she'd arrived at a deeper understanding of how much courage it had taken for him to pursue her, and she considered that courage the best proof of his true love. Liliana said that a man capable of changing the way he is for the love of a woman is a man who deserves to have his love returned. Ricardo Morales didn't forget this conversation, either, and he decided to stay that way forever and for her. He'd never felt himself worthy of anything, much less of such a woman. But he knew that he was going to make the most of the situation, for as long as he could—until midnight should come, and the spell would be broken, and everything would turn back into mice and rats and pumpkins.

For all these reasons, Morales would always remember that on May 30, 1968, Liliana was wearing a sea-green nightgown, and that she'd gathered up her hair into a simple bun, from which a few dark brown strands had escaped. He remembered that a sunbeam had entered the kitchen window obliquely and lighted up her left cheek with a glow that made her even more beautiful, and that they'd drunk tea with milk, and that they'd eaten buttered toast, and that they'd talked about which pieces of furniture should stay in the living room, and that he'd risen from the kitchen table and gone into the dining room to fetch the plans he'd been drawing up for arranging the furniture in the most harmonious way possible, and that she'd laughed at his mania for drawing up plans for everything, and that she'd looked deep into his eyes and smiled and said he shouldn't spend so much effort on their old furniture, poor thing, because sooner or later they'd have to convert the living room into a bedroom anyway, and that he, slow and distracted or rather beclouded in his adoration for this woman who'd come to him from another galaxy, hadn't understood her allusion but had nevertheless managed to slip his arm around her waist and walk down the hall with her to the street door and kiss her slowly on the threshold and step out, waving his hand in good-bye, not knowing that it was forever.

Cinema

With several strokes of the carriage return lever, Benjamín Chaparro ratchets up the typed sheet and frees it from the typewriter. He takes the page by its edges, holding it with his fingertips as if it were a live hand grenade, and lays it on top of the sixteen or seventeen others that have likewise escaped being balled up and thrown at the umbrella stand. He's mildly thrilled to notice that the typed pages have already attained a minimal thickness and become something of a stack.

He gets to his feet, satisfied with himself. Two days previously, he was in despair, confounded in his search for a beginning and overwhelmed by the certainty that he'd never be able to write his book. And now, that beginning has been written. Well or badly, but written. The thought contents him, even though he remains anxious. He's anxious about how to continue, how to recount what happened to those people. He wonders if that's the feeling writers have when they tell a story, a certain sense of omnipotence as they play with their characters' lives. He's not sure, but if that really is how it feels, he likes it.

He consults his watch and sees that it's seven o'clock in the evening. His back hurts. He's been sitting at his desk almost the whole day. He decides to reward himself for his initial progress with a bit of a celebration. He finds his wallet on a shelf, determines that he's got enough money, and goes to see a movie. What he most enjoys about moviegoing isn't so much the pleasure of seeing one film or another as it is the knowledge that he'll talk to Irene about it the next time he's with her. He'll refer to the movie by the way, in passing, as though reluctantly, and she'll ask him questions about it. They like talking about movies. They have similar tastes. And something tells Chaparro that Irene would like it if they could go to a film together. They can't, obviously. It wouldn't be right. And maybe it's all in his head, anyway. Where did it come from, this idea that she'd like to see a film with him? From his wish that she would. Does he have any reason to be sure she would? No. None. Never.

3

When the telephone in the judge's chambers rang at five minutes past eight in the morning of May 30, 1968, I was so deeply asleep that I incorporated the sound into the dream I was having, and only at the fifth or sixth ring did I manage to open my eyes. I didn't pick up the receiver right away, as my entrance into the waking state was traumatic enough without the added strain of carrying on a telephone conversation.

Besides, I was quickly distracted by Pedro Romano, who began leaping and whooping all around me. The said Pedro was celebrating, and with a certain perverse logic I accepted my role in his celebration, miming annoyance and rubbing my eyes before answering the phone. We'd spent the night there, in the judge's office, sometimes sprawled in the big, dark, leather armchairs, sometimes dozing at the desk, faces down, heads on arms. When he started jumping around, Romano kicked the tray with the dinner dishes, and one of the cups we'd used bounced off the tray and rolled to the foot of the bookcase. Before answering the phone, I hesitated for a few more seconds, which I spent hurling mental insults at our jackass of a judge, because he insisted on making us man the office all night during the fifteen days when his court was in session. One week fell to Romano's section and the other to mine, but what to do about the problem of the fifteenth day? Judge Fortuna Lacalle, the dumb prick, had reached a Solomonic decision: he would fuck up both our lives. Each case was assigned to one of our court's two sections according to the police precinct where the case originated, except when serious crimes—namely homicides—were involved. Those were the responsibility of the section on call, but on the fifteenth day, serious cases were assigned to the sections based on the time when the first police notification came in. Romano was raising his arms in victory and shouting, "Eight-oh-five, Chaparrito, eight-oh-five!" because if the telephone in the examining magistrate's office was ringing at that hour, it couldn't be for any reason other than to report a homicide, and what Romano was celebrating was simply the fact that it was after eight o'clock, and so, since the odd hours were his and the even hours mine, he'd avoided taking on a complicated, laborious investigation by five short minutes.

Now that I think about it, and now that I'm writing it down, I can see how profoundly cynical our attitude was. You would have thought we were in some kind of athletic contest. Not for a moment did we stop and think that if that telephone was ringing, whether five minutes before or five minutes after eight, it was because someone had just killed someone else. For us, it was simply a matter of office competition, and the loser had to bust his butt. We'd see which of us was the lucky one, which of us was cool. As things turned out, it was Romano. And although in those days I hadn't yet come to loathe him—a period of time, not very long, was to pass before he started showing me what a despicable creature he was—I felt a burning desire to swat him across the head with the telephone. Instead of doing that, I assumed a look of exasperation, coughed to clear my throat, picked up the receiver, and solemnly said, "Examining magistrate's court. Good morning."

4

I went down the steps to Talcahuano Street, cursing my fate. In those days, I was still pondering my reasons— or rather, reproaching myself—for not having finished my law degree. On such occasions as this one, my reproaches sounded pretty convincing. I'm twenty-eight, I'd tell myself; had I completed my studies, I'd have ten years' experience in the Judiciary, and I could already be the clerk in charge of some other court, instead of being stuck, bogged down, *mired* in that goddamned examining magistrate's court as deputy clerk and chief administrative officer. And then, later, a prosecutor, why not? Or a public defender, just as good. Wasn't I sick of watching as whole battalions of cretins started out from positions like mine and then moved up through the judicial ranks, making careers, climbing the ladder, taking off? I was, indeed I was.

My complaint ought to have a medical name. *"Deputy Clerk's Complex.* Attributed to a judicial employee who, because he lacks a law degree, can rise no higher than deputy and chief administrator to a clerk and, although he exercises considerable power over secretaries, underlings, and interns, will never in his fucking life ascend beyond that position in the hierarchy and therefore grows thoroughly frustrated from seeing others, sometimes more capable than he but generally, and to an infinitely greater degree, assholes, pass him by like rockets on their way to jurisprudential stardom." A pretty definition, worthy of being submitted to specialized legal journals, though they'd probably reject it because of that part about the guy's "fucking life," or because of that other part about "assholes," or—most probably—because the editors of those publications are lawyers themselves.

Adalberto Rivadero, a deputy clerk who was my first boss when I started out as an intern, told me a supreme truth: "Look, Chaparrito. Courts are like islands; you can land on Tahiti or Alcatraz." The old master gazed down at me from the height of his grizzled years, the same sad elevation that I have now attained, and his face clearly indicated that he felt more like an inhabitant of the latter island. "And another thing, kid," he added, looking at me with the sorrow of one who knows he speaks the truth but knows also that the truth, in this case, is useless. "The island depends on the judge you get. If you get a nice guy, you're saved. If you get a son of a bitch, things get complicated. But the worst are the assholes, Chaparro. Watch out for assholes, my boy. If you get an asshole, you're screwed."

As I went down the steps, trying to figure out which bus I should take, Adalberto Rivadero's maxim—which deserves to be cast in letters of bronze and prominently displayed next to the blindfolded statue that stands in front of the Palace of Justice—was echoing inside my head. Because on May 30, 1968, I already knew I was screwed. I worked in an examining magistrate's court, formerly well run, but now in the hands of an asshole. And an asshole of the worst kind: an asshole eager to make a rapid ascent. The asshole who believes he's reached the apex of his possibilities tends to reduce his actions to a minimum. He senses, at least obscurely, that he's an asshole. And if he thinks he's at the peak of his career, he feels satisfied, and at the same time he's afraid. He's afraid others will see, simply by looking at him, that he's an asshole. He's afraid of screwing up in such an obvious way that others will notice, if they haven't already, that he's an asshole. And so he gives himself over to stasis. He reduces his movements to a minimum and lets life carry him along, and therefore the people in his employ can do their jobs in peace. They can even couple their knowledge and experience with his inertia and make him appear to be smart or, at least, a little less of an asshole.

But the asshole who wants to advance his career poses two difficulties. To begin with, he's bursting with energy,

filled with enthusiasm, abounding in initiatives, which
flow from him as from a fountain and which he wishes
to present to his superiors openly and frankly, so that
they will realize what an undervalued diamond they hold
in their hands, a man relegated to a position inferior to
his moral and intellectual deserts. And this is where the
second difficulty arises: this particular category of asshole compounds temerity with obliviousness. For if he
cherishes the dream of advancement, it's because he
feels worthy of it, and he may even go so far as to consider himself unjustly treated by life and by his fellow
men if they deny him the fulfillment of his intrinsically
legitimate aspirations. That's when the asshole's obliviousness and drive make him dangerous. They raise
him to the level of a threat, not so much to himself as to
others—and, more specifically, to those others who are
under his orders, one of whom, to take a random example, must abandon the warm hospitality of his office and
betake himself to the scene of a crime. And it's precisely
for that reason that he leaves by the Talcahuano door and
goes down the steps spewing a stream of expletives.

That was me, the victim, harboring deep in my heart
the suspicion that the judge who wanted to play the diligent schoolboy before his superiors on the Appellate
Court wasn't the only asshole in this story, no, but that
there was another asshole, who—because he was pusillanimous, or because it was convenient, or because he

was distracted—had failed to complete his legal studies and as a consequence was never going to advance
past deputy clerk, and who was therefore like a train up
against one of those big wood-and-metal buffer stops,
an unequivocal sign that tells you you've come this far
but you'll go no farther, my man. Shunted off, end of
the line, that's it. And from then on, he knew, he'd see
a long parade of clerks, who would give him orders he'd
have to obey, because the clerks, lawyers as they were,
would be his superiors, and there would be a long parade of judges, too, who would give the clerks orders
they would then pass on to him. I was complying with
just such an order, according to which, whenever a homicide case came in while we were on duty, the deputy
and chief administrator of the clerk's office whose turn
it was had to betake himself to the scene of the crime in
order to oversee the work of the police.

Once and only once, trying not to seem arrogant, had I
dared to consult my illustrious magistrate about the use-
fulness of such diligence, since the Federal Police were
responsible for carrying out the first phase of the investigation. No matter, His Honor declared; that was the
way he wanted it done. This was his entire response, and
in the ensuing silence, I felt the special wretchedness of
one who must not so much as allude to what everyone
in the room knows, which in this case was that our new
judge was an imbecile, and that the clerks weren't going

to say a word. The clerk of Section No. 18 hasn't got the slightest intention of opposing the judge, I thought, because having discovered, and how, that his new boss is a first-class, black-belt asshole, the said clerk is preparing to bring to bear all the influence he can muster so that he can set sail for some other island, where calmer breezes blow. And as for Julio Carlos Pérez, I said to myself, your immediate superior, the clerk of Section No. 19—your section—he's highly unlikely to notice that the judge is an asshole because he's one as well, and to a superlative degree, and consequently, you are screwed. So what can you do? Nothing. You can't do anything. Or you could, at most, make a novena to San Calixto and pray that the chief asshole may succeed in his ambitions and get a quick promotion to the Appellate Court, and perhaps, once he's there, he'll calm down, he'll feel fulfilled, and he'll pass into another category of asshole, accomplished, satisfied, peaceful, and contemplative, the kind that can be found occupying some of the most illustrious offices in the Palace of Justice.

But that hadn't happened, and there I was. As I asked the vendor at a news kiosk which bus would take me to the corner of Niceto Vega Avenue and Bonpland Street, I started feeling sick in anticipation of the scene I was going to have to witness. I tried to buck up my courage, if only out of shame, telling myself that I couldn't get weak in the knees in front of the crowd of cops who were sure to be milling around in that apartment, even though it would give me the creeping willies to see a corpse, a new corpse, a fresh corpse, a corpse produced not by the natural law of life and death but by the categorical and savage decision of a murderer who was on the loose somewhere nearby, and then I had my bus ticket out, making sure to keep it so I could get reimbursed for the expense when I got back, and since it would be a while before we reached the barrio of Palermo, I walked all the way to the rear of the bus and took a seat, still cursing myself between my teeth for not having had the drop of discipline, the ounce of fortitude, the dollop of willpower I would have needed to become a lawyer.

5

When I turned the corner and saw the first signs of the vain commotion the police display in such cases, my stomach began to churn. There were three patrol cars, an ambulance, and a dozen cops, coming and going with nothing to do but determined to keep on doing it. As I wasn't inclined to give them the satisfaction of detecting my queasiness, I walked up to the group quickly, reaching for my rear trouser pocket. I held my credentials under the nose of the first officer who barred my path, declared without condescending to look at him that I was Deputy Clerk Chaparro of Examining Magistrate's Court No. 41, and told him to take me to the officer in charge of the operation. The uniformed policeman acted according to a rule whose iron logic allowed him to follow his chosen path without undue difficulty: everyone who had one more stripe on his sleeve than he did must be obeyed; everyone who had one less stripe must be treated like dirt. Although I was totally unadorned by epaulets, my peremptory tone placed me in the first category, and so he saluted me awkwardly and asked me to follow him "into the interior."

It was an old house divided up into several apartments, all of which opened onto a side corridor, ugly but tidy. Geraniums in flowerpots had been placed here and there in the hall in a failed effort to beautify it. Two or three times, we had to move to one side to avoid running into more policemen, all of whom had come out of the second-to-last apartment. I calculated that there must be more than twenty cops on the scene, and once again I was appalled by the morbid pleasure some people find in the contemplation of tragedy. Like train accidents, I thought. I was more or less accustomed to those, because I traveled on the Sarmiento Line every day, but I could never begin to understand the curious onlookers who would crowd around the stopped trains and peer between the wheels and the rails, hoping to glimpse the victim's mutilated body and watch the firemen's bloody work. Once, suspecting that what was actually bothering me was my own weakness, I forced myself to move closer to an accident site, but soon I was horrified beyond recovery, not so much by the atrocious spectacle of death as by the jubilant, festive expressions on the faces of many in the crowd. It was as if the accident were a free show put on for their enjoyment, or as if they had to take in every single detail of the scene so that they could describe it properly to their colleagues at work; they stared with unblinking eyes, engrossed, spellbound, their lips slightly parted in a half-smile. Well, as I crossed the threshold into that apartment, I was sure some of the men inside would be looking out from under the visors of their blue peaked caps with just such expressions on their faces.

The tidy living room I entered contained many decorative objects on the walls and bookshelves. The dining set in the small adjoining room, six chairs and a table crowded together into too narrow a space, had little to do with the small armchairs in the living room and no relationship whatsoever to the style of the decor. "Newlyweds," I guessed. I walked a few steps toward the door that opened to the rest of the apartment, but my way was blocked almost at once by a wall of blue uniforms arranged in a semicircle. Not much brainwork was required to deduce that the corpse was lying in there. Some of the men were silent, others commented loudly to demonstrate their manliness in the face of death, but they all had their eyes fixed on the floor.

"I want to talk to the officer in charge, please," I said; it didn't sound like a request. I searched for the right tone, a little hard-edged, a little weary, to show this bunch of lazy gawkers that I represented a higher authority and they owed me a modicum of respect. My idea was to take the experience gained from the command/obedience tactic I'd used on the cop who blocked my way outside and apply the method at the group level. They turned around to look at me, and the voice of Police Inspector

Báez responded from the other side of the room. A couple of the policemen stepped aside, and I could see Báez, sitting on the double bed.

It was still going to be hard to get to him, because the bed took up almost the whole room, and the body was lying on the floor next to the bed. I couldn't see much more through the narrow passage the cops had made for me, but I figured that if I didn't want to look soft, I would have to stop and contemplate the dead woman.

I knew it was a woman, because the policeman who'd made the call to the court at five after eight had told me—using the strange jargon the police seem to delight in—that the victim was "an unidentified young female." Their supposedly neutral language, their conviction that they were speaking in forensic terms, occasionally struck me as funny, but in general I found it annoying. Why not just come out and say it? The victim was a young woman whose name we didn't yet know and who seemed to be a little over twenty years old.

I guessed that she'd been beautiful, because despite the ugly bluish color her skin had taken on when she was strangled and the predictable distortion of her face, frozen into a grimace by horror and lack of oxygen, there was a majesty about that girl that not even a horrible death had been able to obliterate. I was disturbingly certain the place was crawling with so many policemen precisely because of that, because of her beauty, and because she was lying naked at the foot of the bed where she'd been flung, face up on the bright parquet floor; and I knew some of the men standing around her were thrilled to be able to gaze at her body with impunity.

Báez stood up and walked over to me, skirting the big bed. He shook my hand without smiling. I was sufficiently acquainted with him to know that he liked his work, but he didn't enjoy the suffering from which his work usually arose. If he hadn't thrown the blue crowd of curious cops out of the room, it was simply because he hadn't registered their presence very clearly, or because he knew they were part of police folklore, or maybe a little of each. I asked him if the forensic team had arrived yet. Time would show me that I was never in my life going to meet a cop half so honest and clear-thinking as Alfredo Báez, but that morning, among the many things I didn't know, I didn't know that one, either, and so I took the liberty of becoming indignant about how little care he seemed to be taking to preserve the evidence at the scene of the crime. Had I been a little better acquainted with him, I'd have understood that what looked like indolence in Báez was, in fact, resigned fortitude at finding himself, once again, surrounded by a bunch of dimwits on a one-way trip to nowhere. Báez paged through his notebook and informed me of what he'd been able to determine so far.

"Her name's Liliana Colotto. Twenty-three years old. Schoolteacher. Married since the beginning of last year

to Ricardo Agustín Morales, teller at the Provincial Bank
of Buenos Aires. The neighbor in the next apartment
told us she heard screams at a quarter to eight this morning and looked through the peephole in her door. Since
her apartment's the last one, her front door's not on the
side, it's on the end, and so she can see down the whole
length of the hall. She saw a young man come out of this
apartment. A little guy. Black hair, she thinks, or maybe
dark brown. At this point, she had to blather for a while
about the distinction between black hair and dark brown
hair. I guess the old bird doesn't have much opportunity
for conversation. Anyway, she said the husband left for
work, as usual, very early in the morning, 7:10 or 7:15,
and so it caught her attention when she heard sounds
coming from next door sometime after that. When the
man came out of this apartment, he didn't shut the door
behind him. So the old lady waited a few seconds until
the street door closed and then stepped out into the
hall. She called to the girl, but there was no answer."
Báez flipped over the last page. "That's it. Well, except
that she peeked through the door and saw the girl lying
there, as you see—very still, the neighbor said—and then
she called us."

"The guy who went out—could it have been her
husband?"

"According to the old woman, no. She said the husband is fair-haired and tall, while this guy was short,

and his skin was very dark. By the way, the whole time she was positively itching to badmouth the girl for letting a visitor in twenty minutes after her husband left. Ah, right, he hasn't been notified—I have to give him the bad news. If you want, we can go together. He works in the . . . I've got it right here . . . in the Capital branch."

We heard steps entering the apartment and a few murmured greetings.

"Well, there you are," Báez said to an obese man carrying a briefcase. "Start whenever you like, we don't have a thing to do."

It didn't look as though the other was going to answer, because he took his sweet time about it. He stared at the body for a good while. He squatted down. He stood up again. Then he laid his briefcase on the bed and took out a few instruments and a pair of rubber gloves. At last, speaking without emphasis, he said, "Why don't you go fuck yourself, Báez?"

"Because I'm hanging around here like an asshole waiting for you, Falcone."

The medical examiner seemed not to think further conversation necessary. He began his work with a close examination of the corpse. He spread the young woman's legs delicately, as if she could still feel his touch and suffer from it. He felt around on the bed, located his briefcase, pulled it closer, and extracted a kind of cannula and a test tube. To avoid shock, I turned my eyes away. On the chest of drawers were a vase of artificial flowers and a framed photograph of an older couple. His parents or hers? A crucifix hung on the wall above the bed. On each night table stood a small, heart-shaped picture frame containing a photograph of a young bride and groom, both looking nervous but self-possessed.

I imagined them in the photographer's studio on their wedding day. They clearly didn't have much money, but she'd probably insisted on performing such rituals. I felt like a creep for nosing about her home and her past like that; it was almost as if I were looking at her as she lay cold and naked on the floor of the bedroom. At last, puffing a little, Falcone stood up straight again.

"Well?" Báez asked.

"Raped and strangled. I'll confirm that later in the lab, but there's no doubt." As Falcone spoke, he pulled open the door of what looked like a secondhand wardrobe, chose a neatly folded blanket—a light coverlet, obviously for summer use—and spread it over the girl's body with swift, precise movements. I assumed that the doctor lived alone, or that his wife made him make the bed. In any case, I appreciated his respectful gesture.

"The fingerprint crew's on the way. You think there are any prints left? Or have this pack of loiterers touched everything in sight?"

"Stop it, Falcone, I'm not that fucking stupid." Báez defended himself, but he seemed more bored than offended. "I'm going to see the husband at his work," he announced, and then he turned to me. "You coming?"

"Yes," I said, accepting the invitation and trying not to let my voice reveal how desperate I was to leave the scene. Any excuse would do.

The door was blocked by three or four policemen, talking loudly. "That's enough, goddamn it!" Báez thundered. If an opportunity to chew out his subordinates presented itself, Báez, like all senior police officers, seized it, as if shouting at underlings were an extraordinarily effective and economical way of making them meek and submissive. "Get out of here! Go do something useful! Whoever I catch screwing off gets weekend duty!"

The cops moved away obediently.

6

I had a strange feeling when we entered the bank. It was a big, square room with wide, cold marble panels on the walls. Spaced at regular intervals across the ceiling, a series of ancient, glass-shaded lamps hanging at the end of narrow black tubes poorly illuminated the vast room. An unbroken line of tall counters, made of gray Formica and topped by glass panels, separated the area reserved for employees from the public space. A bored janitor was cleaning the glass around the circular openings through which the bank's customers made themselves heard. I hated enormous rooms, and I thought it must be horrific to work every day in a place like that. I even went so far as to comfort myself by recalling the office of the court where I worked, its shelves crammed with files from floor to ceiling, its narrow passages, its faint aroma of old wood.

But the strange feeling had to do with something else. As soon as I went through the door, following Báez, I cast a quick glance at the twenty or so employees; even at this hour, when the bank wasn't yet open to the public, they were already at their desks, absorbed in their work. It was as if no one had yet been selected to receive the awful news we were bringing—not, at least, until the guard who'd opened the door for us walked across the room, lifted the hinged section of one of the counters, stepped into the area reserved for bank personnel, and directed his steps toward the desk occupied by the person we'd asked for. I looked from one employee to the next, wondering which of them was Morales. I tried to remember the wedding photograph on the night table in his bedroom, but I couldn't, maybe because I'd looked at it too hurriedly, or too apprehensively.

I felt that tragedy was hovering above those twenty lives and hadn't yet decided to descend on one. A ridiculous notion, of course, because only one of those men could be Ricardo Agustín Morales. None of the others. All of them were safe from the horror we were there to communicate to him alone. But as long as the guard didn't stop beside one of them as they worked, each of them (each young one, at any rate) seemed like a valid target, a potential victim of fearful chance, a possible recipient (against all odds, past all predicting, beyond all the certainties with which humans bear, every day, the terrifying knowledge that everything we love can be extinguished from one moment to the next) of news that would unhinge his life.

The guard passed several desks and leaned down to speak into the ear of a young man who was tallying checks on a huge adding machine. Across the distance that separated us, I was starting to feel sorry for the guy, but all of a sudden, events seemed to corroborate my theory of a catastrophe hesitating before swooping down on its target: the young fellow with the checks raised his hand and pointed to a door in the back, and it was as though that gesture of stretching out his arm had saved him from the impending misery of having lost his wife in a most brutal way.

Báez and I looked where that arm was pointing, and almost as if in a synchronized theatrical movement, the door in the rear of the enormous room opened to reveal a tall young man with slicked-down hair combed straight back, a serious little mustache, a blue jacket, and a tightly knotted tie. In the last moments of his innocence, he walked toward the desk where the guard and the young colleague with the checks waited, eyeing him curiously.

The guard spoke to the tall young man and indicated that we were looking for him. Now, I thought, at this exact moment, that boy has just entered an endless tunnel, one he'll probably stay in for the rest of his life. He looked in our direction. At first he seemed surprised, but his surprise immediately turned to suspicion. The guard must have told him that Báez and I were both policemen. It's always the same—people want the simplest image possible. A policeman is something everybody knows. A deputy clerk in an examining magistrate's court, Criminal Division, belongs to a more exotic species. So there we were, ready to plunge our knives into the lad's jugular, and he was looking at us, not sure yet whether or not he should be worried.

I walked over to the hinged counter as the young man approached it from the other side. I'd decided to introduce myself but then to let Báez do the talking. There would be time later to explain which of us was the policeman and which the judicial employee. Besides, Báez seemed to be used to communicating abominable information. As for me, when it came right down to it, I had no reason to be there at all, no fucking reason to be a witness to how one goes about shattering a young banker's life. And if I *was* there, I owed the privilege exclusively to that jackass Judge Fortuna Lacalle and his overriding eagerness to be promoted as soon as possible to the Appellate Court.

7

While the brand-new widower, Báez, and I sat close together in the bank's tiny kitchen, I was reflecting on how odd life is. I felt sad, but what was it, exactly, that was making me so sad? I didn't think it could be the boy's bewilderment, his pallor, or his wide-open, unfocused eyes after Báez told him his wife had been murdered in their home. Nor was it the kid's grief. Grief can't be seen, simply because it isn't visible, not in any circumstances. What you can see, at most, are some of its external signs. But such signs have always struck me as masks rather than manifestations. How can a man express the intolerable agony of his soul? By weeping floods of tears? By sustained howling? Disjointed babbling? Groans? Sobs? I felt that all such possible tokens of grief were capable only of insulting that grief, of belittling it, of profaning it, of placing it on the same level as free samples.

While I stared at Morales's frozen face and listened to Báez talk to him about going to the morgue to identify the body, I believed I understood that the reason we're sometimes moved by another's grief has to do with our atavistic fear that this grief may get transferred to us, too. In 1968, I'd been married for three years, and I believed, or preferred to believe, or fervently desired to believe, or was trying desperately to believe, that I was in love with my wife. And while I contemplated that boy—his body collapsed on a rickety little bench, his small eyes fixed on the blue flame burning on the stove, his hands pressed against his temples, his tightly knotted tie hanging down between his open legs like a plumb line—I imagined myself in his place, in the plight of a broken man whose life was over, and the image horrified me.

Morales's drifting eyes had come to a stop on the flame he'd lit five minutes previously, intending to fix himself some maté, right before our brutal irruption into his life. And I thought I understood what was going through his mind as he gave monosyllabic answers to Báez's methodical questions. The young man couldn't focus on exactly what time it had been when he'd left for work that morning, nor could he remember precisely how many people might have the keys to his apartment or whether he'd seen anyone who looked suspicious hanging around his building. It seemed to me most likely that he was taking a mental inventory of everything he'd just lost.

His wife wouldn't accompany him to do the shopping that afternoon, or any other, nor would she ever again offer him her alabaster body, nor bear his children, nor grow old at his side, nor walk with him on Punta Mogotes beach, nor laugh until she cried at some especially funny episode of *The Three Stooges* on Channel 13. Back then, I didn't know these details (which Morales consented to reveal to me only after some time had passed), but it was evident from the young man's anguished face that his future had just been blown into rubble.

When Báez asked him if he had any enemies, I couldn't help feeling, deep down inside, an urge to burst into sarcastic laughter. Unless there was someone Morales had given the wrong change to or whose electric bill he'd forgotten to stamp PAID, who could hold anything against this guy? He shook his head without emphasis and impassively turned his eyes back to the burner's blue flame.

As the minutes passed and Báez's questions went into details that neither Morales nor I cared about, I watched his expression grow more and more vacant. His features gradually relaxed, and the tears and sweat that had dampened his skin at the start dried up definitively. It was as if Morales—once he'd cooled off, once he was empty of emotions and feelings, once the dust cloud had settled on the ruins of his life—could perceive what his future would be like, what he had to look forward to, and as if he'd realized that yes, beyond the shadow of a doubt, his future was nothing.

8

"It's solved, Benjamín. Case closed."

Pedro Romano said this to me with an air of triumph, leaning his elbows on my desk and waving a piece of paper with some typewritten names on it under my nose. He'd just hung up the telephone. I'd watched his side of a long conversation in which vociferous exclamations (so that no one could doubt the importance of what he was working on) had alternated with long speeches delivered in a conspiratorial whisper. In my initial distraction, I'd wondered why the hell he'd come to my section to use the telephone instead of staying in his own. Then I saw Judge Fortuna talking to Clerk Pérez in his office, and things became clear: Romano was trying to show off. Since I considered myself a compassionate fellow, and since I was, naturally, in the most absolute ignorance as to all the consequences the events of that day were going to have in the years to come, I found Romano's efforts to dazzle our superiors more amusing than annoying. I wasn't tickled so much by the way he was striving to call attention to himself as by the moral and intellectual qualities of the superior for

whom he wanted to stand out. That someone would play
the model employee before a judge might have seemed
to me like fairly pathetic behavior, but that he'd do it
without realizing that the judge in question was an
idiot of the first magnitude who wouldn't even notice
the performance left me speechless. Nevertheless, I
was even more deeply surprised when Pedro Romano
finished his telephone conversation and told me that
the case was solved, showing me a piece of paper with
two names written on it and looking at me as if to say,
*Here, I'm doing you a favor, though we both know I don't
have to, because it's your section's case.*

"Workers," he said. "In Apartment 3. Doing renova-
tion."

Romano evidently thought the telegraphic style he was
using, punctuated by theatrical silences, increased the
drama of his scoop. I asked myself how such a limited
guy had risen to the position of deputy clerk. My answer
was that a good marriage works wonders. Romano's wife
wasn't particularly pretty, or particularly nice, or particularly intelligent. But she was particularly the daughter
of an infantry colonel, and in Onganía's Argentina that
was a significant merit. I recalled the sea of green army
hats at the wedding, and my annoyance grew.

"They saw the girl passing. They liked what they
saw. They started thinking about it," Romano continued, moving on from identifying the perpetrators to

reconstructing the crime itself. "It was a Tuesday morning. They watched the husband leave early. They got up their courage. Then they acted."

Seeing that he insisted on talking like an official telegram, I was on the point of telling him to get the hell away from me. My hopes rose, in vain, when he stopped leaning over my desk, removed his hands from it, and stood up straight. Instead of going away, however, he dropped into the nearest chair. He shifted it closer with a few sudden hip movements, and then, once again, his eyes were level with mine.

"They went too far and wound up killing her."

He stopped talking. Maybe he was waiting for a standing ovation or the flashes of news cameras.

"Who told you about this?" I asked, immediately guessed the answer, and risked saying it: "Sicora?"

"Precisely." Romano's tone included, for the first time, a very slight trace of doubt. "Why?"

Should I light into him or should I let it go? I opted for the peaceful choice. Homicide Lieutenant Sicora was a specialist in avoiding work. He hated contacting people, he detested walking the streets, he loathed the essential duties of an investigator. As far as I could tell, all he had in common with Báez were the whites of their eyes. Sicora worked up his hypotheses from his living room and tended to pin homicide raps on the first poor bastards that came along. What really burned my ass, however,

wasn't Sicora; it was that Romano, dimwit extraordi-
naire, was taking the lieutenant at his word. Sicora was
a lout and an idler, and this was a fact known to the very
nuns in their goddamned cloisters. How could Romano
be unaware of it? And even if he hadn't heard, he still
had the obligation of knowing the proper protocol for
conducting a preliminary investigation.

In spite of all that, I didn't want to get too overheated.
After all, Romano was a colleague, and I'd had enough
experience in the Palace of Justice to know that verbal
wounds are hard to heal.

So I changed the direction of my questions a bit: "But
look . . . wasn't Báez handling the case?"

My delicacy went unrewarded; Romano answered me
with frigid irony. "I don't think Báez is Spencer Tracy,
you know. He can't take on everything. Don't you agree?"

I'd about had my fill of him, and the remains of my
patience were sifting away like handfuls of sand. "No, I
don't agree. Especially if the alternative is to let the investigation be led by a brainless lout like Sicora."

Although I'd just impugned his source, Romano didn't
rise to the bait. Instead, with the air of one who gener-
ously consents to educate another, he grabbed the fingers
of his left hand and started enumerating. "There are two
of them. Workers. They were doing renovations in the
front apartment or the one next to it. They're not from the
neighborhood and nobody knows them. Get the picture?"

Romano paused, as though certain I was enthralled by his arguments. Then, after a show of deciding whether or not to reveal the clincher, he shook his head, thrust his chin forward, and added, "Besides, they're two little dark-complected guys. They look like thieves, if you see what I'm saying."

In those days, whether because I was young or because I was tenderhearted or both, it was hard for me to categorize people I knew as sons of bitches. But every time Romano was around, he seemed determined to make me less inclined to go easy on him. More than once, I'd seen him making fun of people in custody who were dark-skinned and looked poor. I'd also seen him fawning on the more or less distinguished lawyers he had to deal with. I spoke the first words that came to me: "I see. Well, if you want to charge them with being dark, let me know."

I thought about adding, *Hold on and I'll check the Penal Code to see which statute applies*, but for fear of ruining the effect, I decided to keep the naive irony to a minimum. In any case, I could see that Romano was making a fierce effort not to insult me, and when he spoke again, not the smallest vestige of the casual camaraderie he'd started with remained in his voice. "I'm going to the police station. Sicora told me they've got the prisoners ready for interrogation."

"Ready for interrogation?" I'd moved beyond annoyance and was now ready to explode. "That means they've already had the shit beat out of them. I'll go myself. Don't forget, it's my case."

Generally, I disliked the judiciary zeal that led some of my colleagues to use possessives when referring to cases, but the guy had exhausted my patience. My parents had taught me not to call people names to their faces; therefore, I controlled myself, put on my jacket, and left with a curt "See you later." The only indulgence I allowed myself was to shut the door with considerably more force than necessary.

9

I entered the police station with the tough-guy demeanor
I habitually adopted in front of cops, and which usually
gave me good results. I identified myself and waited two
minutes before Sicora came out to meet me, grinning
with satisfaction. Evidently his friend Romano hadn't
thought it necessary to inform him that I was angry.

"They're ready to confess," he said, brandishing two
file folders with various legal documents sticking out of
them. "Sebastián Zamora. Paraguayan, twenty-eight years
old. Worker. Lives in Los Polvorines. The other one's José
Carlos Almandós, twenty-six. Also a worker. He's an Argentine, at least, but he lives in the shantytown at Ciudad
Oculta."

Trying to sound natural, I asked, "Did you put them in
a lineup?"

Sicora looked at me with his mouth open.

"Have you talked about these suspects with the other
witnesses? I mean the ones Báez interviewed."

Overcoming an incipient stutter, Sicora replied, "Not
yet. I called the court, and Deputy Clerk Romano told me

to keep things moving forward. He said he'd take care of informing the husband, and—"

"I'm not talking about the husband," I said, cutting him short. "I mean the neighbor woman who lives in the apartment at the end of the hall, the one who saw the murderer leave and called the police. Or the owners of the other apartments, including number 3, where the suspects were working."

When I saw the disconcerted expression on Sicora's face, I realized that the fellow's idiocy was so vast I'd never be able to apprehend it in its full glory. "You're not telling me you didn't compare notes with Báez, are you?" I asked. The question produced another period of silence, at the end of which I said, "Bring me Báez's papers. And I want to see the two suspects, right away."

Sicora was too stupid to protest or complain about being ordered around by a civilian. He went off to fetch the statements Báez had collected, but he didn't take me to see the prisoners. A bad sign, I thought. I made myself as comfortable as I could at a desk covered with overflowing boxes of documents and pushed practically into the corridor that led to the cells. I started to look through Báez's work and stopped almost at once, when I came to the declarations made by one Estela Bermúdez. I read her statement attentively, took it out of the folder, and put it aside. Then I looked up at Sicora, and I figure my eyes were shooting off sparks.

"Have you gone over the statement from Estela Bermúdez?"

Sicora gazed away, as if trying to recall, or taking time to decide how he should answer; then, almost immediately, he focused on me again, furrowed his brow, and said, "Who's she?"

I was expecting this question. "The woman who lives in Apartment 3, Sicora."

The policeman knew he'd lost his bearings.

"When Báez took her statement," I said, trying to make my voice sound peaceable, because that seemed the best way to humiliate him, "the woman declared that she had two guys working on her apartment, but they hadn't come either Monday or Tuesday. Not on Monday, because it rained all day long, and the work they were doing was outside, on the terrace. And not on Tuesday, because they needed it to be good and dry before they could apply the tar. She said they'd called her up and arranged to wait until Thursday."

I held out the sheet of paper so that he could read it for himself, but Sicora, taking hold of the last shreds of his dignity, counterattacked: "So what? Couldn't they have made that call just to cover themselves, gone to the apartment house anyway, killed the girl, and fled the scene?"

"Look, Sicora, everyone who lives in the building—the woman in Apartment 3 and all the rest—they all stated that the main door, the door to the street, is always locked with a key. When they have visitors, they have to leave their apartment, go down the hall, and unlock the door for them. Didn't you read that? It's in all the statements. And the woman in the next-door apartment, the one who reported the crime—did you read her statement? She says again and again that she saw only one guy leave the scene."

I gathered up the stack of documents I'd made and pushed them across the desk, but Sicora made no move to take them. He kept staring at me, looking more wretched every minute. When I understood the reason why, a shiver ran down my spine, and the order I gave him was peremptory: "Take me to the suspects."

Sicora bounded to his feet as though he'd been sitting on a spring. "It's . . . uh, it's lunchtime. The meals are being served."

I insisted: "I can't wait, and I can't come back later. I want to see them. And I want you to put me in touch with Báez, right away."

Sicora kept dallying for another few seconds. Then he shouted a name, and a police officer emerged from the corridor. Sicora said, "Accompany this gentleman to the cell where those . . . where the two suspects are."

The policeman led me to the end of the hallway, which was flanked by the bars of four pairs of cells. We stopped

in front of the last one on the left. There was no smell of
food. The officer manipulated the door, which opened
with a screech. Inside the cell, the light was on. Two men
were on the hard bunks that ran along each of the side
walls. One of the two was asleep, and when we entered,
he didn't move. The other, who was lying on his back
with his arms covering his face, turned on his side to
look at us. I greeted him, and he mumbled a reply. We
gazed at each other for a moment.

"Call Sicora," I ordered my escort. He hesitated.

"I can't leave you alone in the cell."

I was sick of them. When I spoke again, I raised my
voice. "Call him,or I'll report you, too."

The policeman went away. Trying to keep the rage and
horror out of my voice, I said, "How do you feel?"

The man on the bunk seemed to smile beneath the
layer of dried blood that covered his face below his nose.
He was missing two front teeth, and I was sure their loss
was recent. Speaking as well as he could, he told me that
now he was hurting a little less, but that his companion
had been kicked in the ribs repeatedly and had wept
until he'd fallen asleep a little while ago.

The police officer returned and announced that Lieutenant Sicora had gone out. "Then get me the captain,"
I said.

"He's having lunch."

"I don't give a fuck!" I shouted. It wasn't often that I descended to such a barrack-room level, but I was incensed.

When I returned to the Palace of Justice three hours later, instead of going to my own office, I went to Section No. 18. I walked down the narrow aisles separating the desks and advanced between the rows of tall, bulky file cabinets without a word of greeting to anyone. When I reached Romano's desk—he was sitting at it, absently reading the newspaper—it was my turn to stick a piece of paper under his nose. "Listen up," I said. "I've just come from the Appellate Court, where I filed a complaint against you and your fuckwit friend Sicora for physical coercion and abuse. The medical examiners are conducting an examination of your two suspects right now, on my orders."

I was trying not to lose control of myself. Romano had lowered the newspaper and was trying to think. I kept talking: "I'll bet my balls that the idea of beating the shit out of those two was yours and not that idiot Sicora's. He went along with it so he could play the hero and score points with the court. Fucking jackass. So I've got two recommendations for you. First, if you want somebody worked over, do it yourself. And second, if you're going to beat the shit out of someone, make sure he has some connection to something, because the two guys you brought in are nothing but poor working stiffs."

I turned on my heels and dropped a copy of the complaint on the nearest desk. "When you finish reading
that, send it to my office," I said. All of Romano's colleagues, naturally, were looking at me with the utmost
surprise.

Maybe I should have shut up at that point, but just as
it was hard for me to become really angry, once I boiled
over, I found it equally hard to cool down. So I said,
"You know, Romano, I've always thought you were pretty
much a jackass. But that's not it. Well, yes, you're a jackass, all right, but what you really are, beyond any shadow
of a doubt, is a lowdown, worthless, no-account son of a
bitch."

Back then, I was unaware of the problems that day
had planted like seeds in my destiny, and of the harvest
I'd sooner or later have to reap. I suppose no one can
read, in the fluff of the present, the signs of his future
tragedies.

10

That very evening, during my first private conversation with Ricardo Morales, I made my decision to help him any way I could. We were in a bar at 1400 Tucumán Street, sitting next to the guillotine window that separated us from the sidewalk. Outside, a torrential rain was very gradually letting up.

After chewing out Romano, I'd gone to my office, sat at my desk, and taken deep breaths, trying to calm down. It had occurred to me that the poor widower was probably hurrying over to the court at that very moment, convinced that he was about to learn the truth. And in fact, twenty minutes later, he arrived; I heard two timid knocks on the door of the court and an impersonal "Come in" from one of the young office workers.

Soon the kid who'd waited on Morales came to me and said, "Excuse me, sir, there's someone to see you." I raised my head and spent a few moments thinking that if the new intern was speaking to me so formally, it surely meant I'd crossed the threshold into maturity.

When he saw me approaching the reception area, Morales said, "I got a telephone call at the bank." Maybe he recognized me as one of the two who'd brought him the news of Liliana's death.

"Yes, I know," I replied, incapable of saying anything more precise. I supposed he was going to ask me if there had really been "a major breakthrough" in the case, or if it was true that "the murderers had been remanded into custody," depending on which journalistic style (*Crónica? La Nación?*) that fool Romano had chosen to imitate while communicating his supposed scoop. But to my surprise, Morales contented himself with remaining very stiff, with his hands lightly resting on the counter and his eyes fixed on mine.

That was worse than if he'd asked questions, because his silence struck me as the silence of a defenseless man convinced that nothing is going to turn out the way he'd dared to dream it would. Maybe that's why I invited him to have coffee with me. I was aware that I was violating the most elemental rules of judicial asepsis. I soothed my conscience by telling myself I was doing it out of sympathy for his loss, or I wanted to make some kind of amends for Romano's stupid haste.

We went out the Tucumán Street door and into a fierce downpour that gusts of wind blew sideways. Water was rising in the street when we bounded across it. Morales followed me docilely as I went on, clinging to storefronts and dashing under awnings, trying to avoid getting too drenched. With the same meekness, or apathy, he let me lead him across Uruguay Street, into a bar, and to a table next to the front window. Making a brusque sign to the waiter, I ordered two coffees; Morales accepted his wordlessly. After that, we had nothing to do.

"What lousy weather, huh?" I said, making an effort to climb out of the uncomfortable silence we'd sunk into.

For a long time, Morales stared absently at the flooded sidewalk.

"We sent for you," I said—even though the word "we" tied me to that son of a bitch Romano—"but there's something I have to tell you."

At this point, I got stuck again. How to begin? Maybe I should say, *We got your hopes up for nothing, please excuse us.*

"Don't worry," Morales said, finally turning to look at me with the slightest of smiles on his face. "You just told me."

I stared at him in confusion.

"It was the 'but,'" he continued by way of explanation. I opened my mouth to reply, even though I didn't understand what the widower was trying to convey. Seeing me flail about like a drowning man, he went on: "The 'but.' You just said, 'We sent for you, *but.*' That's enough. I get it. If you had said, 'We sent for you, *and,*' or 'We sent for you, *because,*' that would have been different. You didn't say that. You said 'but.'"

Morales turned his gaze back to the rain outside, and I supposed, incorrectly, that he'd finished.

"It's the shittiest word I know," he said, and then he was off again, but I never for a minute thought we were having a conversation; it was an interior monologue he was speaking aloud out of pure distraction. "'I love you, but . . .'; 'That could be, but . . .'; 'It's not serious, but . . .'; 'I tried, but . . .' See what I mean? It's a shitty word people use to annihilate what was, or could have been, but isn't."

I looked at his profile as he watched the rain come down. I'd figured he was a simple young guy with narrow horizons whose world had just collapsed. But his words and the tone he spoke them in were those of a man acquainted with grief. He seemed like someone who'd always been prepared to suffer the hardest blows and endure the worst defeats.

"That makes things a little simpler for me," I said. Although I felt somewhat ashamed, I found in his knowing melancholy a way to escape from the odd sensation of guilt I was starting to feel.

"Go on, I'm listening." Morales shifted his chair in my direction, as if to facilitate focusing his entire attention on me, or as if he wanted to avoid being hypnotized by the rain again.

I told him everything. I no longer felt obliged to disguise Romano's and Sicora's responsibilities in the matter—as far as I was concerned, they could go straight to hell. I ended my account by explaining that I'd just filed a complaint against the two of them in the Appellate Court, and that I was waiting for the medical examiners' report on the injuries suffered by the two workers.

"Poor guys," Morales said. "What a mess they got dragged into."

He spoke in a tone so neutral, so lacking in emotion, that he seemed to be talking about something totally unconnected with himself. I'd been afraid that Morales would disapprove of my actions and insist on clinging fanatically to the case Romano and that other moron had built up out of the smoke of their own stupidity. But now I was starting to realize that the young man was too intelligent to find solace in any story that wasn't the truth.

"If you catch him, what will he get?" Morales spoke without turning his eyes from the rain, which had finally turned into a thin drizzle.

I couldn't help remembering the relevant articles of the Penal Code, one of which decreed that the punishment in such a case was life imprisonment, while the other provided for a concurrent sentence of imprisonment for an indefinite period of time, as stipulated for anyone who "kills in order to prepare, facilitate, commit, or conceal another crime." I didn't think Morales could be hurt by any hard truth at that point, simply because his soul was so thoroughly wounded that another wound wouldn't matter. I said, "It's first-degree murder. Article 80, paragraph 7 of the Penal Code. The sentence is life imprisonment."

"Life imprisonment," Morales repeated, as if making an effort to grasp the idea entirely.

I took a chance: "Does that disappoint you?" I was afraid I'd sounded insolent, asking him such a personal question. After all, we were two strangers.

Morales looked at me again, and his sudden perplexity appeared sincere. "No," he replied at last. "It seems fair." The young man continued to surprise me.

I kept quiet. Maybe it was my duty to explain to him that unless the culprit had a prior murder conviction, he'd be able to leave prison on parole in twenty or twenty-five years, even if he'd been sentenced concurrently to confinement "for an indefinite period of time," in accordance with article 52. But I had the feeling that such an explanation would increase his grief.

So I said nothing and kept my eyes fixed on Morales, who for his part was staring at the sidewalk. I saw his brow suddenly darken, and he made a sign of vexation. I too looked outside. It had stopped raining, and the bright sun was lighting up the wet streets and reflecting in the puddles as if shining for the first time.

"I hate when this happens," Morales said, all of a sudden. I was apparently supposed to know what "this" was.

"I've never liked to see the sun come out after a storm. My idea of a rainy day is that it ought to rain all day and into the night. If the sun comes out the next morning, fine, but this? This is unforgivable. The sun's butting in where it's not wanted. It's an intruder." Morales stopped for a second and gave me a quick, absent smile. "Don't worry. You're probably thinking the tragedy has scrambled my brains. It's not that bad."

I had no idea what to say, but once again Morales didn't seem to expect a reply.

"I love rainy days. Ever since I was a little boy. I always thought it was ridiculous when it rained and people called it 'bad weather.' Bad weather for what? You yourself complained about the rain when we first sat down, didn't you? But I suspect you were just making small talk because you felt uncomfortable and didn't know how to fill up the silence. Doesn't matter, really."

I kept on saying nothing.

"Seriously. It's only natural. I suppose I'm a rare case, but I believe that rain has a bad reputation it doesn't deserve. As for the sun . . . I don't know. With the sun, everything seems too easy. Like in what's-his-name's movies . . . you know, the singer . . . Palito Ortega. It's that fake innocence—I always find it exasperating. I think the sun gets too much good press. And that's why it irritates me when it barges in on rainy days. It's as though the damned thing just can't stand to let those of us who don't worship it like idolaters enjoy an entire day without sunshine."

By this point, I was staring at him, completely absorbed.

"I'll tell you what I think is a perfect day," Morales went on. He made a few small gestures with his hands, as if he were directing a film. "An early morning sky covered with storm clouds, a certain number of thunderclaps, and a good, steady rain all day long. I'm not talking about a heavy downpour, because the idiots who love the sun complain twice as much if the city fills up with water. No, I'm satisfied with a continuous, even rain that lasts into the night. Well into the night, in fact, so I can go to sleep to the sound of the drops coming down. And if we can get a few additional thunderclaps, so much the better."

He fell silent for a minute, as if he were remembering such a night.

"But this," he said, twisting his mouth into a grimace of disgust. "This is a rip-off."

Morales remained turned away from me, looking out at the street with an expression of great disappointment on his face, and I was able to study his features for a long time. I tended to think that my work had made me immune to emotions, but this young guy, collapsed on his chair like a dismounted scarecrow and gazing glumly outside, had just expressed in words something I'd felt since childhood. That was the moment, I believe, when

I realized that Morales reminded me very much, maybe too much, of myself, or of the "self" I would have been if feigning strength and confidence had exhausted me, if I were weary of putting them on every morning when I woke up, like a suit, or—worse yet—like a disguise. I suppose that's why I decided to help him in any way I could.

11

It was a day in late August, and I was sitting in my corner of the court offices, finishing the paperwork for a prison release.

Although I was well aware that the moment for removing the Morales file from the active docket was close at hand, I tried to postpone that step by employing the oldest and most futile method I knew: I put the case out of my mind. And therefore, because of my ineffective resistance and the ineluctable circumstances, my little games of denial and procrastination were brought to a halt, suddenly and punctually, when the moment arrived.

I noticed that Clerk Pérez was approaching with a case file in his hand. He dropped the dossier on the glass top of my desk, where it landed with a weak splat. Before he turned around and went back to his office, he said, "I'm leaving the Palermo murder with you so you can dismiss it."

In the jargon of our profession, "leaving the murder with me" meant that he wanted me to write up a decision; Palermo was the barrio where the crime had been

committed. Since we had no suspects, we couldn't identify the case, as we usually did, by the defendants' names;
and when Pérez told me to "dismiss it," he was referring
to the precise nature of the decision he expected me to
produce. With no positive leads after three months of
investigation and with no evidence that would allow us to
proceed in any direction, he was requesting that I write a
recommendation to seal the file. End of the line. Good-
bye to the case. A thousand times I'd written up such decisions or, for simpler cases, ordered my subordinates
to do so. But I balked at this one, because as far as I was
concerned, this case wasn't about the Palermo murder,
it was about the death of Ricardo Agustín Morales's wife,
and I'd resolved to help him as much as possible. And up
to that moment, the truth was I hadn't been able to do
very much.

I put aside the papers I'd been working on and pulled
the blue dossier closer. "Liliana Emma Colotto," I read.
"Homicide." I leafed through the pages; their contents
were pretty predictable. The initial police report, with
the statement of the first officer to arrive at the crime
scene after the neighbor called the police. The description of the discovery of the body. The medical examiners'
application to perform an autopsy. The note attesting
to the notification of the examining magistrate's court,
namely me. Me receiving the news, half asleep on the
wide desk in the judge's office, with that prick Romano

jumping around me and celebrating. The statements
Báez collected from the witnesses. The photographs of
the crime scene. I quickly flipped past those; nevertheless, in one of the shots, taken from a point to the right
of the victim's body, I thought I recognized, very close to
her hand, the tip of my shoe. I paged through the autopsy
very fast—those descriptions turned my stomach—but I
lingered over the examiners' conclusions.

Rape . . . death by strangulation . . . and that third
conclusion? I hadn't paid attention to it when we'd
first received the autopsy report, some weeks before.
Although it didn't seem possible, the case was apparently capable of intensifying grief even further from beyond the grave. Suddenly anxious, I continued looking
through the file, but it appeared to contain no more new
information. I came to the brutal charade Romano and
Sicora had conducted with the innocent workers: two
scanty pages of "spontaneous confessions" beaten out
of those poor guys by that pig Sicora. After that, there
was my formal complaint to the Appellate Court, accus-
ing Romano and Sicora of illegal coercion and abuse and
requesting that a medical examiner assess the injuries
suffered by the two arrestees.

I thought of Romano, as I did every time I passed his
empty desk. Right after I filed my complaint, disciplin-
ary proceedings had begun, and he'd been provisionally
suspended from his duties. At first, I'd been afraid that

his staff might bear me a grudge for turning him in; at
the end of the day, we all worked for the same court. But
my relations with them remained so cordial that I was
moved to wonder whether they might not be secretly
grateful to me for having gotten their loutish boss off
their backs. I returned to the few pages left in the file.
The remand of the case from the police to the examining magistrate's court. The statements taken in our
offices from the same witnesses, who limited themselves to verifying what they'd already said. And finally, a supplementary autopsy report (on the results
of some visceral examination that added nothing and
which, in any case, I was too apprehensive to do more
than skim).

On the back of the last page, there was a note in Pérez's
handwriting, dated that same day. Following Judge Fortuna Lacalle's express instructions, Clerk Pérez had
written, "Any case submitted by the police but containing no named suspects or perpetrators must be removed
from the active docket within two months, or three at the
most." Had the judge upheld that principle because he
was methodical, that would have been one thing; but no,
he upheld it because he was mediocre. His real motto
was "The fewer cases, the better." That was the reason
behind his mania for shelving cases as soon as possible
when no suspects had been found, no matter whether
the crime was theft or murder.

I imagined the next step. I would put a sheet of letter-head paper in the typewriter, select the approved heading for such a document, and type up a decision of some ten lines, prescribing a stay of proceedings in the case, citing the lack of suspects, and recommending that the police continue their investigations in order to identify the guilty parties. That last part served to keep up appearances; in practice, the document was the dossier's death certificate, and the case would be archived forever.

I looked though the whole file again. Although Fortuna was a fraud and Romano a suck-up, they were, goddamn it, right. I turned to the autopsy and reviewed its conclusions one more time. I wondered if Morales knew what they were; I figured he didn't. I thought about his young, beautiful wife. Young, beautiful, raped, dead, and left on their bedroom floor.

I had to tell him what was in the autopsy report. I was certain that the young man's heart held an immense capacity for grief, but not much room for deception. Nevertheless, to inform him of what I'd learned and at the same time to reveal that the case was closed, consigned to the archives, seemed excessively cruel; I thought the knowledge might be too great for him to bear.

I took out an eraser from the top drawer of my desk and neatly erased the date written in the margin of the last page. Then, with the slightly faltering delicacy of one who imitates another's handwriting, I changed the date so that the case would remain active for three more months. I stood up and put the file on a shelf where, as I knew from experience, no one would lay a finger on it for decades unless I gave an explicit order to the contrary. Neither the judge nor the clerk would ask any questions about that case. I returned to my desk and spent a long time gnawing the cap of a ballpoint pen and wondering what would be the best way to explain to Morales that his wife, at the time of her rape and murder, was almost two months pregnant.

Telephone

Chaparro knows he'll regret ringing her up, but the possibility of hearing her voice, like everything that has to do with her, attracts him with an irresistible force. And so he gets closer and closer to making the call and regrets it every step of the way, from the moment the notion occurs to him until the moment he hears her pick up the phone.

He starts his approach by telling himself that he needs certain pieces of information contained in the legal proceedings. Does he really need them? At first his answer is yes, because after thirty years, many minor details (places, dates, the precise sequence of events) remain in his memory as little more than a faint blur. But, he immediately objects, such precision is obsessive and disproportionate. Does it really matter whether the case was inactive for five months or six? He's not submitting evidence for a preventive detention; he's narrating a tragedy in which he had the dubious honor of serving as both witness and protagonist. So much strict attention to detail is, therefore, unnecessary. But this admirably balanced line of reasoning does nothing to diminish his obstinate desire to review the case. Two days pass, days during which he barely manages to draft a couple of useless pages, before he's able to admit to himself that the idea of looking over the case file captivates him only because it offers an unobjectionable, crystal-clear excuse for visiting Irene.

She knows—he's told her himself—that he's "writing a book." Fine. After the passage of so much time, it's only natural that a writer would want to check a few details. Terrific. The case is stored in the General Archive, in the basement of the Palace of Justice. What better means of facilitating Chaparro's access to the old dossier could there be than an informal call from the examining magistrate of the court that handled the case in the first place? An unbeatable ploy. It would give him an opportunity to have coffee with Irene and play the part of a writer engaged in his research. Irene likes the project he's embarked on, and she becomes still more beautiful whenever she's discussing something she feels enthusiastic about. On the whole, therefore, the perfect excuse. So why does it make him so nervous, and why does he hold back whenever he's on the point of calling her? Precisely because of that, because it's all a pretext. It's basically that simple. However he looks at it, the whole thing's an alibi for spending time with her. And Chaparro quails before the smallest possibility of exposing his feelings to the woman he loves.

He knows the people who run the archive. Most of them entered the Judiciary after he did. If he presents himself at the reception counter and asks to see a case file, they're highly unlikely to refuse him. And even if they do, he can always ask young García, the current clerk, to make a call from the court and smooth the way for him. So what sense does it make to ask Irene for help?

Well, none at all, except that he'd get to spend five minutes alone with her, protected by an unimpeachable excuse. Without such a screen, he can't. Even though he wants to, it's impossible. He's terrified by the thought that the fire in his guts might be visible from the outside, that he might garble his words or get the shakes or break out in a cold sweat.

His embarrassment is ridiculous. They are, after all, both adults. Why not simply tell her the truth? Why not visit her in her office, without a pretext, and let her know how he feels? They're grown-ups. A few hints should be enough, some courtly gesture that would serve to demonstrate his interest, and Irene could imagine the rest.

Why can't he do that? Because it's simply out of the question. Because Chaparro has spent so many years keeping his feelings to himself he'd rather carry them to the grave than blurt out some awkward declaration, some sweetened, easily digestible version of what's in his heart. He can't just show up and remark, as naturally as can be, "Look, Irene, I wanted you to know that

I've been crazy about you for three decades, including some less intense periods during the many years when we didn't work together."

Chaparro roams like an automaton from the kitchen to the dining room and back. He opens and closes the refrigerator fifty times. Even though sooner or later, in the course of almost every pass, he stops in front of his desk, he's so wrapped up in his dilemma that he can't see those scattered pages for what, despite his fatalistic predictions, they are: the embryo of his damned book.

For the hundredth time, he looks at the telephone, as though the thing could help him decide to act. Suddenly, he takes two steps toward it, and his heartbeat accelerates. He regrets what he's going to do before he's dialed the third digit, but he forges ahead, because he's resolved to fulfill his desire, and at the same time, he rues the decision. He feels, in short, the mixture of cynicism and hope that's the hallmark of his life.

He dials the direct line to her office. He's not the least interested in letting any of his former coworkers learn about this call. After the third ring, someone picks up the phone.

"Hello?" It's Irene's voice. Not for the first time, Chaparro's surprised by this almost imperceptible sign of independence from convention in the woman he adores. At the beginning of their tenure in the vast Palace of Justice, all new employees copy their colleagues and use the bureaucratic formula for answering the telephone: the words "Court" or "Clerk's office," spoken in a monotone, and followed, when one is in a friendly mood, by "Good day." Not Irene.

Ever since her first day of work in the Judiciary, Irene has chosen to initiate her telephone conversations with that warm, familiar "Hello?" as if she were waiting for a call from her grandma. Chaparro knows this, because he was her first boss. He'd just been promoted to deputy when Irene started working in the clerk's office as an intern. He would later come to feel some regret for having decided, when they were first being introduced, not to speak to her in the familiar *vos* form. He'd been brought up to have the greatest respect for women, even very young ones, even those who might walk up to him, extend a hand, and greet him with a laconic "It's a pleasure." His reply had sounded quite formal: "How do you do, Miss? Good to have you with us." At the time, Chaparro was twenty-eight, ten years older than his new employee, and he was convinced that a boss always had to keep the hierarchical rankings clear in dealing with his subordinates. He'd hesitated a little when he looked into her eyes, because the girl looked back at him so intently, so penetratingly, that it was as if his own eyes had been struck by two well-aimed, jet-black beams. He broke the impasse by immediately releasing the hand she'd given him and instructing a secretary to describe the young

intern's basic duties to her. As their court was on call
and overwhelmed with work, they'd assigned the girl to
answer the telephone. After her fourth or fifth "Hello?"
Chaparro had deemed it proper to explain to her, from
the heights of his juridical experience, that it would be
infinitely more practical to answer incoming calls by
saying, "Clerk's Office 19," thus sparing the caller the
time required to overcome his surprise at such eccen-
tricity and to verify whether he'd actually reached the
court. Well before the conclusion of his discourse, Chaparro had started feeling like an idiot, although he wasn't
sure whether that was because of the intrinsic stupidity
of his counsel or because of Irene's demurely amused
expression as she listened to him go on. Nonetheless,
she nodded a few times, as if accepting his suggestion.
Three minutes later, however, when the telephone rang
again, she answered with a "Hello?" as informal and
unjuridical as all the previous ones. There was no temerity in her voice, nor did it convey the slightest defi-
ance. Maybe that was why Chaparro couldn't get angry
at her and considered the matter closed.

All her life, Irene has answered the phone like that,
and so she does on this August day, thirty years after
their first meeting, when Chaparro stops pacing around
his house and circling the telephone and picking up
the receiver and putting it down again who knows how
many times and finally decides—since he can no longer

avoid acting, which is the point he generally reaches before any important decision—to call her at her office and hears the "Hello?" that makes his heart leap in his chest.

Alibis and Departures

Benjamín Chaparro goes directly to the judge's chambers. He doesn't pass through his own clerk's office or through the offices of Section No. 18. So agitated is he by the imminence of seeing Irene that he's afraid everyone will notice how love-smitten he is. He knocks two times. Irene's voice bids him enter. He thrusts his head inside with a gesture of involuntary timidity, the kind he hates himself for. A smile lights up her face when she sees him. "Come in, Benjamín," she says. "Come on in."

Chaparro steps in, feeling his temperature rise. Has his face turned red? The sight of her stuns him as much as it did the first time they met, but he tries to keep her from seeing that when he looks at her. She's tall, with a narrow, fine-featured face. When she was younger, she was a little bony, but the years—and childbearing?—have added a slight, becoming roundness to her figure. They greet each other with a kiss on the cheek. Only when they sit down, one on either side of her big oak desk, does Chaparro release the breath he's been holding since the instant before the kiss. Now he can breathe easy; since he hasn't smelled it, it's possible that her scent won't keep him awake for the next two or three nights. A little embarrassed, as if they've caught each other doing something entertaining but reprehensible, they smile without talking. Chaparro draws out the moment before he speaks, because he sees her blush, and that makes him feel extremely happy. But when she looks into his eyes with an unspoken question that seems to penetrate all his alibis, he feels he's lost the advantage. Better stick to the script, he thinks. So he states his request, and to justify it, he expands a bit on the subject of "his book." He presents (becoming excited as he does so) a summary of the story, which she knows only superficially and by hearsay, that is, from remarks made by Chaparro himself and by other dinosaurs in the court. When he finishes, Irene gives him an amused look and asks, "Do you want me to make a call to the archive?"

"If you could . . . I'd like that," Chaparro declares, swallowing saliva.

"It's not a problem, Benjamín." She frowns slightly. "But look, the people down there know you better than they know me."

Shit, Chaparro thinks. Is his alibi so transparent? He says, "The problem is, the case is ancient history." He's running out of excuses.

"Yes, I know. You told me about it once. It came in after you had me promoted to the eleventh Court, right?"

Is there some second meaning behind that "you had

me promoted"? If there is, Irene's more perceptive than Chaparro would like to believe. In 1967, and more precisely in October of that year, when she'd been working as an intern for two weeks, and not long after he'd definitively abandoned his demand that she answer the telephone as God intended, Chaparro had dreamed about her. He woke up trembling. He was a married man, and at the time he was still doing his best to convince himself that his marriage with Marcela was a good one. He tried to forget the dream, but it recurred on each of the five following nights. The last time, the image of Irene was so vivid and the glow of her naked body so convincingly bright that Chaparro felt like weeping when he woke up and realized that none of it had really happened. That morning, he arrived at the court determined to purge the amorous feelings that were beginning to consume him. He telephoned all the colleagues he was on more or less friendly terms with and lauded the merits of an intern who was embarking on a career in the Judiciary, a law student who deserved a paid position. At the time, Chaparro was already a young man respected and well liked in the profession, and some months later, one of the colleagues he'd contacted called him back with the offer of an entry-level job "for the girl." Chaparro broke the radio silence he'd been maintaining with the young woman and told her the good news. Irene appeared quite happy to hear it, and her joy hurt him a little. If it was so easy for her to go, that meant there was nothing in their clerk's office she minded leaving. Nothing she'd miss. It made sense, he told himself. She was engaged to a young engineering student, a friend of one of her older brothers. Chaparro's passion made him feel uncomfortable in front of Marcela, and knowing that his love was unrequited made him feel lonely as well as unfaithful. He told himself it was best to uproot a plant that put out no shoots and had no future.

Irene moved to her new office in March 1968, shortly before the Morales case came into his hands, and Chaparro lost sight of her. Things were like that in the courts. Someone who worked two floors down from you might as well be living in another dimension. Chaparro had no news of Irene until February 1976, when she reentered his life as the new clerk of his section: she'd obtained her law degree and been appointed to the post. Although Chaparro was a free man, having separated from Marcela several years previously, Irene's return gave him no sort of opportunity to declare himself, even had he dared. When he saw her come through the door of the clerk's office for the first time since 1968, she was preceded by a considerable, six-months-pregnant belly. Because he'd thought the way to spare himself the sting of knowing she had her own life—while his was being ruined—was to close his ears to any news of her, it was only then that Chaparro discovered she'd married her engineering student two years before. The young man was now an engineer, and she was expecting their firstborn.

When Irene returned from maternity leave, it was Chaparro who was gone. It surprised her to learn that her deputy clerk had accepted an open position in the Federal Court of San Salvador de Jujuy, up in the extreme northwest, fifteen hundred kilometers away, but she was given to understand, sotto voce, that Judge Aguirregaray in person had suggested the move to Benjamín. This information was conveyed in a baleful, conspiratorial tone that Irene, even though she wasn't very knowledgeable about political matters, had no trouble interpreting: at some point during the cold winter of 1976, it had evidently become dangerous for Benjamín Chaparro to remain in Buenos Aires.

Over the course of the following years, each of them received news of the other in fragments. Chaparro knew about Irene's continuing climb up the professional ladder: public prosecutor in 1981, clerk of the Appellate Court a couple of years later. In her turn, she heard of his return to Buenos Aires in 1983, when the military dictatorship was in its death throes. He arrived accompanied by his wife, a woman from Jujuy whom he would later divorce. Throughout the decade of the 1980s, contact between Chaparro and Irene was scant, nothing more than a couple of fleeting conversations

after chance meetings in the street. Irene found out that
Chaparro's wife, the woman from Jujuy, was named
Silvia, and that they had no children. He learned that
Irene was still married to her engineer and that they had
three happy, growing little girls.

They met again a few years later, in 1992. Chaparro
had gone through his second divorce some time previously, and he'd persuaded himself that it would be best
for him to live out his days in prudent solitude. Apparently he wasn't made for marriage. He was over fifty
years old. Perhaps the time was right for him to give up
women. He was prepared to do without them. What he
was unprepared for was Judge Alberti's retirement at
the beginning of the year and the appointment of the
new judge, who was none other than Irene.

When they met face to face, in the same office in which
they were now sitting, the two had grinned at each other
like battle-tested veterans surrounded by raw recruits.
"We already know each other," Irene said, smiling, and
the twenty-five years standing like a protective barrier
between Chaparro and the series of dreams that had
shaken the foundations of his soul crumbled into dust,
with nary a trace left behind. The woman had no right
to activate that smile. But she still used "de Arcuri," the
engineer's name, she was still married, and that was the
kind of obstacle Chaparro was disinclined to try to overcome. Not at that point in his life, at least. So he greeted

her with a firm handshake and an atrocious "How are you doing, Your Honor?" thus establishing a sensible distance between them. She accepted the boundary, and for the next two years, even though they saw each other eight or nine hours a day, five days a week, they treated each other with reserved courtesy.

Then, on an ordinary morning, without any preliminaries, Irene started addressing him with the informal *vos*. It was a Monday, and with the naturalness that marked all she did, she merely said to him, "Say, Benjamín, I need you to help me with the release request for the Zapatas. Could you?" Chaparro could. And they went on like that throughout the following years, until he announced his upcoming retirement. Had she been surprised to hear it? The inveterate optimist that lived inside Chaparro tried to suggest to him that a look of muted sorrow and poorly concealed astonishment had transformed Irene's face. But there was no reason for surprise; he figured everybody in the court knew about his plans. So was she simply sad that he was leaving?

Whatever the answer might have been, Chaparro cut his meditations short. He asked himself—he couldn't help it—whether it would be worth his while to confess the truth to the woman he loved, and his reply was no, no way, not possible. Wouldn't declaring his love for her amount to acknowledging that he'd loved her for almost thirty years? Wouldn't it be the same as confessing that he'd spent his life longing for her from afar? Never, he thought vehemently. They hadn't really spent much time together over the course of all those years anyway, Chaparro told himself, but deep in his heart, he knew he'd never stopped loving her, and a combination of chance, common sense, and cowardice had always kept them apart. His silence was his; he owned it. If he spoke, he'd end up sunk in the swamp of her pity. He was determined to avoid such a plight, to avoid hearing anything that sounded like "Poor Benjamín, I didn't know . . ." The mere thought clouded Chaparro's vision with anger and shame. *Let my love die with me*, he inwardly declared, *but don't let it be spoiled.*

"Benjamín? That's the case you're talking about, isn't it?"

Chaparro jumps. Irene looks at him, smiling, questioning, and he wonders how long he's been sitting there like an idiot. Actually, it can't have been long. He's so used to thinking on that topic, a source of both pleasure and pain, that at least he thinks about it rapidly. "Yes, yes," he says. "That case."

"All right, then, I'll give them a call."

Irene pauses a moment, holding his gaze, before looking up the archive's number in her address book. When at last she lowers her eyes to the little book and the telephone, the knot in Chaparro's gut relaxes. With her usual informality, she greets whoever answers the

phone and asks to speak to the director. She has a smile
on her lips, wide-open eyes, and the slightly absorbed
expression of someone who's talking to another person without seeing him. Since she's turned toward the
window with her face in profile, Chaparro can observe
her as he pleases. Nevertheless, he restrains himself. He
knows from experience that if he looks at her too long,
the anguish of being unable to throw his arms around
her and kiss her, meticulously and indefatigably, will
overcome him. So, all things considered, he prefers to
look in some other direction.

"There you go, Benjamín," she says as she hangs up.
"No problem. In the archive even the floor tiles know
who you are."

"Is that a compliment or a joke about my age, Your
Honor?"

She turns serious. Only her eyes keep smiling, very
slightly. "Can I assume you're not going to show your
face around here again until you need us for something
else?"

*If it's a question of needing you, I could stay in this office
for the rest of my life.* That's the answer Chaparro would
give her, if he had enough nerve. Since he doesn't, he
says aloud, "I'll come back someday soon, Irene."

She doesn't reply. Instead she rises from her seat,
moves her face close to his, and gives him a big, loud
kiss on his left cheek. Chaparro can feel the fullness of

her lips, her hair gently brushing against his skin, the warmth of her body so close to his, and he inhales her fresh, wild fragrance, an accursed scent that goes directly to his brain, lodges in his memory, exacerbates his desire for her, and promises him three nights of insomnia, with their attendant days.

Archive

Entering the General Archive always causes the same feelings in him. At first, a heavy sensation, as if he were descending into an enormous tomb. But then, once he's inside the mute, dark, dungeonlike space and walking through the narrow aisles flanked by giant shelves crammed with bound dossiers, he feels a rare sense of security, of shelteredness.

A few steps ahead of him, the archivist who's serving as his guide leads him along. Chaparro thinks about how easy it is for us to detect the passage of time in the physical decay of the people around us. He's known this man for . . . how long has it been? Thirty years? The fellow's surely past retirement age. His left leg has a slight limp. At every step, the sole of his shoe makes a sound like sandpaper on the tiled floor. Why has he kept on working? Chaparro figures that to such a man, after so many years spent guarding a silent catacomb where document-stuffed shelves absorb all sounds, the outside world must seem like some sort of horrible, thunderous, ongoing explosion. Chaparro is reassured by the thought that his companion's not stuck in some prison, he's in a refuge.

They walk in the shadowy labyrinth long enough for Chaparro to become completely disoriented. Then the old archivist stops in front of a set of shelves exactly like the other thousand they've passed and looks up for the first time. Until this point, he's advanced with his eyes straight ahead of him, occasionally turning left or right, moving with the cautious determination of a rat accustomed to the dark. Now he raises his arms to a shelf that looks to be out of his reach. Stretching his worn-out joints causes him to emit a very soft groan. He yanks at a bundle of dossiers identified by a five-digit number, seizes the bundle, and resumes his march. Chaparro follows him to the end of the aisle and turns left behind him. The other aisles are dimly lit; this one's almost dark, so dark that Chaparro stops to give his eyes a chance to adjust. He's afraid he'll end up lost amid towering shelves, as in a well surrounded by blackness. The archivist's footsteps keep fading and become inaudible, as if the old man has entered a foggy sea. After a few seconds, just as the sudden anxiety of solitude is about to take hold of him, Chaparro hears a distant click. The archivist has just turned on a small lamp, which stands on an otherwise bare table. A shabby chair completes the furnishings of the "reading corner" he's apparently getting ready for Chaparro, who's happy to escape the black hole of the stacks.

With two expert movements, his guide opens the bundle of dossiers. He puts the sisal cord aside so that he'll be able to retie the bundle after the visitor has finished with it. Then he pulls out the case file Chaparro has requested. It's in three volumes, each bound together with thin white string. The archivist makes a meticulous pile of the volumes on the wooden table and places the chair appropriately. "I'll leave you here," he says in a high, hoarse voice, the voice of a man who's definitively entered old age. "When you're through, just leave things as they are. I'll put them back in order."

He starts to walk away and then stops and turns around, as if he's remembered something. "To get out, you have to advance diagonally," he said, accompanying his words with vague arm gestures. "Turn left at the first intersection, right at the next, then left again, and so on. If you hear noises, don't worry, it's the goddamned rats. They're everywhere. We don't know what to do about them. Poison, traps, nothing works. Every day, I take out a bunch of dead rats, but every day there's more of them, not fewer. Anyway, they won't bother you. They don't like the light."

"Thanks," Chaparro replies, but the old man has already turned and vanished around a corner at the end of the aisle.

Seamster

In the methodically sewn binding of the three volumes, Chaparro recognizes the expert hand of Pablo Sandoval, and as always when some little thing reminds him of Pablo Sandoval, Chaparro misses him. The best worker he ever had. Quick to learn, stupendously good at drafting official documents, endowed with a prodigious memory. But wait a minute. He's just committed the same injustice he commits every time he recalls Sandoval; he's begun by evoking him as his best assistant ever, by praising him as a boss's dream. And that's wrong. Not that the memory is false. No question about it, Chaparro never had a coworker as good at what he did as Sandoval. But to do justice to the man, Chaparro must remember that he was a good friend who also happened to be an exceptional employee.

There was only one precaution Chaparro had to take when they were working together. At the end of the day, when Sandoval would gather up his things and leave with a "See you tomorrow," Chaparro would wait a few minutes and then stick his head out the window of the clerk's office. If he saw Sandoval crossing Tucumán

Street toward Córdoba Avenue, then everything was all right; his assistant was going home like a good man and a good husband. But if a few more minutes passed and Sandoval didn't appear, Chaparro would prepare for the worst, because he could be sure his employee was on his way to the dives in the vicinity of Paseo Colón, with the irrevocable intention of drinking himself into a stupor. Chaparro would close the window and call up Sandoval's wife, Alejandra. He'd tell her that Pablo was going to be late, but that he, Benjamín, would get him home. She'd sigh, thank him, and hang up.

He'd continue working for a while, usually until well after nightfall. Then he'd leave the Palace of Justice by the security exit above Talcahuano Street and get a bite to eat in a cafe on Corrientes Avenue. Before midnight, he'd take a cab to the Bajo quarter and visit Sandoval's favorite bars, one by one, asking the driver to wait at each stop. When he finally located Sandoval, Chaparro would clap him on the shoulder, dig around in his pockets to see if he had enough money left to cover his last few drinks, and pony up the difference himself. Then he'd load him into the taxi and give the driver Sandoval's address. When they stopped at the door, Alejandra would come out, hurrying to pay the cabbie. Chaparro wouldn't insist on paying, because doing so would violate a tacit agreement between him and both Sandovals. Therefore he would limit himself to helping Pablo to the street door

of his building, where his wife would take over, except for
the times when her husband's state was too pathetic and
Chaparro would be obliged to carry him all the way to
his bed. Sandoval's wife would bid Chaparro good night
with a wan smile and a "Thanks a lot."

The next day, Sandoval would miss work. But he'd return the day after that, with black rings under his eyes
and a look of devastation. When Sandoval was in such
a wretched state, Chaparro knew the man couldn't
work as he usually did. He'd be useless, as if the alcohol had erased his memory centers and short-circuited
his intelligence. At times like those, Chaparro would
set his assistant to binding case files. Without a word,
he'd put the white thread and the upholstery needle on
Sandoval's desk. On his own, Sandoval would carry the
equipment to a table near the shelves where loose case
documents were stacked and then go to work in a way
that was a joy to see. With a surgeon's movements, an
artist's grace, and the solemnity of an officiating priest,
Sandoval gave the impression of a consummate book-
binder. When he finished with a case file, it was bound
into one or more large tomes, each of which looked like
a volume of an encyclopedia. At the end of three or four
days, after the worst of his depression was over, Sandoval would approach Chaparro and, with a smile, return
the needle and thread, as though discharging himself
from rehabilitation.

He died early in the 1980s, while Chaparro was in San Salvador de Jujuy. The thought of embracing Sandoval's widow and paying his final respects to Sandoval himself was sufficient reason for Chaparro to spend his good pesos on plane fare, attend the funeral, and above all, put a two-day parenthesis around his fear of being killed by a band of murderers who, besides everything else, were gunning for the wrong target.

Now, nearly twenty years later, Chaparro forgets for a moment what he's come to do and pulls at the string that binds one of the big volumes. Then he releases the thin cord, having verified that it's got exactly the right degree of tension. It's as though Sandoval has left him this wordless message so that Chaparro will remember Pablo, too, as one of the actors in the story he's begun to write. Message received.

Chaparro smiles, thinking that Sandoval, with his subtle intelligence, would have appreciated the sequence of small details, the infinitesimal resurrection, the deserved homage rendered to him two decades later by his friend and boss, and the said boss's tangential, sidelong approach to that homage through a posthumous eulogy to his late assistant's virtues as a seamster.

Pages

Chaparro grabs the first volume and pulls it closer to the lamplight. It contains two cover sheets, one on top of the other, both of thin cardboard. The second sheet displays black lettering made with a felt-tip pen: "Liliana Emma Colotto. Homicide," followed by information concerning the court. But the first cover sheet, the outer one, reads "Isidoro Antonio Gómez, first-degree murder, Penal Code Art. 80, par. 7." Chaparro opens the dossier and finds the same police reports, the same witnesses' statements, and the same forensic analyses he reviewed in August 1968, after he'd been ordered to declare the case inactive for want of a suspect and he'd decided instead to play a first-rate mug's game.

He flips through a few pages. Although he regrets it almost at once, he can't resist the impulse to look again at the photographs of the crime scene. Thirty years later, Liliana Emma Colotto de Morales is still sprawled on the bedroom floor, abandoned, helpless, with fixed, dead eyes and bluish marks on her throat. Chaparro feels the same shame he felt the day of the murder, because he remembers the lascivious stares of the policemen who

stood around the corpse before Báez sent them packing,
and he's not sure whether his shame has to do with those
stares or with his own obscene desire to lose himself, too,
in contemplating the splendid body that has just died.

He turns over the pages of the autopsy one by one,
but he doesn't read or even skim them. He half-closes his
eyes and concentrates on the musty smell the pages release into the archive's still air. They've been there more
than twenty years, bound one on top of the other, and
Chaparro can't help conjuring up an image that has
entranced him ever since he was a child. He imagines
that he himself is one of those pages. Anyone at all. He
imagines himself waiting for years and years in the most
utter darkness, squeezed between the previous and following pages, smooth and soft like them. If you're one of
those pages, Chaparro thinks, the occasional footsteps
that resound in the aisle at monthly or yearly intervals
can't help you measure the passage of time. They're
barely sufficient for plumbing the terrifying depths of
your solitude. All at once, without warning, without
any signs that would allow you to prepare yourself for
the coming upheaval, you feel a shock. Then another
and another. As the uniform mass of paper that protects
or imprisons you is moved from one place to another,
you're disoriented by a sudden, gently rhythmic motion. Then movement stops again, but there's a sound
of pages passing from one side to the other, followed by

the abrupt, blinding wound of light that means your turn—the turn of the page you are, of the page you've metamorphosed into—has come. You don't waste this chance to see the world again, even though, for you, the Creation is reduced to a face, a male face, the face of a mature man with graying hair, small eyes, and an aquiline nose who barely looks at you and immediately turns his head to the following page, the one that for years and years has been next to you, pressed against you, skin on skin, letters on letters. And then a hand moves across the surface to the far corner and lifts the next page and pulls it toward you, and page and hand blur at the exact moment when the light disappears, and you understand that another eternity of darkness and silence has begun.

When Chaparro imagines the sudden hope and catastrophic disappointment his hands are causing in each page as he leafs through the case file, he's overcome by an absurd feeling of pity. But when he reaches page 208, shortly after the beginning of the second volume, he stops; he's arrived at his destination.

It's a four-line court order, typed on his Remington. On this last point, he has no doubt: The *e*'s are all raised a little above the line formed by the other letters, and the bellies of the *a*'s are filled with ink, because the key was worn out.

The document records a court appearance, falsely dated in mid-August 1968, in which Ricardo Agustín

Morales declares that he has information pertinent to solving the crime. A little farther down the page, an order signed by Judge Fortuna Lacalle orders the petitioner to give, under oath, the reasons for his assertion.

Page 209 presents Morales's sworn declaration, falsely dated in early September. In this statement, which is considerably longer than the other declarations, the name of Isidoro Antonio Gómez appears for the first time. On page 210, a new court order dated September 17 directs that official letters be sent to the Federal Police and to the police of Tucumán Province, requesting them "to ascertain the domicile" of the said Gómez and "summon him to appear in court." All these documents bear the signatures of the examining magistrate and his clerk. Judge Fortuna Lacalle's signature is enormous, pretentious, adorned with useless flourishes. Pérez's is small and bland, like the clerk himself.

Chaparro consults his watch. His eyes feel irritated. The table lamp, shining alone in the midst of darkness, has troubled his vision. It's almost noon, and he knows the archivist is going to get nervous if he doesn't see him leave soon. It's unlikely that he'll quote these tedious legal documents verbatim in his book, but they've helped to evoke the climate of those days. They've returned him to the sterile meetings he had with Morales to keep him from losing hope, or at least to inform him, gently and gradually, that the case was going nowhere for lack of a suspect. And they've recalled the unbearable heat of that hellish summer.

Chaparro rises to his feet and puts the three volumes of the case in a single pile. He doesn't turn off the lamp, because he's afraid he'll get completely lost if he tries to make his way back through the dark stacks. He retraces his steps to the entrance, zigzagging in accordance with the archivist's directions. At one of the last turns, when he's almost out of the archive, Chaparro glimpses something that makes him jump. It's the old man, sitting on a chair in one of the narrow aisles, with his legs stretched out and his eyes fixed on the shelf in front of him. Chaparro feels the same icy apprehension that used to come over him during visits to his aunt Margaret, who was blind from birth. At the end of the visit, when night was falling, his aunt would accompany him to the door, turning out the lights along the way to be sure she wouldn't leave one on and "waste electricity for nothing." When the old lady told him good-bye and, a little absently, stretched out her face to receive his kiss on her cheek, little Benjamín would look over her shoulder and see that her apartment was in darkness. The image of his aunt in those pitch-black, endless rooms—eating dinner, for example, or feeling her way along the walls—would follow him all the way to the Floresta station and terrify him until he got on the train.

With a laconic "Good day," Chaparro bids farewell to the archivist and practically runs out of the archive. He goes back up to the ground floor of the Palace, and shortly thereafter he's descending the exterior stairs to Lacalle Street and rejoicing in his return to sun-drenched, noisy Buenos Aires.

Three hours later, he's in his house in Castelar, and if some passerby were to walk down his street, he could hear the frenetic din of a typewriter and see Chaparro's silhouette through the window, bent over his desk, over his keyboard, banging out the paragraphs of what appears to be the second part of his story. But as it happens, no one hears or sees him. The street is deserted.

12

I didn't dare tell him no, even though there was every reason to suspect that a terrible time was in store for me.

It was at our last meeting. Just as we were taking leave of each other, Morales surprised me by saying, "I'm going to get rid of the photographs."

I asked him why, but I had a feeling he was going to explain whether I asked him to or not. He said, "Because I can't stand to look at her face when she can't look back at me. But before I burn them, I'd like to share them with you. Maybe showing you the photos will be a good way to say good-bye to them."

I could have turned him down. I've always hated looking at photographs. But either I didn't have the necessary reflexes, or I was developing a tendency to let the boy have his way, or I was hindered by the same sudden awkwardness I've felt all my life at the prospect of rejecting a request. The one certain thing is that I accepted.

We agreed to meet again in three weeks. It was the beginning of December. The case had been in a box on a shelf since August, and sooner rather than later, I was going to find myself obliged to revive it, review it, and declare it officially dead; no one would be prosecuted. Although the prospect made me sick, the case, Morales, and I (so deep was my commitment in this mess) were all about to hit a concrete wall. Maybe that was why I agreed to look at the photos.

I left the court with no time to spare and quickly walked the block and a half to the bar where we always met. Morales had already taken possession of a large table, and with the calm concentration of a collector, he was taking photographs out of a shoe box and placing them in different piles. I approached him slowly. Looking over his shoulder, I could see his display of grievous memories.

The wooden floor creaked, and Morales turned around to look at me. He was wearing a pair of librarian's eyeglasses and holding a pencil in his mouth. He made a face by way of greeting me and pointed to the seat across from him. When he did so, I noticed that the piles of pictures were turned toward my side of the table, as if we were at a trade fair and Morales wanted to guide me through his exhibit.

"I'm just about ready," he said, pulling a last handful of photos out of the box and starting to distribute them among the piles in front of me.

Every time he placed a photograph on a pile, he took the pencil from his mouth and marked one of the lines on a long, numbered list. There was no doubt that he was a guy who paid scrupulous attention to details. While he was checking off the last pictures, I noticed that his list went up to number 174, and I feared I was going to be very late for dinner. I reproached myself a little for not having called Marcela before I left the clerk's office. Finding a public telephone anywhere near the bar was going to be a royal pain, but I couldn't neglect to tell her I'd been delayed. Why throw another log on the frigid bonfire of our disagreements? It wasn't that we quarreled. No. I don't think we ever went so far as to quarrel. I was apparently the only one of us troubled by the increasing iciness of our relationship.

"I've put them in order for you. These here," he said, handing me the first pile of photos, "are pictures of Liliana when she was a little girl."

I noticed she was already lovely. Or did I see her like that because I clearly remembered the last images of her, the ones in which her beauty persisted, even in the midst of horror? The pictures of the little girl were classics, typical of children's photos in those days. A selection of posed portraits, all taken inside a photographer's studio. No snapshots. Wearing her best clothes, with her hair most carefully combed. I imagined her parents making faces at her behind the photographer's back to provoke some shy smiles that probably turned confused after every blinding flash.

"These are of Liliana as a teenager. Her fifteenth

birthday . . . and stuff like that. Before she came to Buenos Aires, you know?"

"I didn't know your wife was from out of town. Are you
from somewhere else, too?"

"No, I'm from here. I grew up in the suburbs, in Bec-
car. But Liliana's from Tucumán Province. From the
capital, San Miguel. She came here to live with a couple of her aunts a year or so after she got her teaching
degree."

It was obvious that the family had bought a camera,
because now there were many more pictures. On a river-
bank, a group of girls in bathing suits, accompanied by
a matron of indefinable age and rigorous aspect. Two
girls—one of them Liliana—in white pinafores, carrying
the Argentine flag. A small, shaggy, white dog, playing
with a girl who it goes without saying was Liliana.

The photographs of her fifteenth birthday, some of
them printed in a larger format. Liliana, wearing a light
dress and a double-stranded necklace, a bit garishly
made up, with perhaps too much eye shadow. Pictures
of her standing beside each table in the hall, with a different set of guests at every one: a group of venerable old
folks, surely grandparents and grandaunts and -uncles;
a group of girls, some of them familiar from the swim-
suit snapshot by the river; a group of boys, each encased
in a rented or borrowed suit; a gaggle of smaller girls and

boys, perhaps nieces and nephews. Photographs of Liliana waltzing on the improvised dance floor in front of the
tables, with her dad, her grandfather, and her brother,
and then with a multitude of other boys, who were perhaps dazzled by the circumstance of being authorized, if
only briefly, to place a hand on such a beauty's waist.

A picnic in a place difficult to identify. The Palermo
barrio of Buenos Aires was a possibility, but Liliana
looked sixteen, seventeen at the most, and so she must
still have been in Tucumán when the pictures were
taken. A group of girls and boys, lounging on the grass
near a river or stream.

"These are from after we got engaged," Morales explained as he handed over another pile, a small one
this time. In an apologetic tone he added, "There aren't
many. We were only engaged for a year."

I was glad to hear it. I didn't want to seem uncaring, but
I did want to get that ordeal over as soon as possible, and
there were lots of pictures to go. I was feeling the same
mixed reaction I always felt when looking at photographs:
sincere curiosity, a genuine interest in the lives hinted at
in the glossy, eternally silent prints, but also a deep melancholy, a sense of loss, of incurable nostalgia, of a vanished paradise behind those minuscule instants, arrived
from the past like naive stowaways. So, with a great many
images still left to see, I could already feel melancholy
weighing me down. I reached for one of the piles Morales

hadn't yet handed me, as if a deviation from the sequence he'd laid out would somehow give me back my freedom, which, in any case, wasn't useful for very much.

"Those are from when Liliana got her teaching diploma," Morales explained. There was no trace of resentment in his voice for what I'd feared he might take as an impertinence. "After that, she spent a year teaching in Tucumán, and then she came to Buenos Aires."

These were more recent photographs, and the women's hairdos, the men's jacket lapels, the knots in their ties all conveyed a sense of "not long ago" that I found less nostalgic. It was obvious that the girl's family liked to celebrate things. There was always the well-laden table, a decoration of some kind on the wall proclaiming the event, and a great many chairs set out so that the multitude of friends, family members, and neighbors who were present at every such occasion had a place to sit down.

I don't know why I noticed what I noticed. I imagine it was because I've always liked looking at things a little sidelong, focusing on the background instead of the foreground. I stopped turning over the photographs in the stack I was holding and gazed for a long time at the one I'd come to. It showed an exultant Liliana, wearing a light, simple dress, probably a summer dress, standing in the middle of a circle of young boys and girls and showing them her diploma.

I looked up at Morales: "Would you pass me the pictures from her fifteenth birthday again?" I tried to make
the request sound casual.

Morales did as I asked, even though he gave me a
somewhat surprised glance as he handed me the photographs. It was a matter of a few moments to find the
ones I wanted: two pictures from the dancing. One
showed Liliana posing with a fat, bald, smiling gentleman, probably an uncle; in the other, her partner was a
boy whose face was only partly visible, because he was
staring grimly at the floor. I put the two pictures on top
of the pile, which I then set down next to the graduation
photos.

"Now, could you please find me the shots from a picnic you showed me earlier? Taken in a kind of park, with
a lot of trees. Do you know the ones I mean?"

Morales nodded. He said nothing, and for just that
reason, I realized that he'd detected the confused urgency in my sudden requests and didn't want to distract
me by asking for an explanation. When I had the picnic pictures in my hands, I quickly selected two wide-
angle shots that showed the entire group. A long minute
passed.

"What's going on?" Morales inquired, daring to ask
the question even as uncertainty choked his voice.

I had separated the four chosen photographs from
the others, and now I was going through the piles again,

entirely concentrated on finding another shot of a certain face. In the end, two more pictures interested me,
so I wound up holding six altogether. I shoved the other
168 aside rather brusquely. Maybe I should have explained myself to Morales or at least given him some indication that I'd heard his question. But my idea was so
sudden, and at the same time such a gamble, that I was
obscurely afraid it would vanish into thin air if I spoke
it aloud. So, with a sweep of my arm, I cleared a spot on
the table, nearly knocking the entire photo collection
to the floor in the process, and then I placed in front of
him, too hastily for good order, the six pictures that had
struck my eye. At last, in lieu of answering his question,
I asked him one: "Do you know this guy?"

Morales stared at the photographs, obedient but puz-
zled. Never before that Friday afternoon had he paid any
attention to those features, but he was condemned to see
them in front of him forever, even when his eyes were
closed. That was going to happen, but Morales didn't
know it yet, so he simply answered, "No."

I turned the photos toward me, trying not to blotch
them with my fingers. In the two pictures from the picnic, a boy wearing a light-colored T-shirt, dark trousers,
and sneakers, standing close to the extreme left of the
group, offered the camera his profile: very pallid complexion, hooked nose, black, curly hair. Sitting almost
in shadow at a table littered with plates, the remains

of food, and half-empty bottles, the same kid gazed at a couple on the dance floor, and more precisely at Liliana, with her long, straight hair and somewhat too heavy makeup, waltzing in the foreground with an older gentleman. The other photograph from that same soiree gave a slightly better view of the kid; he held Liliana almost at arm's length, his elbows rigid, as though both wanting and fearing to touch her, and fixed his eyes on the floor, not on her face, much less on her promising neckline.

The fifth photograph had surely been taken in the living room of her home. In the center of the picture, the teaching diploma, held up to the camera with pride and a limitless smile by the same girl, namely Liliana, some years older. A group of friends (neighbors?) stood around the graduate, who was flanked by a man and a woman, no doubt the proud parents. And there was the same kid, now a young man, in this case on the right of the shot: the same curly black hair, the same nose, the identical hard expression on his face, his eyes turned not on the camera but on the girl, whose smile lit up the whole photograph.

And then came the last and best picture of the lot (best because of the naked simplicity with which, from out of the frozen silence, it announced the truth that was growing into a certainty before my eyes). This shot showed the same young guy, turned almost completely away from the action (which consisted of the group gathered around the graduate as before, but without the

diploma) and staring at a shelf on the wall beside him.
On that shelf, almost level with his nose, was a framed
photograph filled with the smiling face of the same girl,
the said Liliana Emma Colotto. For the kid gazing at it ·
in ecstatic contemplation, that portrait had an additional advantage: there on the shelf, Liliana was totally
exposed, totally unaware, totally at his mercy. That was
why he didn't even notice that the photographer was
taking another shot, and so all the friends, relatives, and
neighbors looked at the camera except him, lost as he
was in his silent worship, safe from the others' eyes. He
couldn't know, obviously, that another guy, who would
happen to be me, fifteen hundred kilometers away and
several years later, would look at him looking at her,
couldn't know that I'd just found him out, almost by a
miracle (if we think it's good to discover the truth), or
with fatal shrewdness (if we'd rather consider that the
truth is not always the best harbor for our uncertainties), or through an unacceptable stroke of luck (if we
limit ourselves to identifying the links in the delicate
and apparently random chain of events).

For a moment, I thought Morales would remain aloof
from the mental rebellion that was consuming me. But
when I managed to focus a minimal part of my attention
on him, I noticed that he was rummaging around in his
satchel like a diligent schoolboy. He took out a kind of
album, with gilt vignettes on its cloth covers. He opened

it. It held no photographs; the thin cardboard pages, separated by sheets of wax paper, were empty. It took me a while to realize that various marks slightly scored the smooth surface of every page, and then I understood that Morales had removed the photographs from the album before arranging them in piles and offering them to me. But what was he doing now? As persnickety as he was, I thought it unlikely he was searching for a misplaced photo. He was turning over every page, with the precise movements of someone who doesn't want to make a mistake. The album was thick. He stopped on a page close to the end of the volume. There the divider, the sheet of wax paper, was filled with curvy marks drawn in what looked like India ink. At the bottom of the sheet, in a corner, there was a list, apparently of proper names.

Morales raised his eyes to the photographs I'd just shown him. He chose one of the two from the picnic. Lifting up the marked sheet of wax paper, he slipped the photo under it. When the India ink marks perfectly matched the outlines of the figures in the picture, I understood. There was a number written in the space occupied by each figure. Morales laid his finger on the outline at a point under which, barely visible, was the image of Liliana's eternal observer.

"Nineteen," he murmured.

We both turned our eyes to the list of names.

Morales read the heading: "'Picnic at Rosita Calamaro's country house, September 21, 1962.'" Then he ran his index finger down the list until he came to the line he was looking for. "Number 19: Isidoro Gómez."

13

Although he'd already read it twice, once silently when he received it and then again aloud, Delfor Colotto decided to go over it one more time while his wife was out shopping, just to be sure he'd understood it right. He put on his glasses and sat in the rocking chair on the back porch. He read slowly so he wouldn't have to move his lips, but still, if he'd been in front of the house, where anybody could see him, he would have felt uncomfortable.

When he finished, he removed his spectacles and folded the letter along its original creases. The stationery was smooth and very white, unlike the skin of his hands, which resembled coarse sandpaper. He'd understood the letter, despite his initial fear that some of the words, elegantly handwritten in black ink on both sides of the page, could stump him. "Imperative" was the only one that had given him trouble. He'd had an idea of what it might mean, but he'd wanted to be sure, and so he'd picked up the dictionary the girl had left in the house, and that had done the trick: his son-in-law needed help—urgently, a lot, whatever it might take. He'd understood the rest of the letter with no trouble. At the end, his son-in-law had written, "I leave it in your hands," because he was "certain that you'll devise the best way to go about it." And just here was the thorny problem that had kept Delfor Colotto on tenterhooks ever since the arrival of the letter, two days previously: What could that "best way" be?

He got to his feet. The only thing he could accomplish by staying in the rocking chair would be to make himself more nervous. Maybe his plan wasn't a good one, but he'd devised nothing else. His son-in-law should have been clearer in his letter. The older man felt the younger one hadn't told him the whole truth. Did he consider him unworthy of his confidence? Or—worse—did he think he was an idiot because he hadn't finished school? *Don't get worked up about it*, Colotto told himself. Maybe his son-in-law hadn't given him more details because he hadn't wanted to make him even more nervous. In that case, he'd had a point, because the little Delfor Colotto knew and the great deal he imagined were already driving him crazy, and he hadn't slept a wink for two consecutive nights. More knowledge, or a confirmation of what he feared, might well be worse. Besides, he'd always been fond of his son-in-law, even though that "always" sounded a bit exaggerated, because how many times had he seen him? Three, four at the most? So he didn't really know him, but hell, that wasn't the young guy's fault, after all.

These thoughts gave him the impetus he needed. He went into the house and walked to the bedroom. On the back of the chair a shirt was hanging neatly. Colotto put it on over his undershirt, stuffed the shirttails into his trousers, and readjusted his belt buckle. Then he left the house and strolled to the corner, pausing briefly on the way to greet a couple of his neighbors, who were drinking maté on the sidewalk. Dusk was falling, December had let loose one of its infernal heat waves, and some people were trying to find a bit of fresh air outside.

At the corner he turned right. "We're practically on the same street," he thought. And he felt uncomfortable, as though something had been put over on him. He stopped in front of a house just like his and just like all the others built according to the government's plans for residential development. The little yard in front, the porch, the door flanked by two windows, the American-style asphalt roof. He clapped his hands. From behind the house a pair of dogs came running and barking into the front yard, only to be silenced almost completely by a female voice from inside the house. A rather small woman with white skin and light eyes came out onto the porch, drying her hands on the apron she wore over her skirt.

"How are you doing, Mr. Colotto? What a surprise to see you over this way."

"Still here, Miss Clarisa. Hanging on."

The woman seemed uncertain as to how to continue the conversation. "And how's your wife? I haven't seen her around the neighborhood for a long time."

"She's plugging along, you know, getting a little better." The man scratched his head and frowned.

The woman interpreted this gesture as a desire to change the subject, and therefore she raised her hand to open the little black door before she spoke again: "Come in, please, come in. Would you like some maté?"

"No, thank you, Miss Clarisa, thanks a lot anyway." He held up both hands, palms outward, as if softening his refusal. "I appreciate it, but this is just a quick visit. The truth is I was trying to locate your nephew Humberto."

"Ah . . ."

"It's for a job. The supervisor over in the municipal lumberyard asked me to do a little carpentry work on his house, see, and I might need an assistant, and so it occurred to me that maybe Humberto . . ."

"It's really too bad, Mr. Colotto, but it so happens Humberto's gone to help my brother in the country, you know, out there around Simoca."

"Ah, right." Colotto thought things were going too smoothly. The fact that the small talk perfectly suited his plans made him, if possible, even more nervous. "What a shame. The thing is, I don't want to hire someone I don't know, if you see what I mean."

"Oh, sure I do, Mr. Delfor, and I thank you for re-membering him . . ."

"Well, look, Miss Clarisa." Now. It was now or never. "How about Isidoro? What's he doing? Could he be in-terested in a temporary job?"

"Noooo . . ." Her "no" was long, high-pitched, con-vinced, trusting, innocent. "Isidoro went to Buenos Aires almost a year ago, didn't you know that? Well, not a year ago. A little less, to tell the truth. But when you miss somebody, it seems longer, you know how it is."

Colotto opened his eyes very wide, but he figured the woman would interpret that as simple surprise.

"Let me see," she went on. "We're in the beginning of December . . ." She raised her hands to count on her fingers. "So he's been gone around ten months. It was the end of March, you know. I mean, I thought you knew. Well, I guess I don't go out very much, what with my rheumatism and all . . ."

"Of course, Miss Clarisa, of course." (*Almost there, Delfor,* he thought. *Control yourself, for God's sake, stay calm.*) "But I had no idea. I imagined he was working somewhere around here."

"No. There wasn't much work for him last summer. A few little odd jobs here and there. Nothing to speak of. Oh, I used to tell him he wasn't trying very hard. It made him mad sometimes when I said that, but it was true. He'd stay shut up in his room all day, staring at the ceiling. He looked sick, he never went out. Never, not even to have fun with his friends. I'd ask him, what's wrong, Isidorito, tell Mama what's wrong with you, but who can figure kids out? He wouldn't say a thing. And . . . well, he's turned out to be just as reserved as his father, may he rest in peace, and you know, getting two words out of *him* was a real triumph. And so I let him be. He'd put on a long face and stalk around the house like a caged lion. Finally, one day he hit me with the news that he didn't want to stay here anymore and he was going to Buenos Aires. It made me sad at first, you know—my baby, my only son, and so far away. But he looked so bad, so . . . it was like he was angry, you know? So in the end it seemed almost like a good idea for him to go away."

The woman wanted to go on talking, but standing up for so long made her joints ache and obliged her to keep shifting her weight from one leg to the other. She settled for leaning on the porch pillar. "Anyway, I'll tell you something, Mr. Delfor. Every month, he sends me a money order. Every month. With that and my pension, I can get along really well, you know?"

One more to go, Colotto thought. *One more.* He said, "That's just great, Miss Clarisa. I'm happy for you. Look, the way things are these days, finding a full-time job so fast—"

"Right, right," the woman said, agreeing enthusiastically. "That's exactly what I tell him. I say, you have to

run and thank Our Lady of the Miracle, Isidorito. Well,
but I call him Isidoro, because if I don't he gets annoyed.
A miracle, the way things are these days. He should be
grateful. Because when he got there, he had a recommendation from my brother-in-law for a job in a print
shop, but that didn't work out. But then, soon afterward,
in fact right away, he found a job on a construction site.
Not only that, but it seems they're building something
really big, so the job's going to last awhile."

"What a break! It sounds too good to be true, doesn't
it?" Colotto swallowed saliva.

"I know, Mr. Colotto, I know! It's just fantastic! An
apartment building in the Caballito neighborhood, he
said. Down there around . . . around Primera Junta, I
think. Could that be right? Real close to that train, the
sebway or whatever it is. The building's going to have
something like twenty floors."

The woman kept on talking, but Delfor Colotto missed
most of the rest of her conversation, because he was trying to decide whether he should be happy or sad about
what he'd just found out. He made an effort to concentrate on her words and save his evaluations for later. She
was talking about going to Salta for the Miracle Fiesta if
her rheumatism would allow it, because she was very de-
voted to the Blessed Virgin.

"Well, all right, then, Miss Clarisa, I'll be on my way."
Suddenly, he remembered his excuse for being there

in the first place. "And if you hear about anybody who needs a temporary job . . . I mean someone you could recommend, of course."

"I'll keep my ears open, Mr. Delfor. Now I have to tell you, I don't get much news, stuck inside the way I am, but if I hear anything, I'll let you know, and God bless you."

Delfor Colotto walked back home, bathed in the dim glow of the recently installed street lights. It was strange. Two years before, when he was president of the Development Association, he'd moved heaven and earth to get streetlights put up in this part of town. And now, he felt about street lighting the way he felt about almost everything else; he didn't give a shit.

He stepped into his house and looked at the clock. It was too late to go out to the phone booth. That would have to wait until tomorrow morning. He heard the sound of pots and pans—his wife was busy in the kitchen. He decided not to tell her anything for the moment. As he walked to the bedroom, he took off his shirt. He hung it up again on the back of the chair, went back outside, and sat on the porch. There was a very slight breeze.

14

Ten days after the evening with Morales and his photographs, I made an appointment and went down to Homicide to meet Báez. When I opened the door to his office, he invited me in and offered me some coffee, which he sent one of his staff to get. As always happened when I spent time in his company, I let a feeling of respect for him get the better of me, even though I found such admiration uncomfortable.

He was a large man, hard-featured, built like an armoire. He was—how many?—fifteen or twenty years older than me. It was hard to figure his age exactly, because he sported a thick mustache that would have made a teenager look old. I think the thing that aroused my admiration for him was the calm, direct way he exercised his authority. I'd often watched him moving among other policemen with the controlled self-confidence of a pontiff convinced of his right to command. And even though I'd been the deputy clerk of the court for a couple of years by then, I sensed that I would never in my life be able to give an order without my heart jumping into my throat. I don't know what I was more afraid of: that the people under me would resent my directives, that they wouldn't obey me, or that they'd do what I wanted and laugh behind my back, which was almost the most distressing possibility of all. Báez was surely untroubled by such cogitations.

That afternoon, however, I felt I had a slight advantage over the man I admired so much. I was riding a wave of euphoria because of my hunch about the photographs. What had begun as not much more than an aesthetic observation had turned into a lead, the only one we had.

In those days, I was incapable of regarding my life with moderation. Either I considered myself an obscure, invisible functionary, a slave to routine, vegetating monotonously in a post appropriate to my mediocre faculties and limited aspirations, or I was a misunderstood genius, my talent wasted in the tedious exercise of secondary activities suitable for natures less favored than my own. I spent most of my time occupying the first of those two positions. Only rarely did I shift to the second, which I'd have to abandon sooner rather than later, when some brutal disillusion would end my sojourn at that particular oasis. I didn't know it, but in twenty minutes, my self-esteem was going to be wrecked by one such disastrous purge.

I started off by telling him about the episode with the photos. First, I described them, and then I showed them to him. I was pleased by the attention he paid to my

account. He asked me for details, and I was able to sat-
isfy his curiosity on most points. Báez had always shown
great respect for my knowledge of the law. In our conversations, he'd never minded confessing to gaps in his
own familiarity with legal matters (which was another
reason for me to admire him, given that I regarded my
own areas of ignorance as inexcusable shortcomings).
On this occasion, I was venturing onto his turf, and yet
he gave me the impression that he thought I was doing
so for good reason. When I finished showing him the
pictures, I told him about the instructions I'd given Morales: the widower was to write to his father-in-law and
ask him to find out Isidoro Gómez's current location. So
that his nerves wouldn't get the better of him, so that he
wouldn't try to carry out some sort of absurd personal
revenge, the father-in-law had to limit himself to ob-
taining the desired information and passing it along to
Morales. Colotto's mission had been such a success, I
explained to Báez, that I'd ordered Morales to request
a second round of reports from his father-in-law, the
information to be gathered from other neighbors and
from friends that his daughter and Gómez might have
had in common. We'd based the search for the friends
on the list of names accompanying the photographs
of the famous picnic. As I was preparing to lay out the
findings from the second round of reports, which confirmed Gómez's progressive withdrawal, his apparently

precipitous departure for Buenos Aires, and his arrival in the capital a few weeks before the murder, Báez cut me off with a question: "How long ago did the father-in-law pay this visit to the suspect's mother?"

Although a little surprised, I started counting the days. Didn't he want to hear the verified information I was on the brink of revealing to him? Didn't he want to know that a couple of Gómez's friends from the barrio had corroborated my theory that the young man had been secretly in love with the victim for years?

"Ten days, eleven at the most."

Báez looked at the antiquated black telephone on his desk. Without a word to me, he picked up the receiver and dialed three digits. When the call was answered, Báez spoke in a murmur: "I need you to come here at once. Yes. By yourself. Thanks."

Then he hung up and, as if I'd vanished, immediately began a rapid search of his desk drawers. Soon he extracted a plain notepad with about half its sheets missing and began at once to scribble on it, using big, untidy strokes. He looked like a stern-faced doctor writing me a prescription for who knows what medication. If I hadn't been so tense, I would have found the image amusing. Before Báez finished, there were two knocks on the door. A senior subofficer entered the room, greeted us, and planted himself next to the desk. Báez soon put down his pencil, tore off the sheet of paper, and handed it to the policeman. "Here you go, Leguizamón. See if you can find this guy. All the information you might be able to use is on that sheet. If you manage to find him, take care—he may be dangerous. Place him under arrest and bring him in. The learned doctor here and I will see what we can get out of him."

I wasn't surprised to hear him refer to me as a doctor—he meant a doctor of law, of course—nor was I for a moment tempted to correct him. The police prefer to call all judicial employees of a certain age "doctor"; it's nothing to get offended about, and the cops are right to do so. I've never known any profession whose members are as sensitive about honorific titles as lawyers are. What disturbed me was what Báez said next, as he was dismissing his subordinate: "And be quick about it. If this is the guy we want, I suspect he's already vanished into thin air."

15

Báez's words turned me into a pillar of salt. Why was he making such a dire prediction? I remained as calm as I could until the subofficer withdrew, and then, practically yelling, I asked Báez, "What do you mean, 'vanished into thin air'? Why should he?" The policeman's pessimism had caught me so off guard that I'd simply taken hold of his last words and repeated them as a question, without so much as a clue to the nature of his objection. Nothing, not even remnants, remained of my desire that Báez should consider me a perceptive man.

Because he had some respect for me, I suppose, he tried to be judicious in his reply. "Look, Chaparro," he said, lighting a 43/70 and moving his coffee cup to one side, as if it were an obstacle that might impede the passage of his words to my ears, "if this guy is the one we're looking for—and based on what you've told me, it's perfectly possible that he is—don't think he's going to be so easy to catch. He may be a total son of a bitch, but he doesn't seem like a hothead who does things on impulse. Not that there's any lack of those, believe me. We nab lots of hoodlums because they fuck up so bad they might as well pin a sign on their shirts that says, 'It was me, put my ass in jail.' But this guy . . ."

The policeman stopped talking for a moment, as if evaluating the suspect's intellectual capacities and coming to the conclusion that they were worthy of respect. He exhaled cigarette smoke from his nose. That dark tobacco was stinking up the place. I felt my mucous membranes getting irritated, but brainless pride kept me from coughing or blinking, as I would have loved to do.

"The babe he's crazy about goes off to Buenos Aires. He doesn't think about following her—he's not up to that. Or he is, but he needs time before he can leave home." Báez was formulating his hypothesis as he spoke to me. Along the way, he left gaps to be filled in later, but sometimes he stopped his forward progress and resolved a question with precise arguments. "Anyway, there's a good chance he'd already declared himself back in Tucumán. And the girl didn't want to hear it. So he feels enormously humiliated, he wants the earth to swallow him up. I figure that's why he stays there; he doesn't hold her back—how could he?—and he doesn't follow her. Why should he try?"

Báez seemed to assess his theories for a few moments, and then he went on. "Yes, that's it. I'm sure he confronted her, and she rejected him so fast he felt like he was on a bungee cord. And so he went into hibernation. But then comes the news that she's getting married.

He's not ready for that, and he can't react to it, either. What does that mean, 'react,' for this kid? What can he do? He lets time pass. But he's got nothing going on, and he doesn't forget her. Just the opposite. He's in a foul mood all the time. He's angry. He starts feeling he's been swindled somehow. How can it be that Liliana's about to marry some guy from Buenos Aires she just met? What about him? Is he not worth considering? He spends his days thinking about that, just as you told me—or as the kid's mother told the guy you sent to talk to her. The kid lies in his bed all day, staring at the ceiling. And then, finally, he makes a decision. Or maybe it was made long before. Did he spend months thinking about whether or not he was going to kill her, or did he know he'd kill her from the start, and the delay was just because he was getting up his courage? I have no idea, and I doubt we'll ever know. In any case, as soon as he's got everything clear in his mind, he leaves home and takes the Northern Star to Buenos Aires."

Báez picked up the telephone and bounced the switch hook up and down a few times. When the same office employee as before put his head inside the door, Báez asked him for more coffee.

"And you know what? If this kid really is the guy we're looking for, I'd bet more than I've got that he takes his time getting settled. He looks for a rooming house. He finds a job. And it's only then that he turns his attention to the girl. For a few days, he hangs around on a street corner close to her place, figuring out what the newly-weds' routines are. Their outdoor routines, that is, because he can imagine the indoor ones, and they wrench his guts. Sometimes it gets so bad he thinks maybe he should waste them both, the wife and the husband. Can you imagine how a guy must feel when he sees another guy looking happy and contented every morning, and he knows the other guy just got out of bed with the woman he's crazy for? So he goes back there the morning of the crime. He sees Morales leave, waits five minutes, and walks into the house. The main door's open all day long, because the workers in Apartment 3 have to keep hauling rubble out of it in a wheelbarrow . . . Ah, no, that's bullshit. The workers weren't there that day. So the guy rings the doorbell, and the girl answers him through the intercom. She's surprised, sure, but why wouldn't she let him in? Isn't he her childhood friend, her pal from the old neighborhood? Haven't they done lots of things together over the years? She leaves her apartment and goes to open the main door for him. Probably, as she's turning the key, she remembers the way she had to disappoint him when he declared himself a few years ago, and she feels vaguely guilty. It's strange of him to drop in on her without calling first, especially considering he wasn't even at the wedding, but that's no reason to leave him standing outside the door. She's wearing her nightdress, we know, but she's got a dressing gown on over it, so she's decent. And she's young. An older woman might have considered it improper to open the door while wearing such an outfit. But the girl's not that formal. She has no reason to be. As for the guy, the visitor, he doesn't care what she's wearing. The important thing is she opens the door. She says, "Isidoro, what a surprise," and he comes in and gives her a kiss on the cheek. That's why the neighbor woman doesn't hear him knock on the apartment door. Liliana goes to open the street door for him, leads him back to her place, and they go inside. Poor girl."

Báez puts out his cigarette and seems to hesitate over lighting another one right away. He holds off.

"Does he arrive with the intention of raping her, or does he just improvise? Once again, I have no idea, but I'm inclined to suppose he's been chewing over his plan for some time. This boy doesn't do things without thinking. He's collecting a debt, nothing more or less. So screwing her against her will right there, on the bedroom floor, is his way of making her pay off an old debt. And strangling her with his own hands is his revenge on her for having spited him and ignored him, for having left him back in the barrio, alone and sad, a laughingstock for friends and enemies alike. I'm only guessing here, but I have a feeling this Isidoro can't bear to have people laugh at him. That drives him right up the wall.

"So then? So then it's over. How long can he have stayed there? Five, ten minutes. He leaves no trace anywhere. There are a few small scratches on the parquet floor around the body—the girl tried to get away from him before her strength gave out—but he even takes the trouble of going over those marks with a cloth he's found on a shelf, because he wants to be sure to cover all his tracks. (He has no way of knowing that the yahoos of the Federal Police assigned to handle the preliminaries will trample all over the crime scene and destroy any clue that may have escaped him.) He doesn't wipe the door handle, because he remembers he never touched it. You know why I'm telling you that? So you'll know what kind of person this kid is. We found fingerprints from both Morales and his wife on the inside and outside doorknobs, but that's it. Which means that the punk was cool enough, or cynical enough—call it what you like—to go around the apartment with a cloth in his hand, calmly deciding what to wipe down: the floor around the place where he mounted the poor girl, yes; the door handle he remembered not having touched, no. And you know what he did afterward?"

He stopped talking, as if he'd really asked a question he expected me to answer, but that wasn't the case. Nor was he showing off. Nothing like that. Báez didn't waste his intelligence on such foolishness.

"When I first started working in Homicide, back when I was young and just learning the dance, do you know what I had trouble imagining? Not the crimes in themselves, not even the brutal act of killing someone. I got used to that right away. What I couldn't figure out was what a murderer does after committing his crime. I don't mean for the rest of his days, no, but let's say for the next two or three hours. I imagined all murderers shaking in their boots, horrified by what they'd done, with their memories fixed on the moment when they snuffed out another human being's life." Báez snorted and half-smiled, like a man thinking about something funny. "More or less like Dostoyevsky's young character—you know who I mean?—the one in *Crime and Punishment*. He feels remorse. He says, 'I killed the old woman, how can I go on living?'" Báez looked at me as if he'd just remembered something. "Sorry, Chaparro, I'm being stupid. You don't need a lecture from me—I'm sure you've read the book. But most of the time, I'm surrounded by brutes, know what I mean? Just to take one example, try to imagine that retard Sicora chatting about literature. Can't do it, right? Don't hurt yourself—it's not possible. Well, anyway, the point I'm trying to make is that guilt and remorse aren't that common among murderers. Not at all, really. Granted, you find guys so tormented by guilt they could shoot themselves, but lots of others go out to a movie or get a pizza. And I believe this kid, this Gómez, belongs to the second type. Since it's a Tuesday morning, I'm sure he goes on to work, just like any other weekday. He walks over to the bus stop and waits for the bus. And when he gets off, he buys the latest edition of the *Crónica*. Why not?"

This time, Báez pulled out a cigarette and lit it decisively. When I was writing about the fluctuations of my state of mind earlier, I mentioned that I'd arrived for my police interview afloat on a cloud of euphoria. Well, in about twenty minutes, that euphoria had been blown away. Not only did I feel defeated by events, which was a fairly common condition for me, but I also felt guilty. Instead of calling Báez the moment I had the intuition and letting him figure out the best way to close in on the suspect, I'd done everything my own way: I'd let myself be swept along by my spirit of initiative, I'd compelled the poor widower and his poor father-in-law to serve as my flunkies, and I'd made them kick over an ants' nest for no goddamned good reason.

In spite of all that, I tried to reassure myself. Couldn't Báez be exaggerating? And what if Gómez was much stupider than Báez thought? Wasn't there a good chance the guy had let his guard down over the course of all those months? After all, what proof did Báez have for his hypothesis? Nothing more or less than the account I'd just given him.

And another thing: Suppose Gómez had nothing to do with the crime? With childish spite, I hoped that the trail leading to him would turn out to be nothing but a mirage. I got to my feet. Báez did likewise, and we shook hands. "I figure we'll have some news tomorrow," he said.

"All right," I replied, in a tone that might have sounded unnecessarily curt.

"I'll call you."

I left his office pretty agitated, or at least uneasy, and walked back to the Palace of Justice. Although it was contemptible of me, I was more concerned at that moment about not looking like a bungler than about grabbing the son of a bitch who'd done the crime, whether it was Gómez or some other creep.

A little before seven o'clock that evening, the telephone in the clerk's office rang. It was Báez. "Leguizamón's here with his report."

"I'm listening." My wounded-child attitude was absurd, but I couldn't shake it. Besides, I wasn't ready for the call. I'd thought it wouldn't come until at least the following day.

"All right. Let's begin with the bad news. Three days ago, Isidoro Gómez disappeared from the rooming house in Flores where he'd been staying since the end of March. 'Disappeared' is a figure of speech; he paid what he owed in full and left without giving a forwarding address. Same thing with his job. We located the worksite: a fifteen-story building on Rivadavia Avenue, in the middle of the Caballito barrio. The foreman told

Leguizamón that Gómez was a phenomenal kid. Not much for conversation and sometimes unpleasant, but reliable, neat in his work, and sober in his habits. Just a little jewel. But according to the foreman, Gómez came to him a few mornings ago and told him he was going back to Tucumán, because his mother was very sick. The foreman paid him off and told him to come back and see him if he ever returned to Buenos Aires, because he was very satisfied with him."

There was a moment of silence. Although I dearly wanted to hurl the typewriter, the pencil holder, the case file I was working on, and the telephone, I bit my lip and waited.

"And finally, the good news. We can start operating on the assumption that this is our guy, and that he ran because he knew we were tracking him. Leguizamón brought me an outstanding piece of information. The foreman keeps all the workers' punch cards from the on-site time clock. Gómez worked at that building site for eight months. Want to guess how many times he was late? Two. Once by ten minutes, and once by two and a half hours. You know when that second time was? The day of the crime."

"I understand," I said, the gruffness finally gone from my tone of voice. I've never been a bad loser. "I appreciate the information, Báez. I'll use it to bring the case up to date right away, and I'll let you know what documents to send me."

"All right, Chaparro. Good-bye."

"Good-bye. And thanks," I added, as though making amends.

I was about to hang up when I heard the voice on the other end of the line speaking again. "Ah . . . one question," Báez said. He sounded doubtful. "How did you figure this Gómez boy could be our guy? I know the idea came to you when you were looking at the photographs, but what was it in particular that drew your attention to him? Because I've got to tell you, Chaparro, that was a fine catch, it really was. You might just have put your finger on the murderer."

Obviously, Báez was a good fellow. Was his praise sincere, or was he just trying to make me feel less guilty and ridiculous? I weighed my response carefully before I spoke. "I don't know, Báez. I suppose it was the way he looked at the girl, with that sort of long-distance adoration. I don't know," I said, repeating myself. "I guess when there are things you can't say, the words have to come out through your eyes."

Báez didn't answer right away. Then he said, "I understand. I couldn't have expressed it better. You're good with words, Chaparro. You could be a writer, you know?"

"Don't fuck with me, Báez."

"I'm not fucking with you. I'm serious. Well, look, after we get your updated report, I'll call you."

I hung up the telephone with a click that resounded in the silence of the clerk's office. I looked at the clock. It was very late. I picked up the receiver again, dialed the number of the bank where Morales worked, and asked the night guard to deliver an urgent message: as soon as Morales arrived, the guard was to tell him to come to the court so he could sign a statement. The guard promised to pass on the message.

Once again, the sound of the telephone switch hook. I walked over to the bookcase on whose highest shelf, several months previously, I'd camouflaged the Morales case. Standing on tiptoe, I yanked at the dossier, which came down to me in a cloud of dust. I went back to my desk. I didn't go through the case from the beginning again but went straight to the last proceeding. It was a court order from the previous June, directing that a supplementary autopsy report—on the visceral examination—be added to the case file. I checked the calendar, inserted a sheet of paper with the letterhead of the National Judiciary into the typewriter, and began to type out a new document, giving it a fictitious August date.

I hadn't lied to Báez when I answered his last question, but I hadn't told him the whole truth, either. Gómez's way of looking at Liliana had indeed called my attention to him, and I'd interpreted his gaze as a silent, futile message to a woman who couldn't or wouldn't understand it; all that was true. But I'd noticed that look because—and this is what I hadn't told Báez—I myself had gazed at a woman in just that way. It had been fourteen months since I'd first met her, and as I'd often done in those fourteen months, once again on that hot night in December 1968, I bitterly regretted that she wasn't my wife.

16

When I arrived in the office that morning, I had but one prayer: *Please, God, don't let Sandoval come to work loaded today*. I'd been awake practically all night. Not only had I arrived home extremely late (and then guilty, because Marcela was waiting up for me), but it had taken me forever to fall asleep. What would happen if the judge wised up to the fact that I was trying to put one over on him? Was running such a risk worth it? My nerves had rousted me out of bed very early. I must have looked atrocious, because my wife noticed something was wrong and asked me about it at breakfast.

Today, thirty years later, I remember my plan, and it's hard for me to think of myself as its author. What impulse was driving me to take such a risk? I suppose it was my sense of guilt. And then, over and above the risk, there was the uncertainty: If Gómez wasn't the culprit, what was the point of the mess I was about to set in motion? But if he *had* committed the murder, how could I look at myself in the mirror ever again until the day I died without feeling like a coward for putting my security and my job above everything else?

My practical problem wasn't due to the fruitless search for Isidoro Gómez; I'd been in trouble ever since the moment, several months previously, when I'd foolishly broken the rules to avoid sealing the case. At the time, I'd imagined that the judge, once the culprit was under arrest, would be so pleased that he wouldn't bother me about having kept the file active. On the contrary. A round of sufficiently histrionic and cloying flattery, attributing to him all the merits of the capture, would make him abandon his zeal for correct procedure.

But now I'd come too far to turn back, and it was here that I needed Sandoval. That is, I needed the inspired, shrewd, quick-witted, intrepid Sandoval. If I got the drunken Sandoval, I was fucked. By good fortune, while I was sunk in my meditations, in he came, fresh as a May morning, fragrant with lavender, and shining like the sun. I stopped him on his way to his desk and gave him a brief overview of my plan. He was, without a doubt, a brilliant guy. He understood the setup before I was through explaining it. And he was loyal, because he agreed without the least hesitation to join me in my swindle.

Then Morales himself showed up. Without letting him get past the reception area, I had him sign an addendum to his sworn statement. I gave him no details, told him I'd explain what was going on later, and sent him away. Hours passed. When Judge Fortuna Lacalle finally made his entrance into the clerk's office, I remembered my mother's ploys for overcoming anxiety and commended myself to the Holy Spirit. As always, Lacalle looked impeccable: dark suit, sober tie, breast-pocket hand-kerchief playing off against the tie, slicked-down hair plastered to his skull, suntanned skin. I believe observ-ing him led me to develop my theory that stupid people are better preserved physically than others because they aren't worn down by existential angst, to which those with some semblance of mental clarity are necessarily subject. I have no conclusive proofs of this notion, but the case of Fortuna Lacalle always struck me as evidence of the most blindingly obvious sort.

Princely in mien, as always, he sat in my chair and took his Parker fountain pen out of the inside pocket of his jacket. Theatrically exaggerating my own ges-tures, I began to pile case files on the desk, as if giving him to understand that he was going to spend the next two or three hours of his life signing documents. Thank God it was Thursday—he played tennis every Thurs-day at six—which meant that from about three o'clock on, he would be seized by growing impatience with anything that might deter him from his high purpose. Realizing at once the implications of so many files, he opened his eyes wide and made a remark, intending to be funny, about how fast his staff in this clerk's office did their work. I smiled and started passing him cases

with documents that needed signing, presenting each
of them with a florid commentary on their contents. It
was useless—or let's say redundant and superfluous—
information, but the magistrate was too stupid to notice
the wool I was pulling over his eyes.

It was then that Sandoval appeared for the first time,
showing his face from behind the bookcase that gave my
desk a certain minimal privacy. "Your Honor," he began,
addressing Fortuna Lacalle in a tone midway between
unctuous and ironic, but at the same time sufficiently
confidential for the judge to feel like an accomplice rather
than a victim. "When are we going to see you driving a
Dodge Coronado like your colleague Judge Molinari?"

The judge considered him cautiously. Though a block-
head, Fortuna Lacalle had the preservation instinct that
people like him develop to deal with complicated and
hostile realities, and Sandoval, however one looked at
him, belonged to the elusive world of the complex. *He's
going to ask him to repeat the question. He's going to ask
him to repeat it,* I told myself. With a rapid movement I
grabbed the Morales case and opened it directly to page
208, which I had bookmarked.

"What are you saying, Sandoval?" Fortuna Lacalle was
blinking and paying much more attention to my assistant than to the case I'd placed in front of him.

"A writ ordering that the case be reopened, Your
Honor," I murmured, as if I didn't want such a trivial

matter to interrupt the conversation the judge was con-
centrating on.

"Yes, yes," he said, not looking at me.

"Nothing important, Your Honor," Sandoval said,
giving him a roguish smile. "I thought you'd already
seen Judge Molinari's new car. You haven't?"

Lacalle was striving to respond both quickly and clev-
erly, but to succeed at even one of those goals would require great effort from him; achieving both at the same
time was simply impossible, yet he seemed eager to give
it a try. Since an undertaking of such proportions consumed all his intellectual energy, paying attention to
what he was signing proved to be quite beyond his ca-
pabilities. He therefore affixed his ornate signature to a
writ dated July 2, which did indeed order the reopening
of the sealed case at page 201, but which also, in passing, directed the court investigator to secure an addendum to the sworn testimony given by Ricardo Morales.
I pulled the document away from him as soon as he finished signing it—I didn't want him, by some miracle, to
latch onto the fact that he was signing a court order dated
almost four months ago.

"No, I didn't know about it . . . a Coronado?"

"A Coronado, Your Honor. Electric blue . . ." Sandoval smiled absently, as though enthralled by the
memory. "A treat for the eye. Black leather upholstery.

Chrome details . . .Seriously, you haven't seen it, Your
Honor?"

"No. To tell you the truth, it's been a long time since I
had lunch with Abel."

Perfect, I thought, he's got him on the ropes. Sandoval could be cruel with people he didn't like, and the
way he used that cruelty to undermine his opponents
with their own weaknesses was brilliant. As I've repeatedly pointed out, Fortuna Lacalle was an imbecile who
gave himself the airs of an eminent jurist, but over and
above his self-regard, he was dyspeptically envious of
judges who actually deserved their high office. Molinari
was such a judge, and Fortuna Lacalle's desperate wave—
calling Judge Molinari by his first name, as if the two of
them were good friends, as if pretending to a familiarity
that didn't exist—corroborated my belief that our examining magistrate was mad with envy.

I decided to move on to Act Two. I placed before Judge
Lacalle a deposition in which Morales mentioned his
suspicions about Gómez, suspicions based on some fictitious threatening letters that his wife, also fictitiously,
had received before the murder; they'd supposedly been
sent by the rejected lover and later conveniently destroyed by the couple. I'd drafted the document the previous night, Morales had signed it earlier that day, and
now it was attached to the end of some other case. "This

is a witness statement in the Muñoz case, the one concerning the series of frauds," I lied.

"Ah . . . how's that investigation going?"

We're in for it, I thought. Now, for some reason, he was interested in the case. What could I tell him? What could I invent, after removing acts from one case and attaching them to another? And how was I going to justify that witness statement, which I'd made up out of nothing?

"You still have the Falcon, don't you, Your Honor?" Sandoval came to my aid.

"Yes, of course," Lacalle answered, intending to sound gruff.

"Right, right . . . because . . . what model is it? '63? '64?"

"It's a '61." Lacalle was almost curt, but he immediately tried to soften his response: "It's given me so much satisfaction I can't bring myself to part with it."

Sandoval was an artist. We'd laughed behind the judge's back a thousand times, not because of his '61 Falcon (after all, Sandoval and I belonged to the perpetual pedestrian category), but because the vehicle was, for Fortuna Lacalle, a source of suffering, of private anguish. He'd have given an ear for a new car (assuming he could find someone crazy enough to accept the exchange). On his salary, he should have been able to afford such a purchase, but his wife and their two daughters had spending habits befitting princesses, so much so that the poor judge had to fend off the specters of insolvency month after month. Fortuna Lacalle's transparent face showed me that he was caught up in the mental enumeration of all that he could buy if his women hadn't abandoned themselves so totally to consumerism. And the Dodge Coronado, I figured, stood at the top of his list.

I quickly turned the page. Next came official letters, with copies, to the Federal Police and the police of Tucumán Province, directing them to mount a search for Gómez. The letters were dated in October and had been sent again in November. I'd already made those arrangements with Báez. Lacalle signed the documents as if they were receipts from the cleaners.

"You know what?" Sandoval said. He was inspired. "I'm actually not sure Judge Molinari made a good choice with that Dodge." Sandoval moved his hands as if uncertain how to present his dilemma. "You're a connoisseur, Your Honor, you know a lot about this . . ." Sandoval stopped and then apparently decided to trust the judge's intellectual honesty and wisdom. "Which would you choose? A Dodge Coronado or a Ford Fairlane?"

You're a connoisseur, you know a lot about this, I repeated to myself. Sandoval was a genius. Fortuna Lacalle, in reality, didn't know a lot about anything: not automobiles, not the law, not anything else. But since one of the things he didn't know was that he didn't know anything, he enthusiastically launched into a disquisition, for the

benefit of all present, on the innumerable virtues of the
Ford Fairlane and the unpardonable drawbacks of the
Dodge Coronado, thus demonstrating tangentially and
as it were in passing that Judge Molinari wasn't so perfect
after all. He spoke for ten minutes and even made a drawing of—if I understood correctly—the linkage between the
gear shift lever and the gearbox in both cars.

It was marvelous. By the time he stopped talking non-
sense, Judge Fortuna had signed off on a document acknowledging receipt of the police report (drawn up by
Báez, working against the clock, and sent to me that very
morning), according to which the present whereabouts
of Isidoro Antonio Gómez were unknown. Furthermore,
the judge had put his name to a writ ordering that the
request for an investigation into the subject's present
place of residence remain in force, with a view to ob-
taining a statement from the said subject, and he'd also
signed the new official letter to the Federal Police that
followed the extension of the investigation. Sandoval,
who was leaning against a bookshelf and pretending to
be absorbed in His Honor's passionate discourse, spotted my relieved expression and knew the mission had
been accomplished. However, since he was a sensitive
guy, he didn't want to cut Fortuna Lacalle's lecture short,
and so he let the magistrate expound for another two or
three minutes. Eventually, Sandoval thanked him for
his time: "Well, Your Honor, I have work to finish, so I'll

take my leave," and then, shaking his head from side to side in admiration, he added, "You sure know all there is to know about automobiles, Your Honor."

The judge shut his eyes and smiled with a look on his face that was supposed to express modest acknowledgment of the compliment. To make his muddle complete, I then laid another twenty or twenty-five insignificant documents on the desk before him for his signature.

When Fortuna returned to his office, I collected all the proceedings I'd scattered around in different dossiers, ordered them correctly, and placed them in the Morales case file. Now they'd all been signed by the examining magistrate, but they needed to be countersigned by the clerk, and with him it wasn't possible to apply the same strategy. He and the judge were fools in equal measure, true, but I didn't want to press my luck that far. I decided to put my trust in Pérez's basic nature: he was a pusillanimous fellow, and I was sure he'd go along uncomplainingly with any official piece of paper that bore his boss's signature. So that very afternoon I brought him the Morales case as well as the other twenty or so files whose latest decrees I'd just had Fortuna sign off on. I knew, of course, that there was a chance the clerk might catch on to my maneuver. What would so many proceedings, dated in a sequence going back several months, be doing in a dossier like that unless they were part of a maneuver conducted behind his back?

But for that eventuality, I had an ace up my sleeve.
Should Clerk Pérez go so far as to question my good
faith, or should he suspect that there was something
fishy about the bundle of fake documents that Fortuna
Lacalle had just signed, I was going to move directly to
blackmail: I would declare my readiness to tell half the
Judiciary how enviably assiduous he was in his devotion
to the public defender attached to Section No. 3 in the
Federal Criminal and Correctional Court, a lady neither
his legitimate spouse nor the affectionate mother of the
two healthy lads enshrined in the photograph on his
desk. Fortunately, that wasn't necessary. Without a complaint, he wrote his name after every "Before me" that
appeared under the signature of Judge Fortuna Lacalle,
the automotive expert. When it was over, I collapsed
in my chair, exhausted from nervousness. Sandoval
came up to me with a smile on his face and offered the
philosophical reflection he employed only in exceptional and solemn circumstances: "As I have frequently
maintained, my estimable friend Benjamín, on the day
when the assholes of the world throw a party, those two
will welcome the others at the door, serve them refreshments, offer them cake, lead them in toasts, and wipe
the crumbs from their lips."

First and Last Names

Chaparro pulls the finished sheet out of the type-writer with sufficient force to free the page from the platen without tearing the paper and then rereads what he's just written, smiling at the last words. It's a pleasure for him to exercise his memory. He thought he'd totally forgotten what Sandoval said, the sentence at the end of the chapter about "the day when the assholes of the world throw a party," but now the words have risen to the surface, along with a whole string of other memories of Chaparro's past and of the people with whom he lived it.

He stands up and makes a characteristic gesture: using the index finger and thumb of his left hand, he takes hold of the bridge of his nose at the top, almost at the level of his eyes, and squeezes until he feels a twinge of pain. He got in the habit of doing this during his years in the court, when he'd rise from his chair after a long stretch of time spent bending over his desk, and now he repeats the movement here, in his house, after hours and hours of putting together the memories he's sub-merged in, both his own and those of others. Man's a predictable creature, Chaparro thinks, grossly and perpetually equal to himself. He's been making that gesture and many others he doesn't even notice for more than half his life, and he'll keep repeating it until he's lying in his grave.

He thinks about Irene. Why is it he's thinking about her just now, right after thinking about his own death? Does he perhaps associate it with her? No. Completely the opposite. Irene attaches him to life. She's like a debt he owes life, or a debt life owes him. He can't die while he feels what he feels for Irene. It's as though he couldn't be so wasteful as to allow that love to disintegrate and turn to dust like his flesh and his bones.

But he can't unbury what's in his heart, either. There's no way. He's thought and thought about it, but there isn't any way. A letter? That method would at least offer the attraction of distance and thus a safeguard against the possibility of seeing her look incredulous—or worse, offended—or worse, sorry for him—as she reads his words. Presenting himself and speaking to her face to face doesn't even figure among the options Chaparro considers. He thinks a "mature romance" sounds ridiculous, but declaring his love to a woman who's been married for almost thirty years seems more than ridiculous; it seems offensive and degrading.

Common sense, which Chaparro believes he can occasionally locate inside his skull, tells him there's no

reason to be so solemn, so categorical. What's so in-
conceivable about starting a love affair with a married
woman? He wouldn't be the first or the last to do that.
And so? And so that's just it. But then again, what he
has to say to her is not that he wants to have an affair
with her. What he has to say to her, what he needs to
say to her, and what at the same time he'd be horrified if she knew, is that he wants to be with her, forever,
everywhere, and at every hour, or nearly, because he's
sunk into such a state of adoration that he can make no
sense of life without her. But when his thoughts reach
this point, Chaparro stops in discouragement, and in
his mind's eye, the Irene whom he imagines receiving
his desperate confession adopts the same expression
she does when he envisions her reading the letter that
in any case he's not going to write: surprise, or indignation, or pity.

And after that, nothing. Because after the rejection,
there will be no place anymore for even those brief moments he steals from her life, drinking coffee in her office, exchanging small talk with her, pretending he's
dropped in for nothing more or less than a simple chat
between two colleagues—ex-colleagues—who always
had a good working relationship. Irene seems to enjoy
those sporadic encounters, but once he crosses the line,
she'll have no other choice than to ask him not to visit
her again.

All of a sudden, while he's fixing himself some maté, Chaparro is seized by the same guilty desire he's felt so often before, but he immediately quashes it. If Irene suddenly became a widow . . . couldn't she fall in love with him? He has no assurance of such a thing. So it's best to leave the poor engineer in peace, let him keep on enjoying his life and his wife, damn him.

He puts the last typewritten page on the top of the pile and admires its thickness. Not bad for the first month of work. Or is it a month and a half? Maybe so. Thanks to this project, time passes more quickly. A recurring question nags at him: What's he going to call his novel? He doesn't know. He doesn't have the slightest idea.

Chaparro thinks he's no good at titles. At first he considered giving each chapter a title, but he's given up that particular notion. If he can't conceive a name for the whole thing, he's not very likely to come up with one for every chapter. He's already written sixteen, and he's got many more to go.

He's concerned about something else, too: the name under the title, his name, "Benjamín Miguel Chaparro." He finds that it sounds somehow disagreeable. To begin with, didn't his parents notice that the last syllable of his first name and the first syllable of his middle name make an unpleasant rhyme? Mín-mi. It's frightful. And besides, at least two of his names have meanings beyond themselves, and that's a problem. Take "Benjamín," for example. In Spanish, a *benjamín* is a youngest son, like the Benjamin in the Bible; it's a name not for an adult, but for a little boy, for the youngest of several brothers. Why was it given to him, an only son? And besides, it's one thing to be a seven- or eight-year-old *benjamín*, and quite another to be a *benjamín* of sixty. Ridiculous. But that's not all. *Chaparro* means "short and squat." Calling a human being *chaparro* when he stands over six feet tall seems to be a contradiction in terms. A casual browser who comes across a book by "Benjamín Chaparro" (the cacophonous "Miguel" has to go) may well picture the author as a short, fat young boy. Or is that all just too convoluted? Won't most people react more simply? Yes, but it could happen that at least some readers interpret the name literally. And then the author shows up, and the *benjamín chaparro*, the "stocky little kid," turns out to be a big, bearish sexagenarian. Too absurd.

One solution might be to publish the novel under a pseudonym. The thought crosses his mind, but he rejects it immediately. No way. If he manages to publish the thing, and even if he has to pay for a cheap edition out of his own pocket, he wants his name, be it ever so ridiculous, to appear on the cover. He has a simple reason for wanting his name there: so that Irene can see it.

17

After I'd put the official seals on the court order calling for an investigation into the current whereabouts of
Isidoro Antonio Gómez, after I'd placed the dossier in
the file cabinet reserved for cases with fugitive suspects
and informed Morales of the good news, I felt quite satisfied with my valiant intervention and safe from the
aftershocks of the tragedy. So much so that I returned
to my daily routine as the even-tempered boss, the husband home at seven every evening, the nighttime newspaper reader, the competent Judiciary functionary, and
almost forgot about the Morales case.

After a few months had gone by, however, my memory of the matter was unpleasantly refreshed. I had to
give a deposition in the proceedings against Romano
and the police lieutenant Sicora for illegal coercion
and abuse of the two building workers. The statement itself was a formality, a question of confirming
my original complaint and clearing up a few details.
But I was surprised (and disgusted) when the person
assigned to take my deposition turned out to be a very
low-level member of the office staff. This was a bad

sign: the court seemed to be taking it for granted that the case was going to hit a wall and was therefore limiting itself to merely observing convention. What more did they need to put those two worthless bastards on trial? They had my statement, the declarations of two policemen who'd been on duty at the station, and the medical examiner's report on the injuries the poor subjects had suffered. I decided to hope for the best, in spite of the misgivings that haunted me. The judge was Batista, who I thought was an honest guy, and whom I knew a little, since we'd worked together throughout the holiday period one January. Besides, as I've already said, my commitment to the case was no longer as ardent as it once had been.

Some time later, Batista himself summoned me to his office. He smiled as he received me and shook my hand warmly, and when we'd taken our seats, he told me that what he was about to say was absolutely confidential and asked me please not to divulge it, because both our jobs would be at stake. Hell and damnation, I thought. What could be so serious? I guess the judge was uncomfortable, because after hesitating for a few moments, he spit out the whole thing as quickly as possible, as if he wanted to get rid of something annoying and distasteful, right away. Without mincing words, he informed me that orders had come down "from on high" (he completed the image by pointing an index finger toward the ceiling of his office, but I didn't know whether he meant the Appellate Court, the Supreme Court, or the government) requiring that investigation into the murder of Liliana Emma Colotto de Morales be indefinitely suspended and the case closed as unsolved. He added that he couldn't be much more explicit, but that apparently this young man, this . . . Romano, my colleague, had a lot of clout in high places. When he said the part about "a lot of clout," Batista touched his left shoulder with two fingers of his right hand. He wasn't talking about the Appellate Court, or about the Supreme Court, either. His gesture unmistakably signified "high-ranking military officer." Suddenly, I remembered Romano's father-in-law, an infantry colonel, and I understood. How naive I'd been not to have taken that connection into account when I denounced Romano in the first place. What a dope. If I needed something to make me definitively disgusted with Onganía and his military regime, that was it.

"Do you want to hear some more?" Batista asked me.

I said yes, mostly because the judge clearly wanted to talk.

"I had to summon him to make a statement. You know that, right?" I nodded. "And as I'd been advised to do"—Batista looked up over his head—"I chose to take his deposition myself."

We're all cowards, I thought, *it's just a question of who frightens us enough.* When I'd ratified my earlier

complaint, they'd given some entry-level kid with the face
of a fifteen-year-old the task of taking my statement. In a
matter involving the colonel's scoundrel of a son-in-law,
the magistrate had taken the said son-in-law's statement
himself, sweating with fear the whole time.

"You can't imagine, Chaparro," he said. "You can't
imagine how this guy was strutting around. The attitude
he had. He came into my office as if he was doing me a
favor, granting me a tiny portion of his infinitely precious time. When I began to ask him about the case, he
couldn't wait to badmouth a variety of people. Not so
much you, believe me. He mostly had it in for the two
poor bastards who were beaten up on his orders. They
were Indians, they were thieves, they were crafty dev-
ils. They and all those like them should be killed and
the borders closed. And so on. To tell you the truth, I
didn't include in the written statement most of the atrocious things he said, or maybe not any, because if I had
I would've been obliged to send him directly to jail for
public incitement to crime. Just imagine."

At this juncture, the obvious question was, "So why
didn't you do that, Your Honor?" But I didn't ask it. My
stomach turned at the thought of that son of a bitch getting away with such rank malfeasance, but after all, I was
idle and pusillanimous too, in my way.

"Anyway, when I asked him about the two workers, he
denied any connection with what happened to them, and

the matter rested there. I even went so far as to tell him
that if the criminal case was sealed, then the internal
complaint would very likely be quashed, and the Appellate Court would lift his suspension from work."

Wonderful, I thought, *we'll be colleagues again.*

"But to my surprise," Batista went on, "he was totally
indifferent to being reinstated. He told me he didn't
think he could go back to a desk job, not anymore. The
time has come for action, he said, because the country's in danger, surrounded by enemies, atheists,
communists, and I don't know what else. I cut his rant
short, had him sign the statement, and sent him off. I
had no desire to question him about his plans for the
future."

The interview with Batista left a bitter taste in my
mouth. I felt somehow implicated in the injustice done
to some and the sinister impunity granted to others. But
not even then did I imagine, however remotely, the consequences those events were going to have for the story
I'm telling here, and for my own life.

"My own life." I read those words again and ask myself: What was my own life like in 1969? That was the
year when Marcela proposed that we have a baby. She
didn't ask me if I wanted a child. It was as if she extracted a corollary from what had been going on and
then spoke it aloud: "We could have a baby," she said,

one evening after dinner. We were watching the Channel 13 news. When I looked at her and saw she was serious, I got up and turned off the television, which I never thought provided an appropriate background to any conversation. But there was still something wrong. What was the problem with her? Why didn't I feel any enthusiasm for the idea of being a father? "We've been married four years now. And we'll be finished paying for the apartment next month," she added, seeing the look on my face.

Marcela's logic operated along a fixed trajectory, like a wrecking ball. We'd met at my cousin Elba's. Our engagement lasted two years. We spent our honeymoon in Mar del Plata. We had a home loan from the National Mortgage Bank, a one-bedroom apartment in Ramos Mejía, and pretty dishes from the Emporio de la Loza, the "China Emporium." The next step was the one she was proposing to me, if words spoken in such a watery tone could be considered a proposal. Of the two of us, I was the confused one. The reasonable one was her.

I could answer only with evasions. Marcela respected my position, however distant from hers. Whether she did so out of submissiveness or coldness or force of habit, I don't know. She relied on me to give her a straight answer eventually, when I felt like it. To this day, I'm plagued every now and then by the painful certainty that

I lost my chance to have a child. I was on the point of writing "to live on in a child" or "to perpetuate myself." Is that what it means to have a child? I'm never going to know the answer to that. It's another of the questions I'll take with me, unanswered, to the grave.

18

If I put off going home after I ran into Ricardo Morales on an August evening in 1969, it was mostly because I didn't want to have to respond to my wife's question (or proposal, or initiative, or whatever I should call it) on the subject of having a baby. I didn't know what to say to her, because I didn't know what to say to myself. When I left the court that day, I didn't go to the nearest stop for the 115 bus, which was on Talcahuano. I walked across Lavalle Square and sat down for a while under an enormous rubber tree, and when the cold started to get to me, I decided to go to the bus stop on Córdoba Avenue. I got to the Once railroad station around seven o'clock, a time of day when the sea of humanity was at high tide. This didn't worry me; I could use it as an excuse to wait for a train I could find a seat in, no matter how many I had to pass up.

As I was moving at a considerably slower pace than the other commuters, I shifted over to one side of the concourse to avoid being jostled. I walked along, hugging the storefronts of the cheesy shops that abounded in the station. I stopped to look at some handmade posters, many

of them filled with orthographical horrors, I observed
a couple of shoeshine boys, patient as Bedouins, and I
noticed the severe grimaces on the faces of two whores
who were starting their shift. You see many things when
you're not going anywhere. And then I saw him.

Ricardo Agustín Morales was sitting on a high, round
stool inside a little bar, with his hands in his lap and
his eyes fixed on the throng of passengers hurrying to
make their trains. Would I have gone up to him if he
hadn't spotted me first and raised his left hand a little
in a sign of greeting? Probably not. As I've already said,
once my conscience had been calmed and my judiciary
self-esteem patched up by what I considered a bold maneuver carried out under the noses of the judge and the
clerk, I'd gone back with no regrets to my simple, modest routines. Seeing Morales outside of any expected
context—that is, anywhere but his branch of the Provincial Bank or the cafe on Tucumán Street—gave me a start;
I might even say I found it disconcerting.

But he'd seen me. He'd raised his hand and produced
something that resembled a smile. So I went in, held out
my hand, and took the stool next to him.

"How are you doing?" he said. "Long time no see."

Was there some reproach in that last bit, that "long
time"? I protested—in my secret heart—such unfairness.
Why should I have set up a meeting with him? To tell him
that Gómez (who might have been an excellent young

man, after all) had disappeared no one knew where, and that I'd done everything I could? I looked at him. No. He wasn't reproaching me for anything. Facing outward, his feet hooked under the rung of the stool, his eyes still, his coffee cup cold and empty on the counter behind him, he radiated the same aura of unyielding solitude as in almost all of our encounters.

"Oh, I'm getting along," I answered, in spite of my sense that he wasn't expecting a response. "How about you?" These colloquial formalities, empty but safe, provided a comfortable way to continue the conversation.

"Nothing new," he said. He blinked, twisted around a little, verified that he'd finished his coffee, and turned his back to the bar again. He glanced at the greasy-looking clock on the opposite wall. "Half an hour more and I'm through."

I saw that it was 7:30. What work was he doing that would be over at eight o'clock?

"That policeman was right," he said after a long silence. "He didn't go back to Tucumán. My father-in-law is sure of that."

Morales spoke naturally, as if we were continuing an uninterrupted conversation, one of those where you don't have to name names because everybody knows who it is you're talking about. "That policeman" was Báez, "my father-in-law" was the father of his deceased wife, and the person who "didn't go back to Tucumán" was Gómez.

"I'm here on Thursdays. On Mondays and Wednesdays, I'm in the Constitution Square station. Tuesdays and Fridays, Retiro." Every now and then, as he spoke, his eyes followed a passerby. "That's my schedule this month. I'll change it in September. I change it every month."

A rasping voice came over the public address system, drawing out words and swallowing s's, to announce the imminent departure of the 7:40 express to Morón from Track 4. Although I had no intention of taking that train—I didn't want to stand up all the way—the final call seemed like an opportune excuse for me to begin my farewells. Morales's voice stopped me; once again, he plunged into his subject without preliminaries.

"The day he killed her, Liliana made me tea with lemon," he began. I noticed that he was using the verb "to kill" in the third person singular. There was no more "they killed her" or "she was killed," because now, in his mind, the murderer had a face and a name. "'Coffee's bad for you, you have to drink less of it,' she said. I told her she was right. I liked the way she fretted about me."

I suspected that I was going to miss not only the local to Castelar, due to depart in ten minutes, but also several later trains.

"Besides, if you had ever seen her . . ." He stared intently at a short, young guy who was passing in front of the bar but ruled him out immediately and looked around for another possibility. "Whenever my father watched a fashion show or a beauty contest on television, he'd say that the only way to tell whether those girls were really beautiful or not would be to see them when they got out of bed in the morning, without makeup. I never told her this, but the first thing I did when I woke up every morning was to look at her to see if the old man's theory held up. And do you know, he was right? At least when it came to Liliana."

The dreadful voice came through the loudspeakers again to announce the 7:55 train to Castelar, making all stops. I recalled the young woman's features, and I thought he wasn't exaggerating about her beauty. By then, I was just about guaranteed to get home extremely late, but I didn't feel like moving quite yet—at least, not until I could put a name to the emotion I felt, to the feeling that was steadily growing inside me. Compassion? Sorrow? No. It was something else, but I couldn't manage to identify it.

"You know what's the worst of all?"

I looked at him. I didn't know what to say.

"It's that I'm forgetting her."

His voice quavered. I didn't make the mistake of interrupting him.

"I think about her. I think and think about her, all day long. I wake up during the night remembering her, and I stay awake remembering her. But what's happening is that I tend to remember the same things. The same images. So what am I really remembering? Her, or the memory of her I've built up in the little more than a year that she's been dead?"

Poor guy. Why couldn't I get past that "poor guy" in my thoughts about him? It was a worthless label.

"I thought about killing myself, you know? Sometimes I get up in the morning and ask myself why the hell I'm still alive."

At that point, I too was asking myself why I was still alive. How could I reply to him? And at the same time, how could I keep quiet after such a confession, in the face of such distress? I said the first—or only—thing that came to mind: "Maybe you're still alive so you can get your hands on the son of a bitch who killed her." Then I thought it over and felt obliged to add, as if distancing myself from his fanatical certainty, "Whether it's Gómez or somebody else."

Morales considered my response. Either automatically or methodically, he continued to look at the people passing by on their way to the train platforms. After a while he answered me: "I think so. I think that's why."

We both fell silent. If these private stakeouts were what was keeping him alive, that was already a plus. In any case, however, his efforts were doomed to failure. If Gómez was innocent, he couldn't be blamed for anything. And if he was the murderer, it seemed to me very unlikely that we'd ever be able to arrest him. The guy knew he was being sought, and even if he was careless, it would be practically impossible to pick him out in that sea of people. Seen in this light, Ricardo Agustín Morales's stubborn train-station vigils seemed touchingly naive.

I asked him, just to say something, "Do you still live in Palermo?"

"No. I still have the apartment, but I'm living in a rooming house in San Telmo. It's closer to my work and . . . this," he added, as if he found it difficult to come up with a name for the extravagant hunt he was on.

I told him good-bye and assured him that I'd call him if there was any news. While we were shaking hands, he looked at the clock and saw that it was time for him to go, too. He took out a crumpled banknote and laid it on the bar. We went out together, but after a few steps he made it clear to me that he was going in the opposite direction. We shook hands again.

I walked to the platforms. At the entrance a guard punched my pass. Another train I could take was about to leave, this one an express to Flores, Liniers, and Morón, and then making all stops. There were no free seats, but I got on anyway. I'd decided that I had to get home as soon as possible. Although I wasn't completely sure, I thought I'd succeeded in identifying what I'd felt while I was listening to Morales.

It was envy. The love that man had known awakened enormous envy in me, an emotion beyond the pity I felt for him because his love had ended in tragedy. Clinging, not very gracefully, to one of the white hoops that hung over the aisle and swaying back and forth with the move- ments of the train, I knew I was going to walk home from the station and tell Marcela we had to talk and announce my decision to separate from her. She'd probably stare at me in surprise; I had no doubt that such a move would fall well outside the logical sequence of stages in the life she'd planned for herself. I was going to regret it, be- cause I've never liked hurting other people, but I'd just come to the realization that I was hurting her more by staying with her.

When I got home, the table was set and Marcela was waiting for me. We talked until two in the morning. The next day, I put some things into a couple of suitcases and went looking for a rooming house. I took care, however, to avoid the neighborhood of San Telmo.

19

More than two and a half years passed from that day until Monday, April 23, 1972, at 4:45 in the afternoon, when the conductor Saturnino Petrucci hit the switch that closed the doors on the train departing from Track 2 of the Villa Luro station. Petrucci heard the whoosh and snap and saw the incredulous look on the face of a fat, matronly lady as the door slammed shut in front of her nose. Leaning half his body out of the car, the conductor caressed the button with the lettering that read DEPARTURE SIGNAL, but he didn't press it; instead, he pressed the one marked OPEN. There was another pneumatic click, and all the doors in the train slid open again. Thrilled, the woman made a little skip from the platform to the car and sank down immediately into an empty seat.

Saturnino Petrucci, the conductor—gray uniform, thick salt-and-pepper mustache, imposing belly—congratulated himself on not having stooped to the gratuitous cruelty of leaving the fat lady huffing on the platform. How could it even have occurred to him to pull such a rotten trick? The answer to that question was embarrassing, but extremely clear. It had occurred to him as a way of taking revenge. Not on the fat woman, whom he didn't know, but on the world in general. He wanted revenge on the world because he blamed it for the nasty mood he'd been in since the afternoon of the previous day, a Sunday, to be exact. And the proximate cause of his spleen had been nothing more or less than the latest defeat suffered by his favorite soccer team, the Racing Club de Avellaneda. In other words, he'd been on the point of causing a poor woman great inconvenience because of soccer, because of *futból*, that eternal source of joy and torment.

Petrucci felt like an idiot for being so bitter about a soccer team's performance, but feeling like an idiot did nothing to relieve the bitterness. Almost the opposite, in fact; feeling like an idiot only deepened his gloom. A great load of illegitimate, dirty, and undeserved grief was too much to bear for even such a broad-shouldered, die-hard soccer fan as he was. Wouldn't they ever return, the golden years of his youth, when Racing practically grew tired of winning championships? He considered himself a patient, undemanding man. He didn't want to be like those unbearable River Plate supporters, who needed victory after victory to be satisfied. He would have been content with much less. But even "José's team," the team managed by Juan José Pizzuti, was starting to become a distant memory. How many years had it been since Cárdenas's goal and the World Cup? Five. Five long

years. Would another five pass without a championship
for Racing? Or another ten? Good God. He didn't even
want to think about it, as if the mere thought might at-
tract the evil eye and more bad luck.

That Monday had begun with all the repercussions of
the previous day's defeat: the newspaper headlines, the
jokes in the stationmaster's office, the mocking looks
from a couple of engineers. The black fury that had risen
in him, slowly distilled and barely contained, had almost
turned the fat lady into his victim. He looked out the window. He'd be on this train until the end of the line—the
Once station—and then he'd return on the express. He exhaled through his teeth. He'd reached the level of serenity necessary to spare the woman his senseless revenge,
but his foul mood persisted. He didn't want to go home
in such a bad temper, because he was a good father and a
good husband. He therefore opted to work out his anger in
the most honest way he knew: by going after fare dodgers.

He snatched his ticket punch out of his belt, called
out, "Tickets, passes, riding permits," in a singsong
voice, drawing out the last syllables of the words, and
turned to the comparatively few passengers in the car
with him. Experienced at his job, he gave all the men a
quick once-over. Women rarely traveled without a ticket.
There were only six or seven scattered males sitting in
the green leatherette seats. Several of those passengers
reached for their pockets, but two stood up and began

to walk down the aisle to the car behind them. In no hurry, the conductor punched a young mother's white-and-orange ticket; he didn't need to follow the fugitives with his eyes. A quick glance told him that one of them was wearing a sheepskin coat and the other, a short fellow with black hair, a blue jacket. The train was slowing down. Thanking an old man who showed him his pass, Petrucci made his way to the doors, inserted a key into the panel, pressed the OPEN button, and stepped down onto the platform in the Floresta station. The only thing he had any interest in doing there was to locate the two deadbeat riders, who'd temporarily scuttled out of his sight. He spotted one of them right away: the guy in the sheepskin coat got off the train, played dumb, walked over to a tree, and leaned against it. Petrucci favored him with his indulgence. The punk had left his train, and that was enough for the conductor. But what about the other one, the little pecker in the blue jacket? Where was he? Petrucci felt the fury that had simmered inside him all day long boil up again. Was this twerp trying to be a wise guy? He didn't find the conductor's fierce aspect and obvious experience sufficiently intimidating? He felt safe simply because he'd moved to another car? In short, he was taking him for an asshole? Perfect.

Petrucci closed the doors, activated the departure signal, waited for the train to start moving, and released the door he'd blocked with his foot. Then, sensing that it would be a good idea for him to have his hands free, he put away his ticket punch and the key to the door control panel. He began to walk through the car, swaying slightly from the effects of inertia. When he got to the next car, a glance sufficed to tell him that the object of his search wasn't in it. Petrucci went on to the car after that one, but the blue jacket wasn't there, either. The conductor smiled. The idiot had parked his sorry ass in the last car. The door screeched as Petrucci flung it open, and there he was: sitting on the left, the picture of innocence, and looking out the window as if nothing at all was going on. Thrusting out his chest and swinging his shoulders, Petrucci walked down the aisle to him. He stopped beside the young man's seat and murmured gravely, "Ticket."

Why did this dumbass insist on acting like he, Saturnino Petrucci, was the imbecile? Who did he think he was fooling with that surprised look, that sudden start, that pantomime, I'm looking in this pocket, I'm looking in this other one, I'm acting upset because I can't find the thing, I'm clicking my tongue to show I'm worried? Did he think the conductor hadn't seen him run out of the fourth car before they stopped at Floresta?

"I'm sorry, sir, I can't find it."

Sir, my ass, Petrucci thought. He gazed at the young man tenderly and said to him, in the tone of a stern father, "I'm going to have to fine you, little buddy."

And then something happened. Well, right, things always happen. In this instance, "something happened"
means that the subsequent conduct of one of the persons
involved in the dispute had significant consequences
for the story the author of this book is trying to tell. The
young man rose to his feet, drew himself up, frowned,
looked the conductor in the eyes, and said, "Then you
better fine your mama, you fat shit, because I don't have
a fucking penny."

Petrucci was surprised, but his surprise came wrapped
in joy. The kid was a gift from heaven. Racing Club, his
glorious team, had gone down to defeat yesterday. His
colleagues had spent a good part of today making fun of
his sorrow. But this impertinent, foul-mouthed young
man was giving him the possibility of unleashing the
dark feelings that had been growing in him. He raised
an arm and placed it firmly on the kid's shoulder. "Don't
act smart. You're going to get off the train with me in
Flores, young midget, and then we'll see how smart you
are about paying the fine."

"The only midget here is your dick, lardass." The boy
was looking at him furiously. Later, Petrucci would say he
was caught off guard, which was not at all true. The conductor guessed, perceived, almost wished that the kid
would start a ruckus. But the blow the little shit dealt him
was so swift and so well aimed that it landed unblocked,
flush on his nose, and blinded him for an instant. The

kid shook his hand a little, as if he'd hurt it; later, the doctors would diagnose a metacarpal fracture. He twisted himself slightly in order to get into the aisle and elude the conductor's voluminous body. But when he'd just about escaped, he felt a brutish hand seize the collar of his blue jacket and spin him around deftly, so that he was facing the near window. Then another hand grabbed him from behind, by the belt, and both hands lifted him clear of the floor. As the final step in the sequence, the hands slung him against the aluminum frame of the window, which shattered into fragments under the impact of his forehead. He was a sturdy kid. Although stunned, he remained upright, and now he was free of the conductor's grasp. He turned toward him and put up his fists, ready to fight. Maybe if the man in the gray uniform had been somewhat lighter, or if he hadn't belonged to the boxing federation in his youth, or if Racing had won the previous afternoon, the fare-dodging lad would have suffered no further damage in their scuffle. But as none of those was the case, he first received a violent right uppercut in the pit of his stomach that bent him in half, and then a straight right to the jaw that left him dazed. For dessert, Petrucci served him a left hook under the ribs that made tears spring from his eyes.

At that moment, the train stopped. Happy and proud, Petrucci accepted the applause of the small crowd that had gathered since the stop in Floresta. He turned the

key in the panel to open the doors and exited with the
deadbeat rider, practically pulling him off the train by
the hair. Petrucci walked him to the police post that was
almost at the other end of the platform. A few curious
people stuck their heads out of the doors along the way as
they saw the conductor pass, driving the stunned young
man ahead of him. Petrucci spotted the duty sergeant,
greeted him with a nod, and gave him a succinct account
of what had just occurred. The sergeant took the kid into
custody.

"Here's what we'll do," the policeman said, after cuff-
ing his prisoner to a heavy wooden chair. "I'll send him
over to the station to check for prior arrests. He probably doesn't have any, but I want to fuck with him for a
while. He's got to learn to show some respect, the little
piece of shit."

"Sounds good," Petrucci said, touching his nose for
the first time. It was seriously starting to hurt.

"Shouldn't you get that seen to?" the policeman asked.
"I mean, it's looking pretty nasty."

"Yeah, he really got me good, the bastard." They were
speaking in front of the young man, who stared fixedly
at the floor.

The policeman accompanied the conductor to the
door. Outside, the train was still waiting.

"And all because he wanted to play the big guy, the

stupid little jerk." Petrucci felt the need to explain himself. "If he tells me he's broke, or if he asks me please to let him go, I might not say anything, you know?"

"What are you going to do? Kids these days, they think they're entitled."

"Unbelievable," the conductor concluded.

He waved good-bye, closed the doors, and sounded the departure signal. The train didn't start for a few moments, because the engineer was distracted after such a long wait. When Petrucci arrived at Once station, his nose was swollen and bloody. He was sent to the Hospital Ferroviario, the Railroad Hospital, where he was x-rayed and then examined by the physician on duty. "Fracture of the nasal septum," the doctor said. "You didn't pass out?" Petrucci shook his head, as if getting his septum cracked was the most normal thing in the world. "Go home," said the doctor. "I'm marking you down for four days' rest. Come back in on Friday, and we'll see how you're doing."

If fights with fare dodgers came with so much time off, Petrucci thought, he'd try to get in at least one a month from then on. Overjoyed, he went back to Once station and took a train from there without reporting to security. He had to deliver the medical documents directly to the office in Castelar, and he was feeling extremely weary. When he arrived there with his hospital certificates, some of his colleagues came out to welcome him.

"Step aside, boys, here comes the sheriff," one of them said jokingly.

"Don't break my balls, Ávalos," Petrucci said curtly.

"Seriously, macho man, they didn't tell you in Once?"

"Tell me what?"

"The kid you busted. The one who fought with you."

"Yeah, what about him?"

"You know the cops in Flores brought him in to check for priors, right?"

"What? Don't tell me that little asshole has a record."

"Better than that. The fucker's got an arrest warrant out for him. From a court in Buenos Aires, for homicide and I don't know what else . . ."

"I'll be damned." Petrucci's real surprise was mingled with a touch of retroactive fear: What if the kid had been carrying a weapon?

"So now you're some sort of guardian of the law, see?" someone else said.

"Stop with that bullshit, Zimmerman. You should see this boy, he's got a face like a little lamb. And he's wanted for murder? He must be one of those Montoneros or something like that, right?* In any case, I'm going home. I'm wasted."

---

* TRANSLATOR'S NOTE: The Montoneros were a Peronist urban guerrilla group active in Argentina during the 1960s and 1970s.

They exchanged lethargic farewells. While walking to the stop for bus 644, Petrucci figured the day hadn't turned out so bad, after all. That stupid young punk had lifted him right out of his bad mood. And the timing of his four days off was fantastic, just what he needed to finish installing the subfloor in the back room. He'd been given some horse painkillers, according to the doctor, so his nose hardly hurt. And surely, sooner or later, Racing would win a championship again, after all. He wondered how long it would be before that happened.

He took a seat on the bus. He felt something in his pocket that turned out to be the piece of paper Ávalos had handed him. "The kid's name," his colleague had said. At the time, Petrucci hadn't given it a second thought, but now he was curious. He unfolded the paper and read, "Isidoro Antonio Gómez." The conductor crushed the paper into a ball and dropped it on the dirty floor of the bus. Then he settled in for a brief nap, careful to keep his nose well away from the window. Should the two come into contact, he was sure he'd see stars, and his nose might even start to bleed again.

20

When I had him in front of me, the suspicion that I'd built a skyscraper out of thin air returned. Could this kid with the placid expression and the relaxed stance, as if the fact that his hands were manacled behind his back affected him little or not at all—could this kid be guilty of murder?

After spending two or three days almost motionless and practically incommunicado, sick from eating jail rations and disgusted with being dirty and nervous and cooped up in a cell, many people in custody are pictures of distress, their faces marked by forced submission to the capricious will of others.

Not Isidoro Antonio Gómez. Naturally, he bore signs of the confinement he'd been in since the previous Monday: the rancid odor of unwashed human flesh, the incipient beard, the sneakers with no shoelaces. There was, moreover, the cast on his right hand, plus the greenish bruise above his right eyebrow, souvenirs of his scrimmage with the bellicose conductor on the Sarmiento Line.

I was consumed with doubt. Could someone who knew himself to be guilty of murder remain so calm? Maybe he hadn't even been told why he'd been arrested and brought to the Palace of Justice for questioning, which meant there was still a possibility that he thought all this was a mere procedure, however overdone, a consequence of his having ridden a train without a ticket and fought with the person in charge of curtailing such behavior. *No*, I thought; he was clearly an intelligent guy, so he must have known he was there for some other reason. But if he was guilty, how to explain why he'd let himself get involved in such an outrageous scene? I concluded that he was either innocent or a thoroughly callous son of a bitch.

My head was spinning at a thousand revolutions per minute. If he was innocent, why had he gone into hiding in late 1968? And if he was guilty, why had he acted with such egregious stupidity that he got himself arrested?

When I'd arrived at the clerk's office that Tuesday, the day after Gómez's detention, the news was already waiting for me, and Bácz himself had confirmed it over the telephone. We'd agreed to let the guy marinate for two more days, until Thursday, mostly to give me time to figure out how I was going to go about getting a statement out of him, and also so I could discuss the case at length with Sandoval. No one else who worked with me had half his powers of discernment.

During the previous three years in the court, few things had changed. We'd been able to get the wretched Clerk Pérez off our backs—he'd been promoted to public defender—but losing our boss that way had left a bitter taste, because it appeared to confirm our belief that a certain level of congenital stupidity, such as the kind he displayed like a flag, could augur a meteoric ascent in the juristic hierarchy. As for His Honor, Judge Fortuna Lacalle, we hadn't been so lucky. He was still our judge, and he was still an asshole. But, even worse, it was 1972, and being the friend of a friend of Onganía's no longer provided a very effective push up the road to the Appellate Court. If Fortuna hadn't been able to reach his goal when the mustachioed general's star shone brightest, his current chances were practically nil. And so he continued to vegetate in his old position. The good news was that he'd recovered from his insufferable mania for showing off to impress his superiors. He let us work, signed where we told him to sign, and abandoned his pointless insistence that deputy clerks go to the crime scenes in homicide cases. This was all to the good, because in Argentina back then, the number of dead bodies lying about was on the rise.

For all these reasons, seeing that we were (as Sandoval jocularly put it) "bereft of competent leaders," he and I had sat down together to reread the Morales case, which had stopped cold in December of 1968. Now it was three and a half years later, and the court order requiring the subject's appearance had just been served the previous Monday, in the Flores train station.

Sandoval, who was going through one of the longest periods of sobriety I'd ever known him to persist in, based his conclusion on iron logic: "Even assuming he's guilty, Benjamín, the outcome's still doubtful. Unless he puts the noose around his neck all by himself, our goose is cooked."

This was painfully true. What did we have, really, that gave us sufficient cause to try him for first-degree murder? A widower who accused him (fictitiously, as it happened, because we'd invented Morales's statement to use in case Fortuna Lacalle balked at the police reports) of having sent some threatening letters that were nowhere to be found. Some preliminary formalities, turned over to me by Báez, according to which Gómez had left his place of residence as well as his job hours before the police arrived to carry out the investigations outlined in those very formalities. The time card from the suspect's job, which showed that he'd arrived at work very late on the day when Liliana Emma Colotto de Morales was murdered. Pure shit, in other words. We had nothing at all, and even the stupidest defense attorney would go before the Appellate Court and pulverize our preventive detention order, assuming, incidentally, that we could get Judge Fortuna to sign it.

Because of all those considerations, I suppose, I hadn't bothered to call Morales and inform him. To what end? To make clear to him why we'd have to release the only suspect we'd managed to identify in the course of more than three years? The very suspect that he himself was still looking for—I had no doubt of it—in the train stations, on a rotating schedule, every evening from Monday to Friday?

I had Gómez brought to the clerk's private office, which was empty. A replacement for Pérez hadn't been named yet, and for the moment, our documents were being signed for us by the clerk of Section No. 18. I preferred there to be as few witnesses as possible. I myself didn't know why, but I didn't want witnesses, and so I gave orders that I wasn't to be interrupted. I stepped into the office behind Gómez and the prison guard who was pulling him along by one arm. I asked the guard to take off his handcuffs. Gómez sat down in front of the desk and crossed his right leg over his left. He's sure of himself, this little prick, I thought. It wasn't a good sign to see him so calm.

At that moment, I heard the exterior door of the adjacent office open and a chirpy voice sing out a "Good morning" that made my hair stand on end. It couldn't be. It couldn't. Sandoval stuck his head not very far into the office where Gómez and I were sitting and repeated his merry greeting, accompanied by a broad smile. Although he disappeared immediately, I sat staring for a long time at the spot where he'd stood in the doorway. "The worthless, *worthless* motherfucker!" I said under my breath. He was loaded. Uncombed, unshaven, wearing yesterday's clothes, with one shirttail partially hanging out of his pants. That was the reason for the cheery salutation. Although I'd seen him for barely an instant, it had been enough for me to recognize a sight all too familiar from the many years we'd worked together. I tried to remember the previous afternoon. Hadn't I looked out the window and made certain he was on his way home and not bound for the Bajo bars? Or had my head been so focused on today's interrogation that I'd forgotten to check? Either way, it made no difference. We were fucked.

I rolled a sheet of letterhead paper into the typewriter, which I'd carried there from my own desk. I was leery of deviating from even the smallest of my routines. "In Buenos Aires, on the twenty-seventh day of the month of April, 1972 . . ."

I stopped. Sandoval was back in the doorway, as though waiting for me. I glared at him. He couldn't think he was going to participate in the deposition, not in his current state. Since he'd been so foolish as to ruin seven months of abstinence, since he hadn't minded shitting on something he knew was very important to me, and since his condition would no doubt prevent him from

articulating three words with more than two syllables, I
believed he should at the very least put a sock in it and let
me do what I could with Gómez. Either Sandoval read my
expression or a sudden wave of nausea persuaded him to
take refuge at his own desk. In any case, he went away. I
glanced at Gómez and the guard. They both looked thoroughly uninvolved with what was going on and heedless
of my growing desperation. In spite of everything, I had
to admit that Sandoval brought a very dignified and ele-
vated style to his drunkenness. No hiccups, no zigzagging, no staggering into furniture. The most you could
say about his exterior aspect was that he looked like a
worthy gentleman who, for reasons contrary to his will,
had found himself compelled to sleep outdoors.

I decided to ignore all further distractions and concentrate on taking Gómez's statement. I was resolved
to give him a bad time, to treat him as if I knew he was
guilty. Whatever I did, the game was up. In the coldest
and most calmly menacing voice I was capable of producing, I asked him for some basic personal information and communicated to him the reasons why he'd
been brought in. First I explained his rights, and then I
described in broad outline the elements of the case. As
I spoke, I banged away on my typewriter, the same one
I'm using to record these memories. When I finished
typing out the standard opening, I paused. It was now
or never.

"The first question I have to ask you is whether you acknowledge having a connection with the matter under investigation in this case."

"Having a connection" was sufficiently vague. If only he would let something slip out and give me an opening of some kind. I needed something I could hold on to, but I had no expectations. His face might have expressed many things, or nothing, but he certainly didn't show any surprise. He took a while to answer, and when he did, he spoke serenely: "I don't know what you're talking about."

That was it; I was done. Game over. Heads or tails, I lost. There was nothing I could do. I'd tried. I'd even leaned on the police to bring in the suspect before the public defender arrived and started giving him advice. But evidently, either Gómez knew absolutely nothing about the crime or he realized that he had me by the balls and didn't have the slightest intention of letting me go. He was going to confine himself to playing dumb and denying everything until I had my fill of tormenting him in vain.

At that point, Sandoval came in, squinting a little as if trying to focus his gaze. He walked over to me and bent down almost level with my ear. "The Solano dossier, Benjamín . . . have you seen it?" He spoke in a loud voice, almost shouting the words, as if we were separated by sixty yards instead of four inches.

"It's with the cases awaiting signatures," I snapped.

"Thank you," he said, and went away.

I turned back to Gómez. I hadn't yet recorded his categorical denial in the deposition. I didn't want to do so just yet, but I couldn't think how to proceed. I'd tried a direct attack, and it hadn't worked. Would it be worth it to try some more oblique approach? Or was I really just harassing a poor innocent guy?

"Look, Mr. Gómez." I pointed at the dossier, which was lying on the desk. "Why do you think we've kept you in jail for four days on the basis of an order to appear dating from 1968? Just because?"

"You must know," he said, and then, after a pause: "I don't know anything."

For the first time, I thought he was lying. Or was that simply my desire to keep the case from expiring altogether?

Sandoval again. What a pain in the ass. He'd found the damn Solano dossier and was brandishing it in triumph. "Here it is, I found it," he said, putting it in front of me. "Don't you think we ought to issue a summons to the expert who assessed the building before the auction? I mean, because that way we kill two birds with one stone."

Was he accumulating points to win a whack on the head? That was what it seemed like. Didn't he realize I was trying to trap the suspect, which was like trying to trap a fly in a large room? No. No, he didn't realize any such thing, not with the load he was carrying.

All I said was "Do whatever you want."

He left the office, happy as could be. When I turned to Gómez again, his small smile seemed to indicate that my colleague's intoxicated state hadn't escaped his notice. I urged myself not to let him take over the initiative, but my ship was going down, and I didn't know how to jump off of it. I just sat there, typing nothing, not my stupid questions and not his predictable answers. Then I decided to go for broke, all in, come what might . . .

As he could imagine, I said, we didn't arrest people for no good reason. We were perfectly aware that he'd been a friend and neighbor of the victim. We knew he'd come to the capital from Tucumán, filled with resentment, shortly after the girl's marriage. We knew the only day he'd ever been terribly late for work was the day of the murder, and moreover, toward the end of 1968, when the police investigation had begun to close in on him, he'd disappeared without a trace.

Now that was really it. I'd taken my last shot, and all the odds were against me. There was a tiny possibility that he'd be scared or surprised or both at once and decide to cooperate by way of alleviating the problem. I was used to dealing with idiots who, because they couldn't take the pressure of lying, or because they'd seen too many movies where the guilty got their penalties reduced by confessing their crimes, would wind up singing their entire repertoire, "La cumparsita" included, thereby allowing us to revive moribund cases. But when Gómez looked at me, I knew he was either innocent or very clever. Or maybe both. He remained self-possessed, confident, patient. Nothing seemed to surprise him— or perhaps he'd come prepared in advance to parry my pitiful thrusts.

All of a sudden, I remembered Morales. Poor guy, I thought. Maybe it would have been better for the widower if the case had been assigned to someone like Romano instead of me. Romano sure wouldn't have a problem. He and his pal Sicora could preside over one night of torture down in the police station, and by this time Gómez would be confessing to the assassination of John F. Kennedy. After all, his face was already busted up anyway. I stopped and concentrated. Was I so desperate that the methods employed by a contemptible son of a bitch like Romano were starting to seem acceptable?

Something interrupted my digressions. Or rather, someone. For the third time, Sandoval burst into the office where I was trying to take a deposition. On this occasion, he arrived without a case file in his hand. Making himself right at home, he began to rummage in the clerk's desk drawers. He even went so far as to move my right elbow out of the way, very delicately, so as not to hit me with the tall drawer on that side.

"I already told you, I don't know anything," Gómez said. Was there mockery in his voice? "I knew the girl, yes. We were friends, and I was very sorry to hear she was dead."

I looked at the sheet of paper in the typewriter and hit the space bar several times to situate my text correctly. Then I started typing pretty furiously: "Questioned by the court as to whether or not he acknowledged any connection with the events which are the subject of the present case, declarer stated—"

"Excuse me for butting in, Benjamín." Had I heard right? Was that shit-faced jackass Sandoval really interrupting me at a time like this? "But it couldn't have been this kid."

Now I'd had it. Up to here. I considered the possibility of borrowing the prison guard's pistol and filling my associate full of holes. Could it be possible that alcohol had rendered him so totally oblivious? There I was, almost going crazy but trying to cow our suspect with an image of calm authority, and there was my assistant, marinated in booze at eleven in the morning, taking up his defense. "Go back to your desk," I said. Somehow, I managed to speak without insulting him. "We'll talk it over later."

"No, stop, stop. I'm being serious. This is serious." To top it all, must he keep repeating the few stupidities he was able to articulate? "Have you looked at him?" He gestured toward Gómez with an open hand. The latter, perhaps interested, was reciprocating the attention. "This kid couldn't have done it."

Sandoval picked up the dossier, sat on the edge of the desk, and started leafing through the proceedings. "Impossible," he insisted. "Just take a look. Take a look at this. And think about it."

He held out the case file, opened to the beginning of the autopsy. Was he fucking with me on purpose? Didn't Sandoval, of all people, know exactly how much I hated looking at medical examiners' reports?

"This Colotto girl, let's see, right here: 'Height, 5 feet 8 inches. Weight, 135 pounds,'" he read, striking the lines with one finger. "You see?" He smiled an impish little smile and added, "The girl was a head taller than this kid."

The expression on Gómez's face suddenly turned somber. Or at least so it seemed to me after a brief glance, because I'd actually begun to pay more attention to my drunken coworker than to the suspect.

"Besides . . ." Sandoval paused while he paged back and forth through the file. He stopped at the photographs of the crime scene. "I don't know if you took a good look at the woman," he said, turning the dossier around so I could get a proper view of it and trying to focus his baleful eyes on me. "She was beautiful . . ."

He spun the file back around to his side. "A beauty like that," he said, "is like a miracle, out of an ordinary guy's reach." Then he went on as if to himself, in a voice that was suddenly sorrowful, "You'd have to be a real man to get to her . . ."

"Yes, you would! You sure would!" I turned my head. It was Gómez who had spoken. His features had gone rigid; a sudden grimace of contempt had appeared on his lips. And he wasn't taking his eyes off Sandoval. "No doubt, the poor sap she wound up marrying must be a very macho guy! No doubt!"

Sandoval looked at him. Then he looked at me, and shaking his head slightly in Gómez's direction, he said, "Don't pay attention. The kid doesn't understand. You remember telling me yesterday that the victim must have known the killer, because the main door of the apartment house showed no signs of a break-in?"

Fantastic, I thought to myself. It was my last scrap of a clue and I'd been hoarding it like a wild card, waiting for a chance to play it, and this cretin had given it up for nothing. I said, "So?"

Was it possible he was so crocked he didn't notice the homicidal tone of my voice?

"So think about it." The worst of it was that Sandoval looked so lively, so alert; it seemed incredible that he didn't realize how badly he was screwing up. "Do you suppose a woman like this has time, has room in her head, to remember her Tucumán neighbors and open her door to them one Tuesday morning just like that, after who knows how many years of not seeing them and not thinking about them? Not a chance, Benjamín. Seriously."

Sandoval dropped the case file on the desk and spread his arms, as if his theory were successfully proven and his demonstration over.

"Who *is* this guy?" Gómez's question was directed to me, and it sounded aggressive. I didn't answer him, because in a burst of lucidity, I'd begun to grasp what Sandoval was doing and to realize that the one who was groping around and stumbling into things was me, not him.

"But in that case, we'll have to refocus the investigation completely," I pointed out, addressing Sandoval. The doubt in my voice wasn't fake.

"Precisely," Sandoval said, giving me a satisfied look. "We have to look for a tall man. A good-looking guy, I should think, maybe a blond. Someone . . . let's say . . . someone capable of making an impression on a woman like that." Quickly switching to a reserved tone, he added, "Don't you think we should maybe have another look at her . . . at her friends?"

"Stop talking bullshit." Gómez had turned red, and he couldn't stop staring at Sandoval. The bruise over his eyebrow suddenly looked inflamed. "For your information, Liliana remembered me perfectly well."

I jumped. Sandoval looked at him with the indifferent impatience of someone tolerating the mailman who's rung the doorbell and asked for his Christmas tip. He became very serious and said, "Don't be ridiculous, son." Then he turned back to me: "And another thing. According to the autopsy report, the guy who attacked her was a big brute . . . a stud, actually. Listen." He opened the case file and read—or rather, pretended to read, making it up as he went along: "'From the depth of the vaginal lesions, it can be deduced that the assailant is a very well endowed man. Similarly, the neck bruises demonstrate that he is possessed of extraordinary strength in his upper extremities.'"

"There you go, asshole! I fucked her and fucked her good, the slut!"

In a flash, Gómez had leaped to his feet and started shouting, inches from Sandoval's face. The guard, reacting quickly, yanked the suspect back onto the chair and reattached his handcuffs. Sandoval made a movement of disgust, I didn't know whether because of the insult or because of the prisoner's fetid breath. Then he drew close to the young man once again. "Son," he said. With an expression that mingled compassion and weariness, Sandoval looked like a man whose forbearance was being pushed to the limit by an insistent child whom he had no wish to punish. "Don't go swinging at the piñata, today's not your birthday." Then he turned around to me, as though he wanted to continue expounding his theories.

"You pathetic bastard. You can't even imagine what I did to that filthy whore."

Sandoval turned and gazed at him again, with the look of a man gathering together the last shreds of his patience. "Oh, yeah? And what have you got to say? Come on. Let's hear it, stud."

21

During the course of the following seventy minutes, Isidoro Antonio Gómez spoke practically without stopping. When he finished, my fingers hurt, but except for a few words with transposed letters, the deposition I typed was almost error-free. I asked the questions, but Gómez spoke only to Sandoval, staring at him intensely as if expecting him to break into pieces or turn into a pile of dust on the wooden floor. As for Sandoval himself, he ran an expressive gamut of grandiose proportions: very slowly, he transformed his initial look of annoyance and incredulity into one that showed greater and greater interest. By the end of the statement, he'd constructed a mask in which there appeared a harmonious combination of respect, surprise, and even a touch of admiration. Gómez ended by discoursing, in breezily pedantic style, upon the measures he'd had to take after talking to his mother on the telephone and learning that Liliana's father had been inquiring about him.

"The foreman on the worksite almost croaked when I told him I was quitting," he said, speaking to Sandoval like an experienced and patient pedagogue. He'd

regained his serenity, but he didn't give the slightest indication of wanting to take back any of his earlier
declarations. "He offered to recommend me to people
he knew. I turned him down, of course—I didn't want to
give the police a way of locating me."

Sandoval nodded. He stood up, sighing. He'd spent
the whole time barely perched on the edge of the desk,
listening with folded arms. "To tell you the truth, kid, I
don't know what to say. I would never have thought . . ."
He pressed his lips together, making the face we make
when we're about to give in to the evidence. "Maybe it
happened the way you say . . ."

"It did!" Gómez's conclusion was comprehensive, tri-
umphant, categorical.

I struck the keys a few last blows, closing the deposition with the usual formulas. Then I stacked the pages
and pushed the pile toward him with a pen. "Read it before you sign it. Please," I said. Without having any idea
why, I too had adopted the calm, cordial tone Sandoval
had used at the end of his participation in the scene.

It was an extremely long deposition, which started out
like an informative statement but immediately turned
into a confession, with all the applicable legal guaran-
tees. I'd included an express mention of the fact that the
suspect was waiving his right to make no declaration as
well as his right to have legal counsel present to advise

him during any declaration. By a strange trick of fate, the public defender on duty that day was none other than Pérez, the eternal moron. Gómez signed the pages of his confession one after the other, barely glancing at them as he did so. I looked at him, and he met my gaze as he handed the pages back to me. *Now you can go fuck yourself*, I thought. *Now it's over for you, sweetheart.*

At that moment, the door opened, and in came the one and only Julio Carlos Pérez, our former clerk and current public defender. Fortunately, I was more skilled at dealing with assholes than with psychopaths.

"What do you say, Julio?" I called out in welcome, pretending relief. "Good thing you've come. We've got a statement of information here that we had to change into a statement of confession. For first-degree murder, no less. An old case, from when you were clerk."

"Ah, what a problem. I was late because there was a hearing in Number 3. So you've already started?"

"Well, actually, we've already finished," I said, as if excusing us, or excusing him.

"Uh . . ."

"Anyway, we discussed the case with Fortuna, and he told us to move ahead with it, and he'd bring you up to date on the proceedings later," I lied.

As usual when faced with any eventuality beyond the pale of his daily routines, Pérez didn't know what to do. In some part of his brain, there must have been a suspicion that he ought to take some initiative. It seemed an appropriate moment to offer him a decorous solution.

"Let's do this," I proposed. "I'll add you in at the end and say you joined the deposition after it began, and that will be that. Provided, of course," I added after a short pause, "that your defendant agrees."

"Uh . . ." Pérez hesitated. "I guess it wouldn't be possible to start all over, would it?"

I opened my eyes wide and looked at Sandoval, who opened his wide, too, and finally we both looked wide-eyed at the guard. "Excuse me, counselors," he said, prudently including all of us in the lawyerly brotherhood. "It's getting late, and if you want the prisoner transported back to the police jail, the trucks are about to leave . . . I don't know. It's up to you."

"Another day over there in the police lockup? And still in solitary confinement? That seems too irregular, Julio," said Sandoval, suddenly concerned for the suspect's civil rights.

"Right, right." Pérez felt comfortable doing what he was best at, namely concurring with somebody else. "Well, if the accused has no objection to the foregoing proceedings . . ."

"No problem," said Gómez. His tone was still haughty and aloof.

I handed Pérez the pages and a ballpoint. He accepted the pages, but he preferred to sign them with the handsome Parker fountain pen that was one of his most precious worldly treasures.

"Take him back to the station," I instructed the guard. "I'll send somebody along with the official letter to the Penitentiary Service and an order to remand your prisoner to Devoto."

While he was being handcuffed again, Gómez turned to me and said, "I didn't know there was so much work here for drunken losers."

I looked at Sandoval. By this point, we had what we wanted: a signed confession, and Gómez in deep shit. Anyone else—me, for instance, to cite the nearest example—would have taken advantage of the opportunity to exact a modicum of revenge. To remark to the lad, say, that he'd just fallen for a trick that only a conceited jackass like him would fall for. But Sandoval was beyond the reach of such temptations, and therefore he confined himself to gazing at Gómez with a slightly bovine expression on his face, as if he hadn't completely understood the kid's comment. The guard gave Gómez a light push, and he started walking. There was a click as the door closed behind them. Almost immediately afterward, Pérez left, too, saying something about another obligation he couldn't postpone. Was he still carrying on his affair with the female public defender?

When Sandoval and I were alone, we looked at each other and remained silent. After a while, I extended my hand to him.

"Thanks."

"It was nothing," he answered. He was a humble guy, but he couldn't hide his satisfaction with the way things had turned out.

"What was that part about the perpetrator being 'a very well endowed man' with 'extraordinary strength in his upper extremities'? Where did that come from?"

"Sudden inspiration," Sandoval said, laughing contentedly.

"Let me take you to dinner," I offered.

Sandoval hesitated. "I appreciate it, thanks," he said. "But my nerves are still zinging, and I think it would be a better idea if I took a little time to relax by myself."

I understood perfectly well what he was referring to, but I didn't have the courage to tell him not to go. I went out into the main office and charged one of my subordinates with drawing up the official letter to authorize Gómez's transfer to Devoto Prison, having the worthless Fortuna sign it, and delivering it to the police station where Gómez was being held. There would be time enough afterward to inform the judge of what had taken place.

Sandoval, eager to be gone, picked up his jacket and waved a sweeping good-bye to everyone in the clerk's office. Before he left, however, he carefully tucked his shirttail back into his trousers.

I looked at the clock and figured I'd give him two hours' head start. No, three. Inadvertently, I glanced over at the shelf that held cases waiting to be sent to the General Archive. Luckily, Sandoval would be able to occupy himself during his recovery with a good deal of sewing.

22

On the day following Gómez's confession, I went looking for Morales. I didn't try to see him at the bank or reach him by telephone. I counted on finding him at the Once train station. I thought it would be worthy and fitting for the poor man to learn of his great enemy's arrest precisely while conducting one of his improvised stakeouts in hopes of catching him. Although Morales's efforts had been in vain, I was sure, even after three and a half years, that he was still on the hunt. Going there to tell him the news seemed to be a way of including him in our accomplishment.

The little bar was almost empty. A quick glance through the window was enough to assure me that Morales wasn't there. As I was about to turn and go, a thought occurred to me. I stepped inside and walked to the cash register. The man in charge was tall and fat, and he looked like one of those guys who have seen everything and can no longer be surprised.

"Excuse me, sir," I said, smiling as I approached him. It always bothers me a little to go into a place of business where I have no intention of buying anything. "I'm looking for a young man who comes in here a lot, I think several evenings a week. He's got dirty blond hair. Pretty pale complexion. A tall, skinny guy with a straight little mustache."

The fat man looked at me. I suppose one of the prerequisites for running a bar in Once station is the ability to identify crazies and con men at once. Apparently and silently, he concluded that I fit neither of those two categories. Then he nodded slightly and looked down at the counter, as though searching his memory. "Ah," he suddenly said. "I know who you mean. You're looking for the Dead Man."

It came as no shock to me to hear Morales referred to in that manner, and there wasn't the slightest hint of jest in the fat man's voice. He'd simply reported an objective characterization based on certain obvious signs. A customer who comes in at least once a week, always orders the same thing, always pays with coins, and spends two hours in silence, unmoving, looking out the cafe window, might indeed seem to share some qualities with a dead body or a ghost. Therefore, I didn't feel I was being disloyal or sarcastic or excessive when I answered, "Yes."

"He's been in here once this week already, you know." He paused, as if trying to recall another circumstance that he could relate to Morales's last visit. Then he said, "It was Wednesday. Yes, Wednesday. The day before yesterday."

"Thanks," I said. So Morales was still making his rounds. I wouldn't have expected anything else.

"Do you want me to give him a message when I see him?" The fat man's question caught me when I was halfway out the door.

After a moment's thought, I said, "No, that's all right. But thanks. I'll come back another day." I said good-bye and left.

The harsh sound of the public address system assaulted me in the dimly lit corridor. Only then did I realize that the last time I'd been in Once station was the evening when I'd run into Morales, a few hours before I put an end to my marriage.

I saw Marcela two or three more times after that, when we were signing papers in the civil court. Poor girl. I reproach myself to this day for having hurt her so much. On the night when I finally decided to leave her for good, I burned the script she'd written for the way her life was supposed to go. I tried to explain. Although I was afraid it might wound her, I spoke to her of love, and I ventured to confess that I found a total lack of it in our relationship. "What does that have to do with it?" was her reply. I don't think she loved me any more than I did her, but her plan allowed no room for uncertainties. Poor thing. If I had died, I would have caused her far fewer complications. The neighbor women holding court in the beauty parlor had no objection to the existence of widows. But an estranged wife, in 1969? Positively appalling. How was she going to get her three kids now, her firstborn son, the doctor, and her house with a garden in the suburbs, and her family automobile, and her Januaries at the beach without a legitimate husband? Sometimes, the grief we can cause without intending to is astonishing. In this case, I suspect that her pain was greater than the sacrifice I refused to make to avoid hurting her. On that early evening in 1972 when I went back to Once station, a sense of guilt weighed me down, and after it came sadness. Except for the few impersonal meetings I've mentioned, I never saw her again. Did she find someone with whom she could set out once more on the path she felt prepared to travel, the one that would lead her, without surprises, to an old age without questions? I hope so. As for me, or as for who I was that evening, I exited the station onto Bartolomé Mitre Street and walked home to the little apartment I'd rented in the Almagro barrio.

23

Eventually—on the following Tuesday, to be exact—I found him. The same blond hair, perhaps a little thinner than it had been at our last meeting. The same gray extinguished eyes. Sitting just as before, with his hands immobile in his lap and his back to the bar. The same straight mustache. The same low-key obstinacy.

I told him the whole story from the beginning. I chose (or maybe it just came out that way) a calm, measured tone, much calmer and more measured than the one Sandoval and I, once his hangover subsided, had employed to gloat over our success. Something told me that the little bar was no place for such emotions as triumph, euphoria, or joy. The only part of my account where I let myself get a little more vehement, a little adjectival, a little gesticulatory, was when I described the magisterial intervention of Pablo Sandoval. Of course, I avoided quoting the two or three hair-raising phrases with which Gómez had dug his own grave, but I spoke clearly enough to do justice to the splendid way Sandoval had tricked us, both Gómez and me. Finally, I revealed that Judge Fortuna Lacalle had signed a preventive detention order for first-degree murder without objecting to so much as a comma.

"So now what?" Morales asked when I'd finished talking.

I told him that the investigative phase of the case was almost over. By way of solidifying it even further, I said, I was going to order that a couple of witnesses' statements be expanded and a few more tests made, and I'd also initiate some small legal maneuvers intended to prevent a clever defense attorney from complicating our existence. In a few months (six, or eight at the most), we'd conclude our indictment and send the case to the sentencing court.

"And then?"

I explained that a year could pass, or two at the outside, before a final sentence was handed down, depending on how fast the sentencing court and the Appellate Court worked. But I told him there was nothing to be concerned about, because we had Gómez dead to rights.

After a long silence, Morales asked, "What will he get?"

"Life in prison," I declared.

That was a somewhat thorny subject. Would it be worthwhile to point out that Isidoro Gómez, no matter how severe his prison sentence, would probably be eligible for release in twenty or at most twenty-five years? I'd kept quiet about that on another occasion and did so this time, too; I didn't want to cause Morales any more suffering. He sat sideways on his stool, facing me, heedless at last—maybe for the first time in three and a half years—of the flood of people streaming toward the platforms.

As if he were able to read my thoughts, Morales turned back to the window. His stool squealed on its axis. Ingrained habits don't go away so easily, I reasoned. But something had changed. Now he was looking at the passersby without insistence. I waited for another question, but it never came. What could have been going through his head? After some thought, I believed I understood him.

For the first time in more than four years, Ricardo Agustín Morales didn't know what to do with the rest of his life. What was left for him now? I suspected that the answer was nothing. Or, worse yet, that what was left for him was Liliana's death. And apart from her death, nothing. Something else happened for the first time that evening: Morales was the one who got to his feet and brought our meeting to an end. I stood up as well. He held out his hand. "Thank you" was all he said.

I didn't answer him, limiting myself to looking him in the eye and shaking his hand. Although at the time I didn't realize this, I had accumulated several reasons for thanking him, too. He put his hand in a pocket and came out with the exact change to pay for his coffee. The fat man behind the bar was absorbed in *La oral deportiva*, a sports talk radio show. He wasn't sufficiently aware of us to perceive that he'd just lost a customer. Morales walked to the door and turned around. He said, "Please give my best to your assistant . . . what did you say his name was?"

"Pablo Sandoval."

"Thanks. Please convey my respects and tell him I appreciate his help very much."

Morales barely lifted his hand, turned around, and disappeared into the seven o'clock throng.

Abstinence

Would that be the best conclusion for the story he's telling? Yesterday, Chaparro finished recounting his second meeting with Morales in the little bar in Once station, and now he's tempted to let his book stop there. It's cost him a mighty effort to bring the tale around to this point. Why not be satisfied? He's described the crime, the investigation, and the discovery of the murderer. The wicked is imprisoned and the good is avenged: a happy ending, of a sort. The half of Chaparro that hates uncertainty and almost desperately longs to be done with his project suggests that he's reached the perfect stopping point; he's managed, more or less, to tell the story he proposed to tell, and he feels that the voice he's found to tell it is adequate to the purpose. The characters he's created have a startling resemblance to the flesh-and-blood people he knew, and those characters have said and done, more or less, things the real people said and did. His cautious side suspects that if he pushes ahead, everything will go to hell, his story will overflow its banks, and his characters will wind up acting at their own whim without sticking to the facts, or his memory of the facts, which in this case amounts to the same thing, and all his efforts will have been in vain.

But Chaparro has another half, and a strong desire to be guided by it. After all, it's the part of him that felt the urge and made the decision to write what he's written so far. And that part constantly reminds him that the story didn't end where he's ended it, that it kept on going, that he hasn't yet told it all. So why is he so tense, so nervous, so distracted? Is it simply that he's unsure of how to continue? Anxious about being in the middle of the river and unable to make out the other bank?

The correct answer is both simpler and more difficult, and that's because for three weeks he's heard nothing from Irene. Well, why should he? There's no reason why he should, he acknowledges, and he falls to cursing her, himself, and his goddamned novel. Once again, he begins to circle the telephone, distracted from his book merely because he's busy inventing a series of more and more unlikely excuses for calling her up.

This time, it takes barely two days of fasting, insomnia, and literary inaction before he picks up the phone and dials.

"Hello?" It's her, in her office.

"Hello, Irene, this is—"

"I know who this is." Brief silence. "Are you going to tell me where you've been all this time?"

Another silence.

"Are you there?"

"Yes, yes, sure. I've been wanting to call you, but . . ."

"So why didn't you? You didn't have any more favors to ask me?"

"No . . . I mean, yes . . . Well, it's not exactly a favor, I just thought maybe you'd have time to read a few chapters of my novel, that is, if you want to, of course . . ."

"I'd love to! When are you coming?"

After their conversation is over, Chaparro doesn't know whether to be happy about Irene's enthusiasm (and about the fact that he's going to see her very soon—next Thursday—and about the way she recognized his voice before he told her who he was) or terrified because he's offered to bring her some chapters to read. And why would he make such an offer? Because he's stuck, that's why. Chaparro suspects that no serious writer would be prepared to show his work in such an unfinished state.

In any case—and this is unusual for him—he realizes that it doesn't bother him very much to think he might not be a serious writer. What's much more important is that he's going to have coffee on Thursday with Irene.

24

Isidoro Gómez languished in Devoto Prison for an entire month before finally deciding to go to the showers. In all that period of time, he hardly closed his eyes, and when he did, it was only in snatches, and only during the day; he spent his nights sitting erect on his bunk, with his fists tight and his eyes fixed on the other beds, prepared to repel any assault by his fellow inmates. For most of the daylight hours, he sat in some isolated corner or perched on the sill of one of the big, heavily barred windows, blatantly staring at the other prisoners. Throughout the whole course of a month, he never lowered his guard and never changed his aspect, which was that of a fighting cock, ready to do battle.

On his thirtieth day in Devoto, having at last made up his mind to wash, he marched resolutely—chest inflated, brow furrowed—down the aisle that separated the two rows of bunks and led to the showers. He was pleased when another prisoner seemed to move a little to one side as he passed.

Calmer now, and surer of himself, Gómez stood next to a wooden bench with gray slats and took off his clothes.

He walked across the damp floor of the shower room and turned on a faucet. The jet of warm water striking his face and streaming down his body gave him an agreeable sensation of well-being.

When he heard someone clear his throat behind him, he spun around and clenched his fists in a movement that might have been tenser and faster than he would have liked. Two prisoners were standing in the entrance to the shower room and looking at him. One of them was tall and heavily built, big as a house in fact, with dark skin, dark hair, and the appearance of a dyed-in-the-wool criminal. The other, a fair-haired, skinny fellow of average height with light skin and eyes, stepped forward a few paces and held out his right hand in greeting. "Hello," he said. "So you're finally washing off all that grime, darling? Excellent. I'm Quique and this is Andrés, but everybody calls him Snake." Quique's way of speaking was well mannered and affable.

Gómez backed up against the wall and raised his guard a little higher. His fists were tightly clenched again. "What the hell do you want?" he asked, using the sharpest and most aggressive tone he was capable of producing.

The other apparently didn't notice or chose to ignore Gómez's reaction. "Think of us as your welcoming committee, babe. I know you've been here awhile, but what could we do? Today, though, I can see you're loosening up a little. Am I right?"

"Loosen up your ass."

The blond prisoner appeared genuinely surprised. "Oh! Please, please, what manners! Would it hurt you to be a little nicer? Acting like a mean jerk isn't going to get you anywhere around here."

"What I do or don't do is none of your fucking business, faggot."

Quique opened his eyes and mouth very wide. Then he turned to his companion, as if inviting him to intervene or asking him for an explanation. The big man, who'd been leaning in the doorway, drew himself up before he spoke: "Shut your trap, shrimp, or I'll pull your tongue out through your ass."

"Stop, Andrés. Don't you start talking like that, too. Obviously, the poor—"

The blond prisoner was unable to complete his sentence, because Gómez gave him a sudden, hard push, driving him into the wall, where the back of his head banged against the tiles. He let out a shriek and slid down to a seated position. A furious grimace twisted his friend's face, and in two strides he was standing in front of Gómez, fully clothed and two heads taller. "I'm going to kick the shit out of you, you dumb little punk."

"Fuck your mother, big black fag—" Gómez's retort was cut short. With one blow, the large, dark-haired prisoner struck him down, and before he could get back up, a ferocious kick in the chest left him gasping for air. He tried to crawl away, slipped on the soapy water that covered the floor, and curled up into a ball, protecting his head and chest with his arms as best he could. The swarthy prisoner, holding on to a faucet to keep from slipping in his turn, began to kick Gómez in the back with the fierce indifference of a man booting a ball against a building. From time to time a muffled moan could be heard. Several curious prisoners, attracted by the commotion, gathered around the shower room, summoning others with their shouts to come see the show. One of the first to arrive hissed to get Andrés's attention and then handed him a large knife: "Here, Snake. Take it, man! Open him up and get it over with!" The big fellow accepted the weapon, taking hold of it carefully so as not to cut himself.

"Stop, Andrés! Don't do anything crazy!" The blond prisoner's voice was a desperate prayer, uttered as he tried to get to his feet.

"Cool it, Quique." The swarthy prisoner's voice was gentle, affectionate, ever so slightly amused, as if his comrade's distress touched him. He turned back to Gómez, whom he'd left writhing in pain, and discovered that his opponent had taken advantage of the pause to rise to a sitting position. He was holding his stomach with both hands; his back hurt him even more, but he had no way of touching it. Snake hesitated, apparently unsure whether to continue the punishment or heed his companion's pleas. Some of the onlookers urged him to carve the fresh meat with his knife.

Because Gómez's kick to his ankles was surprisingly violent, or because it caught him unawares, or because his feet were too close together on the soapy floor, Snake pitched sideways as if the ground had ceased to exist beneath him. He instinctively thrust out his arms to break his fall, but as he was still grasping the knife in his right hand, upon impact the blade sank into his palm and wrist. Now it was his turn to cry out in pain. His blond companion leaped to his aid and almost immediately stood upright again, his hands and shirt covered with blood and a howl of panic in his throat.

As several figures rushed toward Gómez, who was still on the floor, lying on his side, he watched them getting closer, and then another kick, this one in the jaw, stopped his vision.

25

Three days later Gómez woke up in the prison infirmary. It took him a while to remember who and where he was. When the male nurse saw him move, he called two guards, who without much ado sat him in a wheelchair and set out for a part of the prison that inmates seldom saw.

At the end of the little excursion, the guards wheeled Gómez into an office where a man seated at a bare table and smoking a cigarette seemed to be waiting for him. Except for a thin strip of hair on both sides of his head, the man was bald, but he had a thick mustache. He was wearing a dark jacket over a shirt with a wide collar and no tie. The guards pushed Gómez's wheelchair in front of the table, left the room, and closed the door. The prisoner didn't speak. He waited for the man to finish his cigarette. Gómez kept silent not only because of his confusion and surprise, but also because the mere act of swallowing saliva hurt his throat so much that he was afraid moving his lips and tongue would cause him intolerable pain.

"Isidoro Antonio Gómez," the other said at last, speaking slowly, as if carefully selecting his words. "I'm going to explain to you why you've been brought here." As he spoke, he played with the hinged top of his cigarette lighter. His chair must have been comfortable, because it allowed him to lean back far enough to put his feet up on one of the corners of the table.

"Son, my goal in this friendly meeting is to figure out the answer to a question: Are you an intelligent guy, or are you a hopeless moron? That's my entire purpose, nothing more or less," the bald man said, and only then did he look at the prisoner. The sight seemed to shock him very much, but then again, everything about him seemed exaggerated. "Shit," he said. "What a mess they made out of you, boy. Goddamn . . . but okay, look. The thing is, I have to make a complicated decision, and in order to make it, I need to answer that question I mentioned. Do you understand?"

There was another pause, and then he opened a notebook that lay on the table beside him. Gómez hadn't noticed it before, but now he saw that it was filled with writing.

"Ever since the cell guards rescued you in the shower room, I've taken a strong interest in your case. You got off easy, you know. If Snake doesn't give himself that atrocious cut, then the others don't call the guards to help him, and instead, my friend, he and his pals open you up, you bleed to death like a butchered pig, and that's the end of the story. You may not believe it, but I was already

familiar with your case. I didn't know you, obviously, but
I knew your case, at least the first part of it. I had to read
the rest to bring myself up to date. God, talk about co-
incidences. I know it sounds asinine to say it's a small
world, but I'm more and more convinced that it's true."

He flipped rapidly through the notebook until he found
a page that interested him. From then on, he turned the
pages more calmly, speaking as he did so. "All right, let
me come to the point. That girl you killed . . . a nasty
business, buddy, a mighty nasty business. But none of
mine. As a matter of fact, I don't really give a damn about
it. But I noticed you didn't leave any incriminating evidence at the scene, and afterward, when the police were
looking for you, you vanished completely, you just flat
stopped showing up anyplace where people might know
you. Am I right? And then you spent three years on your
best behavior so no one would have an excuse to fuck with
you. So I think about all that and I say to myself, this is
an intelligent guy. And then I read on, you see, and I find
out you got busted for fare-dodging on the Sarmiento
Line and fighting with a conductor, and I say to myself,
this guy's an asshole. But on the other hand, I consider
the fact that the boys in the examining magistrate's court
don't have anything, or hardly anything, they can tie you
to the crime with, and I say to myself, all right, he can't
spend his life looking over his shoulder, this is a guy who
thinks logically. And then I read still further, and I learn

about your deposition in the clerk's office and how you
sang your heart out like you were Carlos Gardel, and so I
feel justified in concluding, my friend, and I speak with
all due respect and consideration, that you're as dumb as
a fucking post. But I keep on reading, and I find out some
more stuff, you know? Because that's what I do, I find
out things, it's the way I am. It's how I live. And I find out
you wound up in Devoto and spent a whole month with
your ass intact, and that sets me thinking again. This kid
must be some kind of smart, I think. But then I read that
you got a visit from Snake and Quique Domínguez, two of
the sweetest guys around, and a married couple to boot,
until death do them part, the only thing they're missing
is a pair of golden wedding bands, and the best idea you
can come up with is to react like a fifteen-year-old virgin who feels disrespected, you punch out poor Quique
and fix it so Snake has to kick the shit out of you to save
face after such an insult. And listen, what I just told you
about Snake and Quique is common knowledge, even
the people in the corner bakery know it. If you didn't cop
to that after living with those guys for a month, Gómez,
I'm going to be forced to return to my earlier thoughts
about you, the most, shall we say, pessimistic thoughts,
namely that you're a total and incorrigible asshole."

The bald man paused to catch his breath and then
went on. "Gómez. Put yourself in my place. It's not a
simple call. Should I consider how much nerve it took to

try to dominate the situation the way you did? Or should
I think about what a dumb ass you were to pick a fight
with those two lovebirds, who do less harm than a mixed
salad? I don't know . . . I don't know . . . And another
thing I have to take into consideration is the fact that
you're a lucky guy. I believe some people are born under
a lucky star. You don't? I do. I think some guys naturally
have a lot of luck, and some guys naturally have no luck
at all. And the way I look at it, you were born under a
lucky star. Why? Let's put it like this: you kill that girl,
you skate; the cops start looking for you, you skate;
you're about to get killed in the shower room, you skate.
Now I know, if I want to look at the bad side, I can just
think about what an idiot you were to get yourself busted
on that train, and how your brain stopped working at the
deposition, and how you got it all wrong in the shower
room. But the thing is, over and above a tendency to act
like a jackass on occasion, you're still a lucky guy, you
follow me? And that's an important attribute in a pro-
spective employee."

He paused again and lit another cigarette, first offering one to Gómez, who refused with a shake of his head.
Then the bald man said, "You want more evidence of
what a lucky bastard you are? The fact that you're here,
son. Here in front of me, the man who could become
your new boss. What do you think? Look at it this way: *I*

need new people, and suddenly *you* land in here, within my reach, as though you've fallen from heaven."

He gazed at the young man for a long minute before going on. "And another thing, Gómez. You don't need to know the exact details, but . . . I get a real kick out of the idea of using you, because it's a way to fuck with somebody who fucked with me first, you get me?" The bald man shook his head, as if he couldn't comprehend the chain of events that had led to this. "But leave that here, don't think about it, forget it. You'll have enough to worry about with doing the work I'm going to give you and doing it well."

He took a last drag on his cigarette and blew the smoke toward the ceiling. Then he ran his hand over his hairless scalp and said, "I assume you're not going to make me look like an asshole for doing this. Am I right?"

Coffee

If there are sublime moments in life, Chaparro thinks, this is one of them. His inner perfectionist whispers that it could be more sublime still, but the rest of him quickly discards the objection, because he's afloat on an indulgent sea of happiness and affectionate serenity.

Dusk is falling, and he's sitting with Irene in her office. At this hour, the Palace and its surroundings are deserted. They've finished drinking their coffee, and Irene, after a prolonged silence during which they've exchanged questioning glances across her desk, is smiling. These silences are always uncomfortable, but in spite of that, Chaparro very much enjoys them.

He feels that something has moved, or changed, in the past few months, not only in himself, but also and above all in the woman in front of him, the woman he loves. Since the evening when Chaparro decided not to go to his retirement party and instead turned back to the courthouse to ask her if he could borrow his old Remington typewriter, they've met six or seven times, he figures. Always, as today, in the gathering twilight. To avoid appearing too obvious or too ridiculous, he made up excuses for the first two or three of these encounters, but not since then, because Irene, speaking with unusual directness, told him she thoroughly enjoyed his visits and didn't want him to come by only when he had a specific reason. She said that over the telephone, and Chaparro regrets not having seen her face while she was pronouncing those words. At the same time, however, he suspects he wouldn't have been able to bear revealing to her how much her words enflamed him. What's the proper facial expression in such a circumstance?

Not all of Irene's words sound so sweet. Not long ago, trying to deepen their complicity, he ventured to suggest that their evening encounters could lead to gossip. She answered, simply and almost haughtily, that there was nothing wrong with two friends having coffee together. This statement seems to have set them at a painful remove from each other; he feels as though he's been pushed away, compelled to retreat to a respectable and respectful distance. In his intermittent fits of optimism, Chaparro tells himself he's exaggerating, it's not so bad, maybe she said what she said as a way of soothing her own legitimate concern at the possibility of being exposed. Women know how to hide their feelings, how to defuse emotions that often explode inside men and show all over their faces. At least that's what Chaparro believes, or wishes to believe. It's as though women were condemned to understand the world and its dangers better. So it's not crazy to think that Irene, when she answered him that way, might have been carrying on an argument over his head, a quarrel with the world—that is, with everything outside of this office, which smells of old wood, and where Irene, uncomfortable or perhaps ashamed, has just smiled at him.

Chaparro understands her confusion, indeed he does, because it betrays . . . what exactly does it betray? Well, to begin with, the fact that they've run out of things to talk about. Chaparro has already recounted his ups and downs with his book; Irene has told him the latest Judiciary jokes. If they're sitting in silence now, if now, in that silence, they're questioning each other, if they don't break the silence with their questions or their mute smiles, it's because nothing's holding them there except that, except their simply being face to face, letting the time pass with no purpose other than mutual nearness, and that's what's beautiful about sitting and asking each other unspoken questions.

26

On May 26, 1973, Sandoval and I were working late, and although I had no idea of what was going on, the story of Morales and Gómez had just been set in motion again.

It was already dark outside when the door of the clerk's office opened and a prison guard entered. "Penitentiary Service, good evening," he said, identifying himself as though his gray uniform with the red insignia weren't identification enough.

"Good evening," I replied, wondering what time it was.

"I'll handle it," Sandoval said, heading for the reception counter.

"I was afraid no one would be here," the guard said. "Because it's so late, I mean."

"Yes . . . we're usually gone by now," Sandoval said, looking for the seal so that he could stamp the guard's receipt book, which the latter held out to him, indicating the place where he was to sign.

When the document receipt was signed and stamped, the guard said, "So long."

"Good-bye," I replied. Sandoval said nothing, because he was reading the official letter that had just arrived. "What's it about?" I asked. He didn't answer. Was it very long, or was he reading it over again? I asked more insistently, "Pablo, what does it say?"

He turned around with the letter in his hand, walked back to my desk, and handed me the document. It bore the letterhead of the Penitentiary Service, its seal, and the seal of the Villa Devoto Prison unit.

"It says they just let that son of a bitch Isidoro Gómez go," Sandoval murmured.

27

I was so stunned by what he'd just said that I left the paper he handed me unread on my desk. "What?" was all I could manage to say.

Sandoval walked over to the window and opened it wide. The cool evening air invaded the office. He leaned on the window rail, cursing in a tone of boundless desolation: "The goddamned motherfucking son of a bitch."

The first thing I did was to call Báez. I felt a desperate urgency, which together with a certain awkward rage made me want to contact a man I trusted and demand explanations from him, as if he were the person responsible for what had happened.

"Let me see what I can find out," he said, and hung up.

He called back fifteen minutes later. "It's like you say, Chaparro. They released him last night under the general amnesty that's been granted to political prisoners."

"And since when is that son of a bitch a political prisoner?" I yelled.

"I don't have the slightest idea. Don't get so upset. It'll take me a few days to check into this, and then I'll call you."

"You're right," I said, reconsidering. "Please forgive me. The thing is I can't get it through my head why they would let a piece of trash like that go free, and after what it took to nail him in the first place."

"No need to apologize. It pisses me off, too. Don't think this is the only case. I've received two other calls for the same reason. You know, it occurs to me it would be better for us to meet in a cafe. Rather than talk on the telephone, I mean."

"All right, let me know where and when. And thanks, Báez."

"Talk to you later."

We hung up, and I turned to Sandoval. He was still leaning on the window rail, staring blankly at the buildings on the other side of the street. "Pablo," I said, trying to break his trance.

He turned to me and said, "Looks like there aren't many things you can feel proud of, are there?" Then he shifted back to the window. I think that was the moment when I realized how much his stellar performance at that little bastard's deposition had meant to him. And the sort of medal he'd privately given himself had just been shattered to pieces. I knew that his face, which he kept turned toward Tucumán Street, must be wet with tears. At that moment, the sorrow I felt for my friend was stronger than my outrage at what had just happened with Gómez.

"What do you say we go out to dinner somewhere around here?" I asked.

"Great idea!" he said, unable to restrain his sarcasm. "You want me to teach you how to drink whiskey until you pass out? The problem is who's going to get in a taxi and come looking for the two of us."

"That's not what I meant, moron. How about going to your place? We can have dinner with Alejandra and tell her the whole story."

He looked at me like a kid who'd asked to be taken to the movies and been offered, as a substitute, a boiled lollipop. I think the devastation he saw in my face made him come back to his senses, because in the end, he said, "O.K."

We left the official letter from the Penitentiary Service on my desk, turned off the heat and the light, locked all the locks, and went down to the street. It was late and the door leading to Tucumán was already closed, so we had to leave from the Talcahuano exit. We waited for the bus, but then Sandoval told me he'd be right back. He hurried over to a flower stall and bought a bouquet. When he returned, he said bitterly, "If we're going to be good boys, we may as well go all the way."

I nodded. The bus arrived immediately.

28

Báez and I hadn't seen each other in two years, not since Judge Fortuna Lacalle's delirium regarding his imminent appointment to the Appellate Court had subsided.

"All right, my friend. The information I'm about to give you isn't to be repeated. These days, ever since they let all those guys go free, Devoto's a real mess and dangerous to boot."

I indicated my assent. I knew the policeman wasn't going to waste time with references to the general chaos that both of us accepted as an essential aspect of the reality we were doomed to live in, mutually assuming that its complexity was beyond our understanding. Báez went on, "This seems to be more or less what went down. You all transferred Gómez to Devoto in June 1972, right? They put him in one of the prison barracks . . . I don't know . . . let's say it was Number 7. A few weeks later, our friend Gómez pulls a Gómez: he starts a fight in the barracks and almost gets himself killed. It seems he decided to act like a badass with the two least offensive guys in the barracks and got the shit kicked out of him."

As I listened to Báez, I felt a certain pleasure at the thought that Gómez had suffered because he'd made a bad decision.

"But this Gómez apparently has a special guardian angel. Instead of getting stabbed, say, forty-five times and croaking on the floor of the shower room, he manages to give one of the guys attacking him a bad cut with his own knife. A big commotion ensues. The other prisoners are afraid their comrade's going to bleed to death, so they call the guards, and the guards take away the wounded guy *and* Gómez. He's not exactly unscathed, but he's saved himself. And here we reach the first curious feature of this affair, because you know where the whole incident is reported, the fight, the injured inmates, the big ruckus? Nowhere. Two prisoners, Gómez and the other guy, are pretty badly hurt, but neither of them is taken to the hospital. They're treated right there, in the prison infirmary. There's not a single administrative report, and not one statement is taken, not from any guard and not from any inmate, either. What there is—the only thing there is in Gómez's file—is an order of transfer to another barracks, dated two weeks later, when he's released from the infirmary. You're probably thinking, that's only logical, because if he gets sent back to the barracks he was in before, they'll make mincemeat out of him. Well, maybe so, maybe not. If he has to return to the barracks where they beat him up, maybe he's a lot less cocky when he gets there, and maybe he becomes somebody's sweetheart for the sake of protection, and everything's peaceful. In any case, it doesn't go down like that. What winds up happening is he's put in the barracks reserved for political prisoners. Now, this was the point where I really got confused. What relation could Gómez and his crime of passion have with militant leftists, with the FAR and the ERP and the Montoneros? And on top of that, political prisoners go before a special tribunal, they aren't tried in ordinary criminal courts like the others, you follow me? Gómez's case doesn't have anything to do with that, I told myself."

He paused to slosh around what was left of his coffee and swallow it in one gulp. The cup looked ridiculously small in his huge paw. I knew we'd eventually get to the heart of the matter. That was the difference between Báez and the other cops I knew: the others would have stopped their investigations right there, at the limit of the logical possibilities. Not Báez.

"All right," he went on. "What I've told you so far was more or less easy to find out. From that point on, everything got more complicated. First of all, I know I mentioned the special tribunals, but I don't know that much about them, I don't have much contact with the antiguerrilla section. The guys doing that work have set up something like a separate clan. They strut around looking mysterious, if you know what I mean. Then, in the second place, ever since the amnesty the other day, they've been tearing down the whole circus tent they put up, so for the time being, they're out of work. And you know how it goes—in the middle of a big fucking mess like the one we've got, you can always find someone nostalgic and resentful who wants to tell you about the terrible shit that's going on."

He raised his hand to order another cup of coffee.

"Well. It seems the government set up a little intelligence center inside the prison. I'm confused about the details, and I don't know if the unit was run by the secretary of intelligence or the Ministry of the Interior or the War Ministry. But it doesn't make any difference, because the people involved in those kinds of operations come from all over, from many different departments. Anyway, they set up this little espionage thing inside the prison so they could keep an eye on the "cadres," which is what they call the guerrillas. They were panicked by the thought that something like the breakout at Rawson Prison could happen there. You with me?"

It was like listening to the plot of a thriller, and Báez was an accomplished storyteller, but I still didn't understand what all this had to do with Gómez, and vice versa. When I asked Báez that question, he said, "We're getting there, my friend, we're getting there. But if I don't explain this first part, you won't understand the rest. So the guy in charge of the intelligence operation in Devoto

Prison called himself Peralta. He tried to infiltrate some of his men into the political prisoners' barracks. Risky thing to do, you had to be careful. It seems one or two of Peralta's guys got fingered and returned to him as stiffs. Because of that, he had the bright idea of recruiting some ordinary prisoners for the job. Does that sound dangerous? It sure was, but not for him. In the worst case, one less prisoner. In the best, a direct eyewitness. It was almost like hooking up the damn 'cadres' to a microphone, you know? Like one of those little devices you see in spy movies. Are you following me? Gómez gets recruited while he's in prison. None other than Peralta himself enlists him to do the spy work. And look, it wasn't just him. It seems there were four or five of them in all, but I'm not sure."

He paused for a moment while the waiter served us again.

"And this was where I had to ask myself why Gómez was picked to be one of the spies. That's the question that bugged me. The rest, everything that came afterward, wasn't so hard to figure out. Gómez must have carried out his assignment—after all, he's a pretty bright guy, and cold as a statue when he's not flying off the handle. A little gem like that doesn't come along every day. All right, I don't really know how much of a gem he was, but if he survived in that barracks until May, he must have been doing something right. Why not keep using him on the outside? As for getting him out, that's not a problem. No special procedure required, it just happens. The prisoners know there's going to be an amnesty, and when they draw up the lists, they gladly include Gómez, with all the honors. And if they don't, there's still no problem, because Peralta's people can just add his name. So in any case, he walks."

Báez started to pay the check, but I stopped him and put some money on the table.

"But the real question goes back to before his release. What made this Peralta decide to employ Gómez? The first thing that caught his attention was the guy's nerve, the way he went into the lion's den practically doing the roaring himself. Secondly, as I said, it's a free shot for Peralta; if things go bad, he loses nothing. And in the third place . . . are you ready for the best of all?"

Judging from the bitterness in the cop's tone, "the best" was going to be, in fact, the worst.

"Here it is. If all the things I just told you weren't enough to make the boss, Peralta, decide to use Gómez, once he asked for the particulars of the thug's case and learned more about it, then he had no more doubts. Gómez became a top choice right away. The reason was there, Benjamín, there in the case file."

Well, fuck, I thought. Could what he was about to tell me be so bad he had to try to soften it by using my given name for the first time in his goddamn life?

"Using that kid was a brilliant way to fuck you over."

His words absolutely confounded me. What could *I* have to do it? So far, Báez's story had sounded logical. Depressing, but logical. But his last remark didn't jibe with the rest, somehow. It was like a nightmare you don't think is a nightmare at first and then it begins to turn into one at precisely the moment when it moves past the limits of logic and reason and becomes incomprehensible and disturbing.

"When I couldn't find out anything more about Gómez, it occurred to me to try working from the other end, so I decided to check out his boss, the Peralta guy. It stood to reason that investigating a government intelligence operation inside a prison would be a little complicated, but actually it turned out to be not so hard. They're still Argentines, after all, and if you scratch around a little, you realize everything's cobbled together with wire. If it weren't, Peralta's description and his real name wouldn't have been so easy to find out."

The waiter picked up the money from the table and very slowly started to produce my change, as if trying to persuade me to let him have it as a tip. I dismissed him with a wave of my hand.

"It appears that he's a person around your age, Chaparro. Bald, with a thick mustache—they say it's like mine—and not very tall. He was skinny when he was younger, but now, I'm told, he's moving toward obese.

And you know what? He worked in the Palace of Justice for several years. In an examining magistrate's court. Have you guessed yet?"

It couldn't be. It wasn't possible.

"Yes, indeed. Think the worst, my friend. If you do, you'll generally guess right. He worked with you in Examining Magistrate's Court No. 41. He was the deputy clerk in the other clerk's office until 1968, when he was indicted for illegal coercion and physical abuse of suspects in custody. Nothing came of the indictment, because it was quashed from above. The guy's father-in-law seems to have carried a lot of weight—he was a colonel or a general or something like that—and he used it to get the guy a job in intelligence. Have you placed him yet? His name's Romano."

29

"No, it can't be. What bad luck!" I said several minutes later, when I finally got over my fit of furious incredulity and accepted that what was happening was, in fact, happening.

Báez was looking at me, maybe waiting for me to let him have the two or three remaining pieces of the puzzle. I spoke about the two building workers and the brutal beating Sicora had given them, practically at Romano's direction and under his orders. Báez listened to me with a mixture of surprise and curiosity, because he'd learned almost nothing about the matter at the time. He'd taken a few days off, days he'd had coming to him, and in his absence, Sicora and the other son of a bitch had handled things down at the police station. He wasn't even sure that the police authorities had ever brought charges against Sicora, as I'd done against Romano in the Appellate Court. I corroborated Báez's information about the indictment of my former colleague, namely that it had come to nothing. He asked me to wait a second, went to the back of the cafe, and talked for a few minutes on the public telephone. When he returned, he told me that

Sicora was dead. He'd died in a car crash on Highway 2 in 1971, so we wouldn't be getting any further information from that source. He snorted and added, "Actually, we're not going to get any further information from any source."

That was the truth. With the amnesty in effect, there wasn't any way of proceeding against Gómez. And getting involved with the Secretariat of Intelligence in order to prosecute Romano would be crazy and moreover useless. The two of them were untouchable.

It was all so ridiculous it almost made me feel like laughing, except that it was so evil it made me feel like crying. By bringing charges against Romano for illegal coercion and abuse, I'd given him a chance for a fabulous career—with the help of his fascist father-in-law—in the "Antisubversive Secret Service." And in addition, heaven had granted the worthless bastard the opportunity to take revenge on me. He knew that case was mine, he knew I was trying to move it forward, and he figured that if he put the culprit under his protective wing, he'd eventually be able to place him beyond my reach for good. That's what he'd done, and I hadn't even noticed, not until it was unequivocally too late.

"Poor guy."

Báez's two words floated above the table for a second before they evaporated and silence returned. I didn't reply, but I understood whom the policeman meant.

He wasn't talking about Romano or Gómez or himself or me. He was talking about Ricardo Morales, who lost every time a hand was dealt, every time the dice were rolled, every time the wheel was spun. I tried to imagine his face when I told him the news. Should I go to see him at the bank, or should I make an appointment with him at the cafe where we'd met on previous occasions? The cafe sounded like a better idea. But in any case, how was I going to answer him when he asked me, "What can be done now?" Should I tell him the truth? Should I simply say, "Nothing"?

I dropped a cube of sugar into the coffee dregs at the bottom of my cup and entertained myself by watching the white lump slowly grow saturated and fall apart. "Poor guy," I said as well. It was the only conclusion I could reach.

30

"If you don't mind telling me, I'd like to know how it was that he got released," Morales said, sounding as if nothing could hurt him anymore.

I looked at him before responding; the boy continually surprised me. I kept thinking of him as a boy, I don't know why, because that particular characterization no longer applied. Maybe it was just for the sake of convenience. I'd always thought of him as very young, ever since the first time I saw him, in the Capital branch of the Provincial Bank, where he worked. Back then, he was twenty-four, and clearly little more than a boy. But now, five years later, it was impossible to look at him that way. Not because his dirty blond hair was much thinner— which it was—or because people whom we don't see very often seem more clearly marked by the passage of time, although that appears to be true as well. Morales was no longer young, even though he hadn't yet reached thirty. On either side of his mouth, unremitting grief had dug deep furrows, which his precise blond mustache did nothing to conceal; his forehead, too, was indelibly scored. He'd always been skinny, but now his thinness

had become almost skeletal, as if not even eating could
accommodate any desire, however slight, or procure
him any pleasure, however brief. His cheekbones were
prominent, his cheeks hollow, and his gray eyes deep-
set, as though taking refuge. When I saw Morales sitting
there in front of me on that June afternoon in 1973, I understood that the brevity or longevity of a human being's
life depends most of all on the amount of grief that person is obliged to bear. Time passes more slowly for those
who suffer, and pain and anguish leave definitive marks
on their skin.

As I've said, the young man surprised me. In the
preceding days, I'd pondered whether I should summon him to the cafe or seek him out at his bank, but
the memory of our first interview, when Báez and I
had gone to tell him what we told him, had remained
so vivid that I didn't feel capable of devastating him
again in the same way and in the same place. So I called
him up and arranged to meet him in the cafe at 1400
Tucumán Street. I expected my call to surprise him. For
one thing, we'd had no communication for nearly a year.
What could the deputy clerk from the examining magistrate's court be doing, calling him at his work? Wishing
him a happy birthday? And why would we be meeting
in that same bar? Morales knew perfectly well that it
was going to take two or three years before the final ver-
dict in the Gómez case could be handed down and the

dossier turned over to the sentencing court. If I wanted to fill him in on some minor detail of the case—the formal completion of the indictment or something like that—it wouldn't make sense to arrange a face-to-face meeting. How would any normal person react to such an unexpected and mysterious telephone call? He'd request more information, solicit details, ask questions along the lines of Is it serious? or Can you tell me a little more, just so I can rest easy? Morales did none of that. He listened to me, hesitated a few seconds over whether he could leave work early the following day or would Thursday be better, spoke very briefly with a colleague, and then declared, "Tomorrow's fine." And now there we were, sitting at one of the tables in the back on a chilly Wednesday afternoon.

I'd decided to come to the point as soon as possible, so I said, right away, "I called because I have something serious to tell you, Morales." How could I be so foolish as to feel guilty about what had happened? What did I have to do with the way things had turned out?

"If you called me here so you could tell me they released Gómez, don't bother. I'm already informed."

"What do you mean, 'informed'?" was my ridiculous reaction. I found it uncanny and incredible that Morales already knew what I had planned, uselessly enough, to break to him. But I didn't back off.

"Yes, I already know about it," he reiterated.

I kept quiet then, but I longed to learn how he'd found out.

"It's not such a mystery, Chaparro," he added matter-of-factly. "A few days after the amnesty, a list of the released prisoners was published in the newspaper."

"And what made you think that Gómez's name could be on such a list?"

It was Morales's turn to hesitate for a few moments before answering, as if the question had surprised him. Eventually he made an ironic face and spoke: "Do you want me to tell you the truth? I simply applied the existential principle that governs my life."

I glanced at him quizzically.

"It's my maxim: Everything that can go bad is going to go bad. And its corollary: Everything that seems to be going well will turn, sooner or later, to shit."

Wasn't that the first time Morales had allowed himself to use bad language in a conversation with me? Maybe that was a way for me to gauge the depth of his misfortune. I yielded to an absurd distraction: I imagined Morales's parents addressing their son with raised index fingers and saying something like "Ricardito, no matter what happens, don't ever use bad words. Not even if a bad, bad man rapes and strangles your wife and then goes free." I reined in my imagination and refocused on his words. How could I argue with his axioms? I'd known him for five years, during which time many things had happened to him, and they all appeared to demonstrate that he was thoroughly and incontestably right.

"But seriously," Morales went on, "when you told me Gómez had been caught, and then when you said he'd given himself away and confessed his crime, I thought, 'Well, all right, now at least that's over; he'll rot in prison.' But after I got home, or after three or four days had passed, I asked myself, 'So that's it? Really? As easy as that?' No. It seemed too simple, even after all the crap we've gone through in the last four years. So I asked a lawyer friend—maybe friend's an exaggeration, let's say acquaintance—to tell me what it meant to be handed a life sentence. When I heard that the guy could get out in twenty-five years, at the most, including whatever accessory sentence he might have received, even for an 'indefinite period of time,' I thought that was still pretty good. Obviously, a sentence of life in prison for Gómez would have been too much to expect, considering the way things usually went for me. But I got used to the idea of twenty-five years. I figured that was a whole lot of time, it was the maximum prison sentence you could get in Argentina, and I talked myself into being quite happy with it. Until I realized precisely *that*, that I was happy with it. 'Look, Ricardo,' I said. 'If you imagine you're satisfied, you're dreaming, because any day now, you're going to find out that not even what you've talked yourself into being satisfied with is going to happen.' You see what I mean?"

I saw what he meant. His point of view was intolerably pessimistic. But he wasn't saying anything that wasn't in complete accordance with the facts.

"And so, when I found out that a whole bunch of political prisoners had been granted amnesty on May 25 and released from Devoto Prison, and when I went on to discover that none of them could be tried again for any of the crimes they were doing time for at the moment when they were amnestied, I asked myself the million-dollar question: 'Say, Ricardo, as far as you're concerned, how could the whole state of affairs with that son of a bitch Isidoro Antonio Gómez get worse?' And my answer to myself was, 'It could get worse if the man who raped and murdered your wife appeared in the lists of the prisoners who've been granted amnesty, even though he's not a political prisoner and has nothing to do with politics.' And you know what? Bingo! There he was!"

By the end of this rant, he was practically shouting. A couple of tears shimmered in his wide-open eyes. Then his face grew rigid again, and he looked out at the street. I did the same. It was only after a good while, and in the neutral tone of voice of a man who knows he's beyond harm, not because he's been saved from it but because he's succumbed to it, that he said, "If you don't mind telling me, I'd like to know how it was that he got released." I told him what had happened just as Báez had related it to me. I also explained that Sandoval and I had

found out only when the official letter from the Penitentiary Service came, and I described Sandoval's reaction,
too. I'm not very sure why. I suppose I imagined that
knowing how upset a couple of honest guys like Báez and
Sandoval were might make Morales feel less abandoned
by God, or by fate. When I finished, there was another
long silence. The waiter brought the check to a nearby
table, and I took the opportunity to order another coffee.
When asked if he wanted another one as well, Morales
shook his head.

I hesitated. I'd been deliberating about the next step,
but I hadn't managed to persuade myself to take it. But
since I feared that it was now or never, I forged ahead.
"It's very difficult for me to tell you this, Morales," I
began stumblingly. "I mean, I . . . a man in my position . . . what I'm about to say isn't something I'm even
supposed to think about, but . . ." I went on, chasing
my tail like a puppy. "I'm referring to the possibility
that . . ."

"Better not say it. Stop right there. I know what you're
referring to."

I hesitated again. Did he really understand what I
meant?

"Let's suppose you say, 'Look, Morales, if I were you,
I'd find him and put a bullet in him,' and I listen to you
and I go and do it. Wouldn't you feel guilty?"

I didn't reply.

"And bear in mind, when I say guilty, I don't mean because the son of a bitch winds up dead. I think we agree he's a worthless rat. What I mean is I believe you'd start feeling guilty for my sake. You understand me?"

I didn't reply to that, either. I didn't know what to say.

"It would be funny. Say I go and kill Gómez; two minutes later, I bet, I get put in jail for life. Do you have the slightest doubt about that?" He turned toward the door. A very young couple, a man and a woman, were coming in. "I don't. No doubt at all."

He gazed distractedly at the young people. They looked as though they hadn't been together long; the electric pleasure of recently discovered love radiated from both of them. Was Morales envying them? Did they perhaps evoke for him his own past with Liliana Colotto?

"No, Chaparro," he said, finally picking up the thread again. "Nothing's so simple. Because aside from . . ." Morales seemed to be having difficulty finding the words he wanted, but it also seemed that he'd thought the matter over again and again. "Let's suppose I kill him. Do I gain anything? Do I settle anything?"

After a pause I said, "Maybe you get your revenge."

What would I do in his shoes? I genuinely didn't know. But the fundamental reason why I didn't know was that I'd never felt for any woman what Ricardo Morales felt for his deceased wife. Or perhaps I had, but for a woman

I don't intend to say a word about in these pages. Perhaps if I'd thought about her, about this other woman—my only secret worthy of the name—I would actually have been able to comprehend Morales's love for his wife. I'm sure I would have been capable of anything for her sake, for the one I loved. Then again, she'd never belonged to me the way Morales and his wife had possessed each other, so my story wasn't really comparable to his. His wife had been real, palpable, his own, and she'd been wrenched from him. And because the thought of that was so horrific, I reiterated what I'd said: "Maybe killing him would be vengeance for you."

Morales maintained his silence. He reached into the pocket of his sports coat and pulled out a pack of Jockey Longs and a bronze cigarette lighter. He must have noticed my surprise at seeing him smoke. "I'm a man who makes decisions slowly," he said with a slight smile. "You didn't know I was a smoker, right? Before I met Liliana, I used to smoke like a chimney. I gave it up for her. How can a man light a cigarette if the woman he loves asks him not to, for their sake and the sake of the children she wants to have with him?" He emitted the choked snort that was his version of laughing. "As you'll agree, it doesn't make much sense for me to keep my lungs clean now, docs it? I'm smoking like a vampire, just like before. Assuming, of course, that vampires smoke a lot.

Anyway, until today, I hadn't started doing it in public again, I didn't dare smoke in front of anyone. You're the first. Take it as a sign of friendship."

Once again, I made no reply.

"And as for killing him . . . what do you want me to say? It seems too easy, doesn't it? I had a lot of time to think about that over the years, with all the hours I spent looking for him in train stations. Suppose I'd found him—what would I have done? Shot him full of holes? Too easy. Too fast. How much pain can a guy feel after someone's emptied a revolver into his chest? Not much, I think."

"At least that's something."

Why did my side of our conversation feature arguments that sounded so stupid, so meager?

"It's something, but very little. Too little. Now, if you can guarantee that I shoot him four times and don't kill him but leave him a bedridden paraplegic and he lives to be ninety, then I'm all for it."

Something in his tone sounded false, as if he were a man unaccustomed to exercising cruelty, not even hypothetical, purely verbal cruelty, but still he wanted to impress me in his new role as Morales the sadist.

"But let's go back to my maxim, Chaparro," he said. "Most likely, I'd send him to hell—presuming it exists—with my first shot and miss him entirely with the other three. And then I'd be sent to jail for life (it goes without saying, I wouldn't get any probation) and live past ninety. Gómez gets off easy, he's free from everything before he hits the ground, and I'm in the joint for half a century, envying his luck. No, seriously. Dying can be too easy a path to take, believe me. Things are never simple."

He stubbed out what was left of his cigarette and, with automatic movements, lit another one, the last one in his pack.

"That's why I thought prison, all things considered, was the best possible outcome. All right, it wasn't going to be for life. It wasn't going to be for fifty years. But thirty years or so, the idea of him pissing in a prison cell for thirty consecutive years—that didn't seem so deplorable, don't you agree? But . . ." He gave a resigned sigh. "That didn't happen either. And look, it wasn't the ideal punishment, we're in agreement on that. It was, at most, the best possible one, given the circumstances. And here's where the corollary of my maxim comes in. Since sooner or later, everything has to turn into shit, God moved a couple of pieces and let that son of a bitch get away scot-free."

He was talking so loudly by the end that the young lovers paused in their conversation and looked at us. Morales fixed his eyes on the tabletop and brought himself under control.

"I don't know how to help you," I said. It was the truth. "I sincerely would like to make things easier for you."

"I know that, Benjamín."

It was the first time he'd called me by my given name. A few days before, it had been Báez. What strange channels of solidarity did that horrible story open up?

"But you can't do anything. Thanks all the same."

"No, don't thank me. Because I'm serious: I don't know how to help you."

Morales shredded the silver paper of the cigarette pack he'd just finished. "Maybe you can on some other occasion. For now, I'll say good-bye." He stood up and took a few bills from his pocket to pay for his coffee. Then he held out his hand and said, "Seriously, thank you for everything you've done. I'm truly grateful."

I shook his hand. When he'd left, I sat back down and gazed for a long time at the loving couple, who remained heedless of everything that was not themselves. I envied them profoundly.

More Coffee

For whatever reason (and Chaparro has no intention of investigating whether that reason is just an old friendship or something deeper, more encouraging, more personal, and more a great many other things), Irene takes pleasure in his company, and not solely in his descriptions of the fledgling writer's trials and tribulations. And so, for some reason, they're face to face again, with her desk between them. For some reason, she's smiling a smile different from her common, ordinary smiles, which in fact, Chaparro thinks, are never either common or ordinary. But they're not like this, not like these, which she bestows on him when they're alone together in her office and evening is coming down.

Because he fears he's dreaming uselessly again, he gets nervous, looks at his watch, and starts to stand up. Irene proposes another cup of coffee, and he, with the utmost awkwardness, points out that they've already drunk all the coffee, that the pot in the electric coffeemaker is empty, and that the machine itself is off. She offers to go into the kitchenette and make some more and he says no, although in the next instant he regrets being such an imbecile. He could have said, "Sure, thanks, I'll go to the kitchen with you," but he didn't, and he reproaches himself so fervently for missing his cue that he sits down again, as though that might be a method of undoing the gaffe. But then he thinks there may be no harm done; maybe she simply wants more coffee, that's all, maybe there's some piece of gossip she wants to pass along, that's all, because when you consider it, there's nothing unusual about drinking coffee with a friend and colleague of many years in the court, nothing unusual whatsoever.

But as it happens, they both sit back down, and their conversation revives, a piece of flotsam he can cling to in the midst of all these uncertainties. Without knowing how it happened, Chaparro finds himself remarking to Irene that he spent the other day reading and correcting his drafts; it was raining outside, he tells her, and he was listening to Renaissance music, which he very much enjoys. He stops in embarrassment precisely when he's on the point of saying, as he looks her straight in the eyes, that the only missing element, the addition he needed to consider himself saved and in a state of perpetual grace, was her, her in the armchair next to his, or maybe reclining and reading at his side, and his hand, his fingertips, gently caressing her head and leaving shallow furrows in her hair. Although he didn't say that, it's as if he did, because he knows he's turned as red as a tomato. And now she gives him a look, an amused or affectionate or nervous look, and finally she asks him, "Are you going to tell me what's wrong, Benjamín?"

A fainting sensation comes over Chaparro, because he's just noticed that this woman asks one thing with her lips and another with her eyes. With her lips, she's asking him to explain why he's blushing and squirming in his chair and looking up every twelve seconds at the tall pendulum clock that stands against the wall near the bookcases; but with her eyes, besides all that, she's asking him something else. She's asking him what's wrong, what's wrong with him, with him and her, with him and the two of them, and she seems interested in his answer, she seems eager to know, maybe anxious, and probably undecided as to whether what's wrong with him is what she supposes is wrong with him. Supposes, or fears, or hopes, Chaparro's not sure which, because that's the mystery, the great mystery of the question in her gaze, and Chaparro suddenly panics, he springs to his feet like a maniac and tells her he has to go, it's getting very late. Surprised, she rises as well—is she surprised and nothing more, or surprised and relieved, or surprised and disappointed?—and Chaparro practically flees down the hall, flees past the tall wooden doors of the other offices, flees across the diagonal checkerboard of black and white floor tiles, and catches his breath again only after climbing into a 115 bus, miraculously empty at that peak hour of early evening. He goes home to his house in Castelar, where the final chapters of his story are waiting to be written, one way or another, because he's beginning to find the situation intolerable, not Ricardo Morales's or Isidoro Gómez's situation, but his own, which has nearly ruined him, which has bound him to that woman, that woman sent to him from heaven or hell and now lodged inextricably in his heart and his head, that woman who's still, even at this distance, asking him what's wrong, with the loveliest eyes in the world.

Doubts

"On July 28, 1976, Sandoval went on a monumental bender that saved my life."

Chaparro rereads the opening sentence of his new chapter and hesitates. *Is that a good way to start this part of the story?* he wonders. He's not convinced, but he can't come up with anything better. Of the various objections to the sentence, the strongest concerns precisely the idea he's trying to convey. Can a single human action—in this case, a monumental drinking binge—be the cause that changes another's destiny, assuming that such a thing as destiny exists? Besides, what does "saved my life" mean? Chaparro doesn't like the phrase, which sounds trite to him. And something else: What guarantee is there that what prevented him from returning home on that June night was Sandoval's drunken rampage and not some other indiscernible series of circumstances?

Be that as it may, the sentence makes a plausible opening and will likely remain. Sandoval was one of the best guys Chaparro ever knew, and he's pleased to think he didn't wind up at the bottom of a ditch with two bullet

holes in the back of his neck that night because of Sandoval, even if only because of Sandoval's weaknesses.
And since Chaparro didn't want to die then, nor does he
now, he'll permit himself to declare unequivocally that
Sandoval's titanic booze-up "saved his life."

Chaparro finds himself in a predicament similar to
the one he was in at the beginning of his novel, when
he didn't know how to start telling his story; now he
doesn't know how to go on. Various images assail him
all at once: the spectacle of his trashed apartment; Báez
seated across from him in a dive in Rafael Castillo; a
shed with a big sliding door standing in the middle of
a field; a solitary road at night, illuminated by power-
ful headlights and seen through the windows of a bus;
Sandoval thoroughly destroying a bar on Venezuela
Street.

However, he figures his current narrative standstill
will be less difficult to resolve than his initial paraly-
sis. After all, he personally lived through the chaos his
life turned into, so he doesn't have to imagine what it
might have been like for someone else. And besides,
those things didn't happen to him simultaneously, but
successively. They were stunning, in some cases even
heartbreaking, but they occurred in a chronologi-
cal sequence he can hold on to. The best way to continue telling his story, he concludes, is to respect that
sequence.

First Sandoval wrecks a bar on Venezuela Street. Then Chaparro finds his apartment in shambles. After that, he talks to Báez in a foul-smelling joint in Rafael Castillo. Then he takes a front seat on a night bus. And later, many years later, he stands before the big sliding door of a shed, in the middle of a field.

31

On July 28, 1976, Sandoval went on a monumental bender that saved my life.

He'd looked dreadful the entire day. When he arrived at the office, he greeted no one and set immediately to work checking a ballistics report, a triviality he could ordinarily have dispatched in twenty minutes; it took him five hours. At the end of the day, after everyone else in the office had gone home or over to the law school, I tried to engage him in conversation, but it was like talking to a wall. As usual, he spoke only when he felt like it.

Eventually he said, "My aunt Encarnación, my mother's sister, called me this morning." Then he paused; his voice was shaking. "She said some men came and took away my cousin Nacho yesterday. They were soldiers, she believes, but she isn't sure. They kicked down the door in the middle of the night and busted up everything in the place. They were dressed in civilian clothes, she said."

He fell silent again, but I didn't say a word. I knew he hadn't finished.

"The poor old woman asked what could be done. I told her she should come and stay with us, and meanwhile I went with her to the police station to file a complaint." He lit a cigarette before going on. "What else could I do? What could I tell her?"

"You did right, Pablo," I ventured to assure him.

"I don't know." He hesitated again. "I felt like I was deceiving her. Maybe I should have told her the truth."

"You did right, Pablo," I repeated. "If you tell her the truth, you'll kill her."

The truth. It can be so fucked up sometimes, the truth. Sandoval and I had a long conversation about the whole problem of political violence and repression, which had grown especially acute since Perón's death. Currently, fewer bodies were being dumped in empty lots; the murderers had evidently perfected their methods. As workers in the criminal justice system, we were too far removed from the things that were happening to know details, but sufficiently close to guess them. You didn't have to be a fortune-teller. Every day, we saw people being arrested or heard news of other arrests. However, the people taken into custody were never put in jail, never brought before a judge, never remanded to Devoto or Caseros.

"I don't know. She has to find out sooner or later."

I tried to recall Nacho's appearance. I'd seen him a few times when he visited the court, but his features escaped my efforts to bring them into focus.

"I'm leaving," Sandoval said, suddenly getting to his feet. He put on his jacket and headed for the door. "See you later."

Oh, fuck, I thought. *Here we go again.* I opened the window and waited. Although several minutes passed, I didn't see him cross Tucumán in the direction of Viamonte Street. I felt a little guilty. I remembered something I'd read: "Flooding in India leaves forty thousand dead, but as I don't know them, I'm more concerned for the health of my uncle, who suffered a heart attack." Somewhere in a military barracks or police station, Nacho was being tortured with cattle prods and beaten to a pulp, but I wasn't as distressed on his account as I was for his cousin Pablo, my friend, who had gone off to drink himself into a coma.

Was I selfish and unfeeling, or were we all? I consoled myself by thinking that I could do something for Sandoval, even though there was nothing I could do for his cousin Nacho. I wonder if I was right. Anyway, I decided to give my colleague the usual head start: I'd go looking for him in three hours. I sat down to correct an order of preventive detention. On second thought, two hours seemed better. Three might be too many.

32

As I was going down the steps to Talcahuano Street, I
hesitated for a moment. I was carrying a good bit of
money in my pocket, because I'd planned to pay the final
installment on my apartment after work that evening—
the notary's office stayed open late—but out of fear that
the detour would take too long and I wouldn't be able to
find Sandoval, I decided I'd look for my friend and postpone my payment until another day. I patted my jacket
to make sure the money was snug in the inside pocket
and flagged down a cab. We drove up and down Paseo
Colón, but I couldn't locate Sandoval. The taxi driver,
who seemed to be in a good mood, offered me a long,
off-the-cuff disquisition on the simplest and most ex-
peditious way to solve the country's problems. If I'd
been less worried and less focused on finding the bar
Sandoval was in, maybe I would have asked the cabbie
for some clarification of the logic linking such asser-
tions as "The military knows what it's doing," "Nobody
here wants to work," "They should all be killed," and
"The River Plate club under Labruna is the example to
follow."

I had the driver cruise the side streets and eventually found Sandoval in an extremely nasty bar on Venezuela Street. I paid my fare, handing the money to the enlightened analyst of our national condition and waiting for him to give me change. Somewhat annoyed by my stinginess, he began to dig around in one of his pockets, and while he did so, I savored a tiny taste of revenge. By this point, I was no longer in a hurry. There was little chance that Sandoval would stand for being hauled out of the ugly little tavern before eleven o'clock, and now it wasn't much past nine.

I sat across from him and ordered a Coca-Cola. The barman offered a Pepsi instead, and I accepted. I'd never seen Sandoval drink like that. It was genuinely frightening, though at the same time, you had to admire his staying power. Evenly, without excessive gestures, he'd lift a full glass to his lips and empty it in one or two swallows. Then he'd stare into the space in front of him and feel the hot liquid as it made its way down to his guts. A few minutes later, he'd fill the glass again.

It was almost midnight, and thus far I hadn't succeeded in getting Sandoval out of his seat, although I must confess that I hadn't tried very hard. From experience, I knew he'd go through an initial stage of drunkenness in which he'd become irritable, fiercely concentrated on his own thoughts, and then he'd reach a second level, more placid and relaxed. That would be

the moment for me to carry him off, but on this particular evening, the transition to the second stage was a long
time in coming. I got up and went to the men's room.
While I was standing in front of the urinal emptying my
bladder, I heard a crash of broken glass, followed by a
series of shouts and the sounds of running feet on the
wooden floor.

I dashed out of the bathroom, nearly wetting myself
in the process. At that hour, fortunately, there was no
one left in the place but three or four regulars, who were
looking on with more interest than fear. Sandoval was
brandishing a chair in his right hand. The owner of the
establishment, a short, powerfully built guy, had come
out from behind the bar and was stalking Sandoval.
Probably because he was afraid of getting whacked with
the chair, the bar owner maintained a certain distance
between him and his drunken customer. Behind the
bar, I could see the broken mirror, the broken bottles,
and shards of glass scattered on all sides.

"Pablo!" I called to him.

He didn't even look at me. He remained focused on
the barman's movements. Nobody spoke, as if the duel
the two were engaged in had roots too deep to be reached
by words. Suddenly, without further preliminaries, Sandoval's right arm moved in a wide semicircle and he
hurled the chair at one of the windows that looked out
on the street. There was another enormous crash, more

running feet, more shouted insults. At this point, the bar owner stopped hesitating. It seemed to him that his drunken enemy, now disarmed, would be easy to subdue, and so he tried to rush him. He didn't know (as I did) that Sandoval's reflexes were not so easily dulled, despite his bloated appearance, or that he'd practiced boxing at a gym in Palermo ever since he was a kid. And so, when the proprietor of the bar got within his range, Sandoval caught him with a left hook to the jaw that flung him backward and left him sprawled on one of the empty tables.

"Sandoval!" I screamed.

Things were moving from bad to worse. He looked at me. Was he trying to place me in the strange and belligerent context he'd created? He picked up another chair and walked a few steps in my direction. *That's it*, I thought. *Just what I need to crown the evening: an all-out brawl with my assistant in a lowlife dive on Venezuela Street.* But Sandoval had other plans. With his free hand, he gestured to me to get out of his way. I stepped aside. The chair passed before my eyes at a respectable height and velocity and smashed into a glass sign advertising a brand of whiskey: a mature-looking gentleman sat in an armchair in front of a chimney fire and sipped the liquor from an elegant little glass. We'd seen a sign like that before, in some other bar in the area, and it was a piece of advertising that Sandoval detested, as he himself had informed me in the course of a previous bender.

With this final chair attack, which Sandoval probably considered an act of justice, his destructive impulses seemed to have been exhausted. The bar owner must have made the same assumption, because he jumped on him from behind and both of them fell to the floor and started rolling among the tables and chairs. I went to separate them and, as is the usual outcome in such cases, received several blows myself. I wound up sitting on the floor, clutching Sandoval against my body and shouting to the barman to calm down; I'd make sure my friend kept still, I said.

"We'll see about that," the fellow said at last, getting to his feet.

His cold, menacing tone of voice scared me. He went over to the cash register. I figured he'd pull out a pistol and start shooting at us, but I was mistaken. What he pulled out was a telephone token; he was going to call the police. The two or three remaining customers, who hadn't deemed it necessary to intervene, realized his intention and left the place in haste. I looked around. Was it possible that there was a public telephone in this hole in the wall? There was not. The proprietor of the little bar gave us a series of murderous looks as he headed for the door. The last thing we needed that night was to end up in the slammer. I stood up. Sandoval looked like a man unaware of his surroundings. I went out after the bar owner, who was walking toward the Bajo. I called to

him. Only after my third try did he turn around and
agree to wait for me to catch up. I told him there was
no need to call the cops; I'd take care of everything. He
gave me a skeptical look, for which he had his reasons.
The broken storefront window must have been worth a
healthy sum, and I seemed to recall a number of splin-
tered tables and chairs, not counting those that Sandoval had turned into missiles. I insisted, and the owner
finally agreed to return to the bar. We walked back in
silence. When we arrived, I couldn't fail to understand
why the guy was mad. His front window was lying in
pieces on the sidewalk, and inside, signs of damage
were visible everywhere.

He spread his arms and looked at me as though asking for an explanation, or as if he'd changed his mind
and now considered his recent indulgence excessive and
unwarranted.

"How much will it cost to repair all this?" My question lacked conviction and emphasis, as he must have
noticed.

"Well . . . a whole lot. Just look around."

I've never been any good at bargaining. I go from feeling like a sadistic exploiter to feeling like a dimwitted
sucker, and vice versa. And that situation—with Sandoval sitting on the floor in front of the bar, leaning back
against it and calmly drinking from a bottle of whiskey

(he'd somehow managed to get his hands on an intact
survivor of the recent disaster), and with the bar owner
clinging to the possibility of calling the police like an
ace up his sleeve—absolutely surpassed anything I might
have imagined.

He named a ridiculously high figure, practically
enough to renovate his nasty little dive from the foundations up. I told him I wasn't close to disposing of that
kind of capital. He answered that he couldn't accept so
much as a peso less. A relatively smaller figure crossed
my mind: the sum of the roll of banknotes I still had in
my inside pocket. In my deluded state, I'd thought the
roll represented the cancellation of my mortgage debt,
but now, trying to sound final, I offered the sum to him.

"All right," he said, giving in. "But pay me now."

He must have doubted that a guy like me, a guy who
went around playing guardian angel to a hopeless drunk,
could be carrying that amount of cash. I held it out to
him. He counted the bills and seemed to grow calm.
"Help me put things back in some order. If I leave the
place this way, I'll have to spend tomorrow cleaning up,
and I'll lose the whole day."

I agreed. We shifted Sandoval off to one side so he
wouldn't be in the way, swept up the broken glass, stowed
the broken tables and chairs in a little storeroom located
on the far side of a filthy patio, and redistributed the

undamaged furniture. Not counting the mirror and the
window, I believe the bar owner came out ahead. After
all, that glass advertising sign for whiskey had been an
appalling thing to look at. You could almost say Sandoval
had been right to pulverize it.

33

We took the only taxi whose driver was brave enough to pick us up. At three in the morning, and with the signs of our recent combat clearly visible (Sandoval's shirt was missing all of its buttons; I had a superficial but conspicuous cut on my chin), we can't have looked like a very trustworthy duo.

The whole way, I kept my eyes fixed on the meter. I knew exactly how much money I had left, and it wasn't a lot. The first taxi had cost me a bundle, though it was nothing compared to the small fortune I'd laid out for the damage Sandoval had done to that wretched little bar. I didn't want to arrive at his house and have to ask Alejandra for money.

Poor girl. She was waiting in the hallway, protected by a mantilla she'd thrown over her nightclothes and her dressing gown. Before we went in, I paid the cab fare. Alejandra told me to ask the driver to wait so that he could take me home. She didn't know I was flat broke, and naturally, I didn't tell her; I imagine I muttered some excuse. Between the two of us, we got Pablo inside and to bed. After that chore had been accomplished, Alejandra offered me a cup of coffee. I was about to refuse, but she looked so helpless, so sad, that I decided to stay awhile.

She wept silently when I gave her the news about Nacho. Pablo hadn't told her anything. "He never tells me anything," she declared, raising her voice. I felt uncomfortable. The whole situation was very complicated. I loved Sandoval like a brother, but his addiction aroused more impatience than compassion in me, especially when I saw the anguish in her green eyes.

Green eyes? An alarm went off inside my head. I bounded to my feet with a start and asked her to see me to the door. She wondered where I expected to find a taxi at that hour of the morning. It was past four, she said. I told her I preferred to walk. She replied that I was crazy if I intended to walk all the way to Caballito in the middle of the night, with all the things that were happening lately. I said there wouldn't be any problem. Whatever the situation, all I had to do was to show my Judiciary credentials, and that was that. It was the truth—I'd never had the slightest difficulty in that respect. Of course, I'd been prudent enough not to flash any such ID in a wrecked bar, with my court colleague sipping whiskey on the floor beside me.

She walked me to the door, told me good-bye, and thanked me. Often, in the twenty-five years that have passed since then, I've wondered about my feelings toward Alejandra. I've never had a problem acknowledging that I admired her, I appreciated her, I pitied her. But was I in love with her? Back then, I couldn't answer that question, and I continue to think that it isn't pertinent. I've never been able to desire my friends' wives; I'd find that unforgivable. Believe me, I don't consider myself a moralist. But I could never have looked at her as anything other than my friend Pablo Sandoval's wife. If at some point I *did* fall in love with another man's wife, I was careful not to strike up a friendship with the husband. But I promised myself not to speak of that woman here, so let's come to a full stop.

I walked across half the city on that cold July night. A few cars and a military patrol in a light truck passed me along the way, but nobody bothered me. When I reached my apartment building, it was past six. As always after a sleepless night, my weariness caused me to conflate recent memories with those from the day before, so that images of the fight in the bar, of Pablo's cousin's disappearance, and of the previous morning's breakfast seemed to be part of the same single recollection. At that hour, all I wanted was a warm bath and a two-hour nap that would distance me from everything that had happened. So when I stepped out of the elevator on the fourth floor, I had no idea what was waiting for me.

My apartment door was open, and a beam of light was projected out into the dark corridor. Had burglars robbed me? I walked to the door and crossed the threshold without thinking that the intruder might still be inside, and in fact no one was there. But I reflected on that later, because as soon as I reached the doorway, I was terrified to discover that the apartment was in absolute chaos. Chairs and armchairs were overturned, the bookcases tipped over, the books ripped apart and scattered everywhere. In the bedroom, the mattress had been slashed to pieces and foam rubber littered the floor. The kitchen, too, was a mess. Stunned as I was, I didn't notice right away that my television set and my stereo system were nowhere to be found. So this was the work of thieves, right? In that case, the violence they'd acted with didn't make sense. Eventually, I went into the bathroom, sure of finding it a shambles like the rest of the place. But there was something else, something apart from the shredded shower curtain and the contents of the medicine chest strewn over the bathroom tiles and the bidet faucets turned on full in an attempt to flood the place. There was also a message, written on the mirror in soap: "Chaparro son of a bitch lucky this time. Next time you're meat."

The writing was large and neat, the work of someone who was in no hurry and felt totally in charge of the situation. Something was scribbled at the end of the message, but hard as I tried to decipher it, it remained illegible. I figured it was the signature of the prick who wrote it. What kind of man could act with such impunity, could lord it over others in such a way? Was there someone who had an unresolved issue with me? As I asked myself these questions, I was buffeted by a cold wave of fear.

I went out. With brilliant foresight, I tried to lock the apartment door. Only then did I notice, key in hand, that the lock had been kicked in.

34

After abandoning my trashed apartment on that twenty-ninth of July, I found myself disoriented. Obviously, the perpetrators weren't simple burglars, nor had it been some random attack. For a moment, I thought about retracing my steps and having a word with the building superintendent, but I was terrified by the idea that the people who'd come looking for me the previous night might try again in the morning. I told myself I'd done right to flee the scene at once. But where could I go? If they knew my address, they must also know where my parents lived, or Sandoval, or someone else close to me. I couldn't put myself—or the people dear to my heart—at risk. But I didn't have a cent. And although I was in fact walking on Rivadavia Avenue, heading for the center of town, I had no fixed destination in mind. I checked the street numbers: I was in the 5000 block. So now what?

If I had misgivings about filing a complaint directly with the police, I could go to the courthouse and file it in the Appellate Court, or so I thought. I wasn't sure. Suppose they were waiting for me around the Palace of

Justice? And who the hell were "they"? Who *were* they?
I happened to pass a bar that had a public telephone.
I went in and searched my pockets. One of the four or
five coins I was carrying turned out to be a phone token.
I dialed the number of Alfredo Báez, the only person I
trusted at all.

He was surprised by my call, but—perhaps alerted by
the alarm and haste in my voice—he immediately put my
chaotic tale into some order by asking a few precise, logical questions. It was his idea that we should meet some
hours later on the Pueyrredón Avenue side of Miserere
Square.

I wandered around that part of town the whole
morning. It was almost noon when I realized I hadn't
notified the court that I wouldn't be coming in to work.
With my last remaining coins I bought a token and
called the office. My excuse for not showing up was a
sudden attack of the flu, and I was informed that Sandoval had called in sick as well. As I always did when
I took a day off, I passed along some instructions. I
consoled myself by recalling that our office workload
wasn't very heavy at the moment. I'd have been more
concerned if I'd known that I wouldn't set foot in the
court again for seven years.

Around two in the afternoon, I took a seat on a bench
in the square. At 2:30, I started awake; some guy had just
sat down next to me. I turned my head. It was Báez.

"Your espionage work doesn't require concealment, I see," he said. It passed through my mind that he always liked to fuck with me a little.

"I'm sorry to bother you. I didn't know who else to call."

"Don't worry about it. Tell me what's going on."

I described to him in great detail everything I'd seen in my apartment from when I arrived until I got the hell out of there. My tale wasn't long in the telling, but I do believe I spent more time relating it than living it.

When I finished, he asked me, "What did you say was missing from your place?"

"The TV set and the stereo system."

"And the message on the mirror . . . ?"

"It said they came there to do me in, and I was lucky I wasn't there. Next time, it said."

"They used your name, right?"

"Yes."

Báez contemplated the toes of his shoes for a few moments. Then he turned his head toward me and said, "Look, Chaparro. If this is what I think it is, you're fucked. Just in case I'm right, don't go home, don't go to the court, don't go anyplace where they know you. At least, not until I get in touch with you again."

"And what the hell am I supposed to do in the meanwhile?" On another occasion, I would have been ashamed

to show Báez how vulnerable I was, but in those circumstances, I had no inhibitions.

Once again, he thought for a while. Then he said, "Do
this. Go to a rooming house called La Banderita, on the
corner of Humberto Primo and Defensa. I don't mean
right away. Give me time to go there and talk to the owner.
Then you show up. You say your name is . . . Rodríguez,
Abel Rodríguez, and you've got a room reserved and paid
for. I'm going to give him a week's rent in advance. By the
way, you don't have a penny in your pocket, right?"

"No, I don't, but . . . maybe I could pass by the
court . . ."

"What did I just tell you? Don't even think about going
to the Palace of Justice. And not anywhere else, either.
You put yourself in your room, and you go out, if at all,
only to do whatever shopping you need. Here's some
money—just a few pesos. Come on, take it, don't be like
that. You'll pay me back later."

"Thanks, but—"

"One week. In a week, I should have a pretty good idea
of what this is all about. Things are in such a mess these
days, you never know, but let's hope for the best."

"Can't you tell me anything? What do you think's
going on?" Still today, I'm amazed at what a fool a man
can be when he's as scared as I was back then. Báez's un-
failing tact kept him from making fun of my stupidity.

"I'll be in touch with you. Stay calm."

He started to walk away, but then he stopped and turned back to me: "Is there some really sharp person assigned to your court at the moment, someone we might turn to? I mean somebody with some clout, your clerk, your judge, the other clerk . . ."

"Our clerk's a woman on maternity leave," I said, and the thought of that distracted me for a moment. But I recovered quickly and went on, "The other section's clerk is mentally challenged."

"That's often the case."

"And we have no judge. Fortuna Lacalle retired a while ago, and they still haven't named his replacement. The acting judge is Aguirregaray, from Examining Magistrate's Court No. 12."

"Aguirregaray?" Báez looked interested.

"Yes. Do you know him?"

"He's a great guy. At last, some good news. Take care of yourself. I'll see you in a week, more or less. Don't worry, I'll come to the rooming house."

I followed his instructions to the letter. I pounded the pavement of the city center all day, and as evening was falling, I headed for San Telmo. As soon as I identified myself as Abel Rodríguez, the man who received me at the rooming house—I assumed he was the owner—handed me a key. The room was clean. I flung myself onto the bed without stopping to remove my clothes. I hadn't closed my eyes for a day and a half, and during the course of those thirty-six hours, I'd participated in a barroom brawl, walked across half the city of Buenos Aires by night and by day, gazed upon the complete destruction of my home, and turned into a fugitive, although I didn't yet have a very good idea why. I laid my head on the pillow—which also smelled clean—and fell fast asleep.

35

The bar where Báez had me meet him seven days later backed up onto the Rafael Castillo train station and was a revolting dump. Three shabby gray Formica tables, a bar covered with sinister-looking sandwiches under glass bells, some wooden stools with peeling paint. The entire establishment, tiny to begin with, was made to seem even smaller by the greasy stink coming from a grill, where the chorizo sausages and hamburgers left over from lunch were now dry and cold. A few men, looking pretty down and out, leaned on the bar and conversed in shouts. At intervals of fifteen or twenty minutes, the corrugated iron roof was shaken by the great din of locomotives pulling trains, and a fine rain of dirt fell from the ceiling beams on persons and things. To complete the scene, a jocular broadcast host, abetted by two unhinged female commentators, was hollering from a radio whose volume was turned all the way up.

After a tense week spent hiding in a rooming house at the cost of Alfredo Báez's savings, I wasn't apt to make too many demands. I don't think I complained, but I couldn't help finding my surroundings soul-shattering.

Still, I knew I had to be in a safe place where people were unlikely to look for me, unless they had the cockroaches on their payroll.

I hadn't heard from Báez at all that week, except for a note he'd left at the reception desk to set up our meeting. I got to the appointed place early, so I had time to upset myself by imagining all the things that might have gone wrong in the past seven days. What if Báez had been the victim of a persecution identical to mine? What if someone had attacked him for poking his nose into the wrong places? My nervousness, steadily intensified over the course of a week and augmented by the nauseating smell, the filth, the bellowing at the bar, and the radio shouters, put me on the verge of breakdown and flight. Luckily, the policeman was as punctual as usual; had he not been, I don't think he would have found me. He shook my hand and sat down, making one of the dirty metal-and-leatherette chairs squeak.

"Were you able to find out anything?" I lit into him at once, before he was well settled. I wasn't in the mood for small talk.

Báez eyed me before answering. "Yes. In fact, I've found out several things, Chaparro."

He frightened me. It wasn't what he said, it was the way he was staring at me. His face bore the expression of a man unsure of how to introduce his subject. Could my plight be that grave? I resolved to shorten the way to the raw truth. "Good," I said. "In that case, I'm listening."

"The thing is I don't know where to begin."

"Wherever you want," I said, and then, trying to joke: "We've got lots of time."

"Don't believe it, Benjamín. You don't have so much." As I listened to him, I tried not to let my growing panic show. "You have to take the bus to San Salvador de Jujuy tonight. It leaves at ten minutes past twelve, from Liniers. Under the General Paz freeway."

When I caught my breath again, I asked, almost shouting, "What are you talking about?"

"You're right. I'm sorry. I think I started with the hardest part. Please be patient."

"I'm listening," I agreed, without lowering my guard.

"After our meeting the other day, the first question I asked myself was who in the hell had attacked you. Clearly, it was no random act. That one sure thing, added to all the rest, allowed me to identify them pretty easily."

"What do you mean, 'all the rest'?"

"Everything, my friend," he said. Then, realizing that my anxiety demanded more precision, he added, "To begin with, the way they went in, the time they went in. Do you have any idea how much racket they must have made, breaking all the things they broke? Your common, everyday thieves go about their work more stealthily. Those guys barged in like they owned the place. They didn't give a shit who might hear them. Think about it, Chaparro: a small band of thugs, acting with impunity in the middle of the night. These days, you don't need many more clues to figure out what side they're on, do you?"

I was beginning to understand, but it was incredible. What could guys like that want with me?

"You've come up against one of those groups of outlaws employed by the government, my friend. That's it in a nutshell. You were colossally lucky they didn't catch you at home. If you'd been there, you wouldn't have lived to tell the tale. You'd have been dragged to a car by your hair and thrown into the trunk, and then pulled out of the trunk and tossed into a ravine with four bullets in you."

Báez seemed to withdraw for a moment, silently contemplating the images of what might have been. Then, suddenly, he returned: "Everything points in the same direction. The impunity, the savagery, the operating in teams. Do you know your neighbor in Apartment B? It took me a long time and a bit of work, but I finally got her to the point where she was willing to tell me that she'd looked out of the peephole and seen four men pass her door."

"And what could they have wanted with me?"

"We're getting there, Chaparro. Bear with me. My next step was to establish—or let's say to confirm—that the men belonged to a group connected with Romano or Gómez."

"*What?*" Those two names fell on my ears with a terrifying splat, like a body landing on the sidewalk from ten floors up. "What are you telling me?"

"Calm down, Benjamín. No use getting upset. It was a foregone conclusion. You're not a militant, you're not a public person. You don't work in a field the military's interested in—in fact, I don't believe they give a hoot about Justice. So what reason could there be for a group of guys like that to come busting in on you? They had to have something against you, some old grudge, something personal . . ."

I did a finger calculation before I spoke. "Forgive me for saying this, but that's ridiculous. It's been almost three years since I've heard anything about Isidoro Gómez—not since they released him from Devoto—and not a word about that other son of a bitch, either."

"I know, I know. I thought about that, too. But it led me to the next question. I decided to operate on the assumption that those guys had something to do with your incident, or vice versa, you follow me?"

"I follow you." Was I truly following him?

"So I had to start thinking about their motives for wanting to do you in. I didn't believe they had any new motives, and old ones struck me as even less logical. So I gave all this a lot of thought, and I wound up coming back to the present and focusing on what's going on now. At first I thought it would be really hard to investigate anybody who works with the intelligence services, anybody in that game. Maybe in a serious country, such organizations are hermetically sealed. Or in any case, I suppose they are. But here, they have more holes than a tea strainer. They like to show off—you know?—all that riding around in cars without license plates, wearing sunglasses, exhibiting those Ithaca shotguns like they were their . . . you know what I mean."

He grew distracted again, and a grimace, a mixture of mockery and contempt, appeared on his face.

"So they turned out to be relatively easy to locate. And then, after two or three conversations in which I played the role of the admiring asshole eager to listen to elite macho bullshit, I practically came away with an organization chart outlining their operations."

"I find it hard to believe they can be so obtuse," I ventured to say.

"Believe it. If they weren't such bloodthirsty sons of bitches, you'd shit yourself laughing at them. Let me go on. Romano apparently has his own little group of seven or eight psychos. It seems he was kept on after they closed down Devoto, bad joke that it was. On the other hand, holding on to the guy was only logical. You couldn't expect a worthless lout like him to do any kind of *productive* work."

I tried to follow his explanation, but an image from eight years before—that son of a bitch Romano celebrating, jumping up and down around the judge's desk— kept recurring to me. How could I have failed to notice, back then, that this colleague of mine was a sadist and a murderer?

"Romano's the leader of the group. And generally, he doesn't go out when they vacuum people." He saw the puzzlement on my face. "Sorry. The thugs say 'vacuum.' It means they carry off anybody they feel like carrying off to one of their hideouts."

I nodded. I remembered what had happened to Sandoval's cousin, who had no doubt been put through the same appalling ordeal. Was it possible he'd been abducted just last week? It seemed to me that had occurred in another life, distant and definitively inaccessible.

"In fact, Romano hardly goes out at all. He works inside, doing . . . how do they say it? 'Basic intelligence,' or 'raw intelligence.' Which means he's the creep who directs the torture sessions where they get names out of the detainees. Then he sends out his heavies to pick up the people he wants." Once again, Báez's face darkened. "But the studs I talked to didn't have much to say on that subject. I guess they still have enough sense left not to brag about such stuff."

What Báez was telling me was so macabre, so irrational, so horrific, and it provided such a simple confirmation of what Sandoval and I had guessed, that I knew it had to be true.

"Guess who's one of the thugs who do the street work for Romano . . ."

I remembered Morales and his maxim, according to which everything that can go bad is going to go bad, and everything that can get worse will get worse. I managed to stammer a name: "Isidoro Gómez."

"None other."

"What a son of a bitch," was all I could add.

"Well . . . I think they're just alike as far as that's concerned. Or they *were* just alike, apparently."

"What do you mean?"

"Remember that all this began, supposedly, when those guys trashed your apartment."

"And?"

"And there was a reason why those guys decided to get rid of you when they did. A few years ago, they had no motive."

"I don't understand."

"Of course you don't. Let me explain. A few nights ago, Romano, in a sudden fury, summons his boys and kicks in your apartment door. He can't wait to whack you. Why? That's easy: revenge. Revenge for what? Think about it. What do the two of you have in common? Nothing—or almost nothing. You have Gómez. Remember Cámpora's amnesty?"

I nodded. As if I could have forgotten that.

"Good. Back then—when that happened, I mean—Romano must have felt that he'd busted your balls up and down the line. That's why he stopped fucking with you. Because he figured he'd fucked you enough."

"And then what?"

"And then the other night, he rushes out like a madman to do you in. Why would he do that?"

"I don't understand anything."

"Just wait, we're almost there. It's as if you two were playing a chess game, a kind of challenge match. You shit on him by getting him fired from the court. He gets revenge by letting Gómez go. So why does Romano decide to murder you now, three years later? Simple: because he's convinced you've just moved another piece. Or, more precisely, he believes that you, Chaparro, have just wasted one of his most reliable men, namely Isidoro Gómez."

My face must have revealed that I had no idea what he was talking about.

"Romano wants to kill you, Chaparro, because as far as he's concerned, you just did away with Gómez. That's it."

I was stunned for a moment, but I had to shake it off or run the risk of missing the rest of Báez's explanation. "I'm not saying you did it. I'm saying Romano thinks you did it. They came to your house looking for you on the night of July 28, right? Just imagine: two nights earlier, on the twenty-sixth, somebody killed Gómez. It happened near his apartment in Villa Lugano."

It was too complicated, or the polluted air in the place had finally overcome me.

"Are you all right?" Báez asked, looking worried.

"The truth is I feel pretty queasy."

"Come on. Let's go breathe some fresh air."

36

We walked to the station. Inside we sat on the only bench whose wooden slats were still intact, on the platform where trains stopped on their way into the capital. At that hour they were almost empty. By contrast, on the other side of the tracks, crowds that grew larger as the evening advanced were getting off every train that pulled into the station. The passengers scattered in all directions or ran to catch one of the red buses with the black roofs.

The open air did me good. I could at least think with a modicum of clarity, and I realized I had something urgent to say to Báez. "There's one thing I haven't told you, Báez," I said hesitantly. "You remember back at the beginning of the case, when Gómez figured out we were looking for him because I tried to play the detective?"

"Well, it wasn't that bad. Besides—"

"Yes it was. Let me finish. After the amnesty, I screwed up again, much the same way. I mean, I see now that it was a screwup. At the time, I didn't think so. I didn't think it was anything."

Báez stretched out his legs and crossed his ankles, like a man getting ready to listen. I tried to be as concise as

I could. I was already embarrassed about having looked like a retard in front of him the first time, eight years before. Now I had to play the part of the recidivist retard. After the amnesty, I told him, it had occurred to me to do Ricardo Morales one last favor: to find out where Gómez was, just in case Morales should get up the nerve to blow his brains out. I explained to Báez that I'd conducted the investigation with the help of a cop, an acquaintance of mine, and that it had all been done, naturally, only by word of mouth, without putting anything in writing. Báez asked me the cop's name.

"Zambrano, in Theft," I answered, and immediately asked a question of my own. "Is he an asshole, or is he a son of a bitch?"

"No," Báez said slowly. "He's not a son of a bitch."

"Then he's an asshole."

"Ah, forget Zambrano," Báez said, trying to protect what was left of my self-esteem. "He's not important. Tell me how the investigation turned out."

"Something like two months passed, but in the end Zambrano came up with an address in Villa Lugano. To tell you the truth, I no longer remember what it was. You know how Villa Lugano addresses are. Block so-and-so, Building I don't know what, Corridor something or other, and all that."

"Well, did he do a good job? Did he give you the right address?"

"I don't know. I never checked it out."

We were silent while Báez tried to fit the piece of information I'd just provided him into the puzzle he was working out in his head. "I think I understand now," he said at last. "Romano must have found out. Especially if Zambrano disregarded the necessary subtleties. But since nothing happened, Romano stayed calm. He probably interpreted your search for Gómez as a futile gesture, a sign of your anger and humiliation at losing him."

We fell silent again. Each of us, I imagine, was mentally taking the next logical step in the chain of events. Eventually, Báez said, "You passed that information on to Morales, I suppose."

"As a matter of fact, I didn't. Pretty ironic, huh? I was afraid he'd take it badly or . . . I don't know. In the end, I didn't tell him anything."

An outbound train arrived and discharged another human flood, which surged out of the carriages and dispersed.

"In that case, the widower must have found out the address on his own account. That kid was never stupid," Báez said.

"You believe it was Morales who did the job on Gómez in Villa Lugano?"

"Do you have any doubt?" Báez turned toward me. Up until then, both of us had been looking at the opposite platform as we talked.

"I . . . at this point, I don't know what to think . . . or say, either," I confessed.

"Yes. It was Morales. I'd even say that's been confirmed. I mean, I've got as much confirmation as you can get in such cases. I went to Villa Lugano the day before yesterday and asked a few questions. A couple of neighbors had a few things to tell me. They even remarked that 'some young guys' had already been there, asking pretty much the same questions as me."

"Romano's people?"

"You bet. In a couple of the local taverns, I heard about an elderly couple who had seen everything. So I went to have a word with them. You can imagine how that went. The desire to talk in the supermarket is inversely proportional to the desire to talk to a policeman. I had to threaten them. I had to act very sorry, but I was going to have to take them down to the station to make a statement. If they'd called my bluff, I don't know where the hell I would have taken them. But they eventually gave in, and by the time I left, we were all great pals. They had seen the whole thing. You know how old folks are. Or should I say, how we all are? They get up at dawn, even though they don't have a frigging thing to do. Since there's no television at that hour, they listen to the radio and peep out the window. And that's how they come to see a young man they recognize because they see him around dawn every morning, walking down the street to the building across from theirs,

where he apparently lives. What makes this night different is that another guy suddenly comes out from behind
some bushes and gives their neighbor a mighty thump on
the head with what looks like a pipe. The kid goes down
like a sack, and his attacker—a tall guy, fair-haired, they
think, but they didn't get a very good look at him—anyway,
the attacker takes a key from his pocket and opens the
trunk of a white car parked right there at the curb. The
old folks don't know much about automobile makes. They
said it was too big for a Fiat 500 and too small for a Ford
Falcon."

I searched my memory. "Morales has—or used to
have, at least—a white Fiat 1500."

"There we are. That's the detail I was missing. So then
the tall guy carefully closes the trunk, gets in the front
seat, and drives away."

We kept quiet for a while, until Báez interrupted the
silence: "This Morales kid was always very well organized, it seems to me. You once described how patient he
was, mounting stakeouts in train stations. No chance he
was going to blow Gómez away right there, jump in the
car, and blast off, laying rubber like a fugitive in a movie.
I'm sure he drove him to a spot he'd already selected,
hauled him out of the trunk, shot him several times, and
buried him there."

I remembered my last conversation with Morales, in the
bar on Tucumán Street, and I ventured to disagree slightly

with the policeman. I figured it was my turn to offer a hypothesis. "No," I said. "I think he probably tied him up and waited for him to regain consciousness. The shooting would come later. If not, he wouldn't have been able to savor his revenge." All at once, a question occurred to me: "How about the hospitals in the area? Was any wounded patient admitted that day? Seriously wounded, I mean."

"No. I did a thorough check."

"Then Morales didn't trust himself to leave the guy a cripple." I recounted to Báez the relevant part of my last chat with the widower.

"Well . . . it's not so easy," Báez concluded. "It's one thing to make plans while you're lying in bed, staring at the ceiling because you can't sleep. Carrying out the plan you've fantasized about is a completely different thing. Morales being a sensible, stable kid, he must have thought—I mean, once Gómez was in the trunk—Morales must have thought, a bird in the hand is worth two in the bush. Maybe you're right, maybe he waited for Gómez to wake up."

"Go figure where he dumped the body," I made bold to say.

A train stopped at our platform, but very few people got on or off. As evening advanced, inbound trains grew emptier and emptier.

"I don't believe he dumped him," Báez said, delicately correcting me in his turn. "He must have buried him very neatly, in a place where he won't be found for two hundred years, not even by accident."

An image flashed in my memory: Morales sitting at a table in the little bar, putting the photographs in strict numerical order and arranging them into chronologically organized piles. "That's got to be it," I concluded. "He must have planned the operation and chosen the site months ago." I paused for a while and then spoke into the new silence. "Do you think he did right to kill him?"

A stray dog, skinny and dirty, came up to Báez and started sniffing his shoes. The policeman didn't shoo the dog away, but when he moved his legs, it got frightened and ran off. "What do you think?" he answered.

"I think you're dodging the question."

Báez smiled. "I don't know. You'd have to be in the kid's place."

Those seemed to be his last words on the subject. But then, after a long pause, he added, "I believe I would have done the same thing."

I didn't reply immediately. Then I concurred: "I believe I would have, too."

37

A few hours later, Sandoval and I were sitting in a taxi, barely exchanging a word. It was as if what was about to happen made the two of us too sad to talk, and neither of us felt like pretending; he wasn't going to act happy, and I wasn't going to act convinced.

"Cross under the General Paz freeway," Sandoval told the driver, "and drop us off at the long-distance bus stop."

We got the bags out of the trunk, and I prepared to say my farewells. It was ten minutes before midnight. Sandoval stopped me. "No," he said. "I'm waiting until you're on the bus."

"Don't be ridiculous, go on. You've got to work tomorrow. How do you expect to get home if you don't take this taxi? It's the only one around."

"Yeah, right, I'm going to abandon you in the middle of Ciudadela. No fucking chance." He turned his back to me, spoke to the cab driver, and paid the fare.

We moved the bags and joined a small group of people, who it turned out were waiting for the same bus. "It comes from the south, from Avellaneda, and stops here," Sandoval explained. "You'll get to Jujuy tomorrow night."

"Sounds like a lovely trip," I said sourly.

In spite of everything, when the enormous, gleaming bus arrived and pulled up at the curb in front of us, I couldn't help feeling a wave of childish excitement at the prospect of going on a long trip, the way I used to feel when I left on vacations with my parents. And so I was glad when Sandoval gave me my ticket and I saw that it bore the number 3: first seat on the right. We looked on as a driver wearing a light blue shirt and a dark blue tie shoved my bags all the way to the back of the luggage compartment after checking my ticket and discovering that I was bound for San Salvador de Jujuy. He put the bags belonging to passengers with tickets to Tucumán and Salta nearer the front. It was certainly true that I was fleeing to the farthest corner of Argentina. Sandoval and I had just stepped away when a loud click signaled that the driver had closed and latched the compartment.

We stood to one side of the bus door and embraced. I started to walk up the steps, but I turned around suddenly to talk to him. "I want you to do something," I said, not knowing how to begin. "Or rather, not to do something."

"Don't worry, Benjamín." Sandoval seemed to have anticipated this dialogue. "How am I supposed to get loaded if I don't have anyone to pay for my drinks and bring me home in a taxi?"

"Is that a promise?"

Sandoval smiled without taking his eyes off the pavement. "Come on, let's not exaggerate," he said. "You wouldn't ask so much."

"So long, Sandoval."

"So long, Chaparro."

Sometimes we men feel more secure if we treat those we love a little coldly. I took my seat and waved to him through the window. He raised a hand, smiled, and headed off to catch the 117 bus, which at that hour passed once in a blue moon.

38

Zárate 18. As we headed north, it gave me an uncomfortable feeling, a sense of inferiority or helplessness, to think that all my possessions fit into the three suitcases in the luggage compartment. I hadn't managed to salvage more than a couple of my favorite books, and I had almost nothing in the way of clothes. One of the bits of bad news that Sandoval had brought me at the rooming house was that most of my wardrobe had been slashed to ribbons, especially the shirts and the sports jackets.

I hadn't told my mother good-bye. Or anybody at the court.

Rosario 45. The headlights tore through the darkness, occasionally lighting up signs like that, white letters and numbers on a green background. Were we already in Santa Fe province? How many kilometers was Rosario from the border with Buenos Aires province? If we'd already crossed the province line, I hadn't noticed it.

I tried to sleep from time to time, but I couldn't keep my eyes closed. The days in the rooming house had been a permanent, monotonous void in which time had stretched out like chewing gum. But so many

things had happened in the course of the last day, and I
had learned about so many others, that I felt as if time
had passed from dead calm to whirlwind.

At the end of our meeting in the Rafael Castillo train
station, Báez had given me the address of Judge Aguirregaray in Olivos, about twenty kilometers north of
Buenos Aires. I asked Báez what the judge had to do with
my case.

"That's what I started to explain to you at the beginning," Báez said. "And then I decided it would be best to
leave it until the end."

Then I remembered. "Jujuy?" I asked.

"Exactly. He's an upright guy, and he's got the necessary contacts to arrange your transfer. It was his idea, by
the way," Báez added.

"Why?"

"I don't know. Or rather, I think it would be better if
you got the explanation from him. He's expecting you."

"But the only solution is for me to run like a fugitive?"
I couldn't resign myself to the idea that my life as I knew
it was going to end overnight.

Báez gazed at me awhile, maybe hoping I'd get the
picture myself. Then, seeing I wasn't going to, he explained: "Don't you know what the deal is, Benjamín?
The only way to be sure Romano will stop fucking with
you is to inform him of the truth. I can set up a meeting,
if you want. But if we do that, I'll have to tell him that the

guy who bumped off his little friend wasn't you, it was Ricardo Morales." He paused for a bit before concluding. "If you want, that's what we'll do."

Shit, I thought. *I can't do that. I just fucking can't.* "You're right," I said. "Let's leave things as they are."

We said our good-byes without too much effusiveness. He wrote down the numbers of the buses I would have to take to get to Olivos. At that point, I was beyond worrying about the possibility of looking stupid, so I even went so far as to ask him what color each of the buses was.

It took me more than two hours to get there. By the time I did, another cold day in that awful winter was drawing to a close. Judge Aguirregaray's house was a pretty cottage with a front garden. I told myself that if I ever came back to Buenos Aires, I'd spring for another place in Castelar. No apartments in the city center for me.

The judge in person opened the door and immediately invited me into his study. I thought I heard, in the background, the sounds of children and kitchen activity. The idea that I might have come at an inconvenient time made me uncomfortable, and I told him so.

"Don't concern yourself about that, Chaparro. There's nothing to worry about on that score. But it seems to me the fewer people who see you, the better off you are."

I agreed. After showing me a large armchair, he offered me some coffee, which I declined. Then he began: "Báez has filled me in on all the details," he said, and I rejoiced, because the mere thought of having to repeat the entire story exhausted me. "What I don't know is how much you're going to like the solution we've come up with."

I tried to sound nonchalant when I ventured to say, "Jujuy."

"Jujuy," the judge confirmed. "Báez tells me this thug who's after you, this . . ."

"Romano."

"Romano, that's it. Báez says this Romano is after you because of a personal matter, a kind of private vendetta. Is that right?"

"Absolutely," I conceded. Obviously, Báez *hadn't* given Judge Aguirregaray "all the details." I noted that the policeman exercised prudence even with his friends, and I thanked him in my secret heart, for about the thousandth time.

"So he's siccing his own hoodlums on you, so to speak. I think it's safe to assume they don't have much in the way of logistics beyond their little group."

"A sort of suburban mafia," I said, trying to be funny.

"Something like that. Don't laugh it's not a bad definition."

"Well, what's to be done, Your Honor?"

"Báez and I think what's to be done is we have to send you far enough away that Romano and his boys can't bother you, even if they discover where you are. So that's where Jujuy comes in. Because sooner or later, Romano's going to find out about your transfer, Chaparro. You know how long court secrets last downtown. The solution is to discourage him, to make going after you too complicated."

He paused a moment, listening to the sound of a woman's footsteps in the hall until they turned into another room. Aguirregaray went to the door, delicately locked it, and returned to his chair. "My cousin's a federal judge in San Salvador de Jujuy," he went on. "I know that must sound like the ends of the earth to you. But Báez and I couldn't come up with a better alternative."

I remained silent, eager to hear about the countless advantages of moving to the fucking sticks to live and work.

"As you know, the federal courts are part of the National Judiciary, that is, they operate within our own structure. So what we're talking about is a simple relocation, a transfer. Your position, of course, will be the same."

"And it has to be in Jujuy," I said, trying not to sound finicky.

"You know, even though you may not think so, Jujuy offers some advantages. One is that you'll be 1,900 kilometers away from here, and it will be almost impossible for the bad guys to bother you. And if they still try to get to you, another advantage you'll have is my cousin."

I awaited further explanations on this point. Who was his cousin? Superman?

"He's a guy with pretty traditional ideas. You can imagine. You know how people can be in the provinces." I didn't know, but I was beginning to suspect. "And don't think he's a nice, agreeable sort. Nothing like it. He's almost repulsive, my cousin. And mean as a scorpion. But the main thing is that up there, he's an important, respected man, and all he has to do is to tell four or five key persons that you're in Jujuy under his protection, and then you won't have to worry, because not even the flies will bother you. And if anything unusual happens—say four strangers entering the province in a Ford Falcon without license plates—he'll find out about it at once. If a vicuña on the Cerro de los Siete Colores farts, my cousin's informed within a quarter of an hour. Do you understand what I'm getting at?"

"I think so," I said. *Wonderful*, I thought. *I'm going to live on the frontier and work for a feudal lord, more or less.* But at that moment the image of my wrecked apartment crossed my mind and tempered my presumptions. If I was going to be safe under this guy's protection, it might be a better idea for me to lose the haughty airs and go directly to wherever he was. I remembered the vicarious shame I'd felt years before, when Judge Batista couldn't find the courage to come down on Romano and backed away from that prisoner abuse case. I too was a coward. I too had reached the line I wouldn't cross.

While Judge Aguirregaray was seeing me to the door, I thanked him again. "Think nothing of it, Chaparro," he said. "One thing, though: come back to Buenos Aires as soon as you can. We don't have many deputy clerks like you."

It was as if his words had suddenly given me back the identity I'd lost. I realized the worst thing about my eight days as a fugitive was that I'd stopped feeling like myself. "I'm very grateful to you," I said, energetically shaking his hand. "Good-bye."

I walked to the Olivos station. The trains on the Mitre Railroad were electric, like those on the Sarmiento Line, except that the Mitre trains were clean and almost empty, and they ran on time. But this moment of local envy showed me how much I missed Castelar. Do all those who are in flight from their past feel weighed down by nostalgia for it? In Retiro, I took the subway, got off near my rooming house, and walked the rest of the way.

"There's a guy waiting for you in your room," the desk clerk said to me as I passed. My knees got weak. "He said you knew he was coming. He introduced himself as your bar associate. Is that right?"

"Ah, yes, yes," I said, relaxing with a laugh that must

have sounded excessive to the man behind the counter. Good old Sandoval—he never changed.

He was indeed waiting for me, comfortably stretched out on my bed. We embraced, and I went into the bathroom for a shower. Then we took that taxi, the one in which we barely spoke, to the bus stop in Ciudadela.

39

Lamentably, Sandoval's final illness and death weren't sudden, and those of us who loved him had more than a year to get used to the idea. He himself took it with the same metaphysical sarcasm that he applied to everything. For whoever wished to listen (I mean among those close to him, because he was always restrained or even distant with outsiders), he declared that nobody had been clear-sighted enough to give proper credit to alcohol for its beneficial effects on his body, or to him for knowing enough to treat himself with it in such ferocious doses. It was obvious, he said, that this collapse, this shocking and irreversible physical decline, was due to his abstinence, which had broken the sacred equilibrium formerly produced in him by whiskey. He smiled when he said that, and those of us who'd always badgered him to stop drinking were grateful to be treated with such indulgence. Until the end, or almost, he kept working in the court.

During the last months of Sandoval's life, I spoke frequently with Alejandra—more than with him, to tell the truth. When I did have Sandoval on the line, we confined ourselves (because the high cost of long-distance calls froze us, or because as typical men we considered any outward show of our sorrow basically a sign of weakness) to brief exchanges of small talk, avoiding with expert precision any reference whatsoever that was either very personal or very heartfelt or very melancholy. I asked no questions about his illness; he asked none about my enforced exile in Jujuy. I suppose the impossibility of seeing each other's face as we mouthed conventionalities increased the stiffness of those conversations, but neither of us wanted them to stop.

And so I wasn't surprised when the secretary handed me the telephone one day, saying simply, "Long-distance operator," and through the echo and buzzing that provided the background for every long-distance communication in those days, Alejandra's voice reached me: at first controlled, then shattered by grief, and finally serene, perhaps even relieved.

That night I traveled in an airplane for the first time. The grief I felt had taken on a curious form. I'd had so much time to prepare myself for bad news concerning Sandoval that comparisons between what I was feeling and my previous speculations about what I would feel afflicted me more than the plain and simple grief of having lost my friend.

From high in the night sky, I looked down on Buenos Aires, which offered an imposing spectacle. When

I arrived at the airport, I felt on my own account the same emotional distance I'd felt on learning of Sandoval's death. I wasn't afraid, or even nostalgic. Nor, after six years, was I happy to return. For an instant, a pang of guilt went through me: I hadn't informed my mother about my flying visit. I didn't wish either to prolong it or to sadden her by letting her know that I'd spent a day twenty kilometers from her house, as opposed to almost two thousand, and I hadn't gone to see her. It was better to wait until July, when she'd come to visit me, as she did every year.

The cab driver decided to edify me with a discourse whose object, I soon realized, was to explain why the British would never be able to reconquer the Malvinas with the wretched little fleet they'd just dispatched. I cut him off curtly: "Please don't talk to me. I need to rest." And in case my lack of interest made him suspect me of treason against our country, I added, "Besides, I'm Austrian."

He sank into silence. While he drove me to Palermo, certain memories came into focus. I was almost happy to realize that they were causing me pain, because my coldness during the preceding hours had frightened me. Perhaps that was why I found myself wondering what that prick Romano was up to. Was he still eager to bump me off? This was no minor question—the response to it would determine whether or not I had to keep living in Jujuy—but I didn't know anyone who could answer it. Báez had died in 1980. I hadn't dared travel to Buenos Aires back then, even though four years had passed since Morales's revenge and the attack I'd escaped by a hair. I did, however, write a long letter and send it to Báez's son, because I thought—and still think—that children should know their parents' true value. And beyond that, I was going to feel lost without Báez. That was the main reason why I planned to go from the airplane to the wake, from the wake to the burial, and from the burial back to the plane.

The wake was held not in Sandoval's house but in a funeral parlor. I've always hated the sterile spectacle of our funeral rites, ever since I was a boy. Those gauzy shrouds, the candles, the fearful stench of dead flowers— they all seemed to me like vain artifices devised by bored illusionists to dissemble the honest and appalling bluntness of death. And so I entered the funeral parlor without stopping in the small chamber where the casket lay. Alejandra was getting through the midnight hours by trying to fall asleep in an armchair. I think she was happy to see me. She cried a little and explained something that had to do with the last treatment her husband had undergone, when there was no hope for anything but an impossible miracle. It sounded to me like a story worn out from having been repeated all day long, but I didn't have the heart to interrupt her. When it seemed she'd finished, I ventured to speak: "Your husband was the best guy I ever knew."

She turned her eyes away from me and stared off to one side. She tried blinking several times, but there was nothing she could do to suppress her tears. Nevertheless, she was able to reply, "He loved you so much and admired you so much. I think he stopped drinking so you wouldn't be afraid for him when you weren't here to help him."

It was my turn to cry. We hugged each other in silence, finally able to ignore the false rituals of that place and honor the memory of her husband and my friend.

Afterward, she made me some coffee, and we talked a little about everything. As it was well past midnight, it was highly unlikely that any stray mourners would be coming in, at least not for the next several hours. Family members who hadn't yet done their duty could be expected to show up early the following morning, before the burial service. So Alejandra and I had time to talk. I spent a good while bringing her up to date on my exile in Jujuy; she wanted to know all about Silvia. Pablo had told Alejandra we'd moved in together, but her woman's curiosity required much more information than what Sandoval had been satisfied with in our letters and telephone chats. I began by telling her that Silvia was the younger sister of the clerk in a civil court in Jujuy and then went on to explain that in such a tiny milieu, Silvia and I couldn't help meeting; that she was very beautiful; that the aura I carried around with me in those distant lands, the aura of the mysterious political exile with the obscure past, had perhaps aided my conquest of her; and that I loved her very much. When I finished, I believed I'd said everything, but that was where Alejandra's interrogation began. I did what I could, without ever shaking off my surprise at the vast number of details one woman can wish to know about another. It was getting close to three when I finally persuaded her to go home and get some sleep. Nobody was going to come at that hour, I said. I think she liked the idea of my remaining alone for a while with all we had left of her husband. And I think I too anxiously welcomed the prospect.

There weren't many people at the graveside. A few relatives, a couple of friends, several court colleagues. I didn't know some of them, and the sensation that I was among strangers struck me as perhaps the most convincing proof of my own exile. I took comfort in seeing the familiar faces of some old coworkers, with whom I exchanged greetings and friendly conversation. Fortuna Lacalle and Pérez, our former bosses, were there as well. The retired judge had aged so much that his body seemed to be on the point of breaking into pieces, but his foolish face remained unscathed in the battle against the passage of time. Pérez was no longer a public defender; to the astonishment of all sensible men and women, he was now a judge on the sentencing court.

While the others were returning to their vehicles, I paused a moment to throw a handful of dirt onto the grave. I turned around to make sure there were no witnesses and saw that the rearguard of the departing group was made up of none other than our old clerk and our equally old judge. I picked up a big, wet clod of dirt and started breaking it into pieces. As I threw them, one by one, onto the little mound, I murmured a kind of prayer, a thoroughly profane prayer: "On the day when the assholes of the world throw a party, those two will welcome the others at the door, serve them refreshments, offer them cake, lead them in toasts, and wipe the crumbs from their lips."

When I was finished, I walked away smiling.

More Doubts

"I haven't left out anything," Chaparro thinks as he returns home, carrying a bag of warm bread. How can it not be warm, seeing that they practically open the bakery for him?

He's starting to develop an old guy's habits. It exasperates him to notice them, as others might be disturbed by discovering wrinkles or gray hairs. Until his retirement, sleeping was a reward and a pleasure to which he abandoned himself without reserve and from which he emerged slowly and lazily; now the hours tick away as he lies there, wide awake. So when he's weary of flopping around in his bed and the first light coming through the shutters dazzles his eyes, he gets to his feet, dresses carefully—he's afraid of turning into one of those consummate geezers who go out wearing T-shirts, suspenders, and espadrilles—and walks a block to buy bread.

When he returns, he prepares maté and carries the calabash gourd to his desk, along with two small loaves, which he carefully sets on a plate to avoid scattering crumbs. It strikes him as mildly funny to consider that his two marriages produced, if nothing else, at least some refinement in his domestic habits.

When he sits down, he reads over the last completed section of his book, and as he progresses, he grows increasingly gloomy. For one thing, he's not sure it makes sense to keep those pages at all. Do they contribute to the story he's telling? If the story he's telling is Ricardo Morales's or Isidoro Gómez's, then the answer is no, the last section has nothing to do with them. But if the story he's telling is his own, the story of Benjamín Miguel Chaparro, then it's yes; his flying visit to Buenos Aires in May 1982 can't be excluded.

He falls to questioning himself again about which story he's writing, and he's assailed by fresh doubts as well as by old, reiterated ones. Because if he's writing a sort of autobiography, he's leaving out a slew of persons and circumstances that were very important in his life. As a case in point, what has he said about Silvia, who was his second wife? Little or nothing. He'd have to check, but it seems to him he's mentioned her only in his bothersome previous chapter, the one on Sandoval's death. But after all, what more could he add about Silvia? That they lived together for ten years, the last four of them in Buenos Aires? That she accompanied him when he dared to return to the capital at the end of 1983, when no one was afraid of the military regime and its henchmen anymore? That during those last four years, Silvia was the one who seemed to be in exile, far from her family, her friends, and the society she'd complained about when she lived in it, but which she'd begun to miss the very first day she arrived in Buenos Aires, a city she always found hostile and aggressive?

Chaparro himself helped her pack her bags, borrowed a car to take her to the airport, and then, with the scrupulous care of a notary, sent her whatever items of their mutual possessions she asked for, whenever she asked for them, from an electric toaster to the exquisite edition of *Moby-Dick* they'd bought together on an excursion to Salta.

Then they stopped talking to each other. Chaparro learned that she'd gotten remarried, but he never tried to find out much about the subject. It was around this time that he decided to have nothing more to do with women, that is, with women capable of mattering to him and, therefore, of causing him pain. It seemed so easy in the beginning that he told himself he'd made a wise decision. It had been a mistake to try to share his life with anyone, because in the end, he'd always regretted making the attempt. He'd lost Marcela through sheer boredom and Silvia by her own choice. He didn't want to keep on losing. It was better to withdraw from play. There would always be a woman close at hand, willing to offer him ephemeral pleasure in exchange for some of the same for herself. He's glad he moved to Castelar, as he'd so fervently desired to do before he was forced to leave for Jujuy. The house he's in, the house in which he sits writing his story, looking out into the garden every now and then and occasionally getting up to fix more maté, used to be his family home. Is he going to put that in a novel? It makes no sense. It's better to return to Morales and finish writing the few remaining pages. And after that?

After that, nothing. Well, except for returning the typewriter to the court, to the goddamned court presided over by the Honorable Irene Hornos, may lightning strike her, because everything (distancing himself from women, occasionally getting close to one without any sort of serious commitment, living the life of a methodical widower in Castelar) had worked just fine for him until February 9, 1991, when the recently appointed Judge Hornos came through the door of the clerk's office, returning after an absence of fifteen years.

Chaparro had promised himself he wouldn't let that minx drive him crazy again, because he was fine the way he was. And because he didn't need a new and brutal disappointment, a new plague of insomnia, a new hole in his heart. It was on this account that he greeted her with a cool "How are you doing, Your Honor? It's been a long time," even though he saw her surprised look as she leaned toward him, advancing her cheek for a kiss, and she became confused; expecting familiarity, she found a wall four meters high, without a single crack, and she had to reply to it, "Fine, and yourself? It certainly has been a long time." And then, because the situation made him angry or anxious or sad, or all three at once, Chaparro muttered some excuse about having left a pile of work unfinished on his desk and hurried away. He moved with sufficient speed to escape her perfume, the same scent as always, but he wasn't fast enough to avoid hearing the usual responses to the usual questions, how's your family, Irene, they're well, the girls are too, thank God, and your husband, my husband's fine, he works a lot but his health is great; may lightning strike him, too, that son of a thousand bitches, I beg his pardon because he's not guilty of anything but marrying her, but still, it wasn't right to do this to him, not now, not when he was doing so well, whether alone or occasionally, fleetingly, accompanied.

From here on out, he knows, everything will lose its taste, or worse, everything will taste of Irene—the air and his morning toast; insomnia and the kisses of whatever other woman he happens upon—and so maybe he ought to apply for a transfer, but no, that wouldn't do, because he's not up for changing to another court and a new set of colleagues, so there's no solution of any kind, except to be quiet, let time pass, ignore the fire in her eyes when they meet his, and turn his gaze well away from her neckline when someone approaches her from behind her desk with documents to be signed, and living like that is pure goddamned torture.

No. He's definitely not going to write a novel in which he's the protagonist. He's plenty sick of himself as it is, too sick to delight in contemplating his own navel. But he's decided not to cut the chapter where Sandoval dies. Morales's accursed story is woven together with his own life. Didn't he spend seven years counting goats on the Andean Plateau because he got involved in that tragedy? He doesn't regret it. He doesn't grumble about that part of his past. But that's precisely the reason why he's going to leave everything he's written intact.

And there's another question: Everything he's written—what's he going to do with it? The pages make a pretty pile on his desk, where before there was nothing but a ream of blank paper lying beside his Remington. He should give the completed manuscript to Irene. She likes it when he brings her his writings. In the last month and a half, not a week has passed when he hasn't visited her with a couple of chapters in hand. Is it any good, his novel? She always praises it. Ah, let it be bad. Because if it's good, her praising it means she likes his writing, period. But if it's bad and she praises it anyway, it's because she wants to please him. Chaparro suspects that the reason he writes is to give his work to her; he wants her to know something about him, to have something of his, to think about him, even if only while she's reading. And suppose it's bad and she praises it because she's fond of him, nothing more? That's to say, she may think what he writes repulsive, but she doesn't want to wound him, not because she loves him, not in the way Chaparro wants her to love him, but because she has a soft spot for him as a comrade, as a former boss, as a current subordinate, as an abandoned dog that inspires pity, poor little thing.

Chaparro exclaims aloud, "That's enough of this stupid fucking shit," which in less coarse terms indicates that he must put an end to his meditations and get to work. He hears the whistling of the kettle and realizes that while he's been absorbed in his flights of amorous fancy, the water for his maté has reached the temperature of an erupting volcano. Tossing the water, refilling the kettle, and waiting for it to reach the right temperature allow him to gather the strength of spirit he needs to start writing the final, definitive chapters of his story. Which ends in the middle of a field. In the shed with the big sliding door.

After he pours the contents of the kettle into the thermos, a very thin column of vapor shows him that the water is now at the correct temperature, and Chaparro escapes from his distractions. In his mind, he's traveled three years into the past, back to 1996, the year that marked the real end of the Morales story, twenty years after the false end in which all of them (Báez, Sandoval,

Chaparro himself, and even that son of a bitch Romano) had naively believed.

He leaves the thermos and the gourd with the maté on his desk and goes to the sideboard in the living room. He knows the letters are in the second drawer, each in its envelope. The paper isn't yellow yet, because the letters aren't so old. And even though he's never reread them, he thinks he can remember them pretty exactly, almost verbatim, in fact. But as he doesn't want to take a chance on distorting the truth he holds in his hands, he removes the letters from the drawer to take them to his desk. He plans to quote from them directly whenever he considers it necessary to do so.

Why this obsession with exactness? he wonders. *Just because,* is his first reply. *Because the truth, or Ricardo Morales's own words, which in this case are the ultimate truth, lies in those letters,* is his answer after a moment's reflection. *Because working this way, with documentary proof in hand, selecting what's important and quoting from it, is the way I worked for forty years in the Judiciary,* he adds. *But that first response is also true.*

40

September 26, 1996, was a Thursday like any other, except for the tumult coming from the streets. The first
general strike against the government of Carlos Menem
was to start at noon, and some members of the Judiciary
union who had gathered on the steps of the Palace of Justice above Talcahuano Street were enlivening the scene
by tossing the occasional firecracker. At ten o'clock the
postman came with the mail. Actually, I presume he did,
because my desk was far from the reception counter. One
of the interns brought me an elongated, hand-addressed
envelope. It bore no official seals and had been sent as
certified mail. I stared at the thing, my curiosity piqued
by what looked like a personal message amid the mass
of communications between government departments
that we were used to.

Thus distracted, I looked for my reading glasses until
I realized I was wearing them. I didn't recognize the
handwriting. Had I ever seen that elegant, neat, upright cursive? Not that I recalled. What I did recall (even
though I'd thought I'd never encounter it again) was the

name of the sender: Ricardo Agustín Morales, resur-
rected after twenty years of distance and silence.

Before opening the envelope, I looked again at the address. I was the addressee, all right: "Benjamín Miguel
Chaparro, National First Instance Courts, Criminal Division, Examining Magistrate's Court No. 41, Clerk's Office No. 19." How did Morales know his letter would reach
me here? The untimely missive upset me a little, even
though . . . what exactly was bothering me about it? I certainly didn't hold him responsible for my desperate flight
in 1976. It had always been clear to me that the one and only
cause of my exile was that bastard Romano. Was I disturbed
because Morales was writing me so many years later? No,
not that either. I retained a friendly, almost affectionate
memory of him. What was it, then? It took me a while before the scales fell from my eyes and I saw the real cause of
my agitation. It was that I was so predictable, so monotonous, so like myself that a person could locate me in the
same court and the same clerk's office, doing the same job
at the same desk, two decades after our last contact.

It was a relatively long letter, postmarked in Villegas
on September 21. So he'd left the capital. Had he been
able to rebuild his life? Sincerely wishing that he had, I
began to read.

First of all, I beg your pardon for importuning you
after such a long time.

Chaparro paused and made a very simple calculation. It had been, in fact, a total of twenty years and a few months.

> If I have not written to you in all these years, the overriding reason was my fear of creating even more problems for you than I had already caused. I learned of your move to San Salvador de Jujuy a few months after it took place, when I communicated with your court by telephone. Although I did not inquire into the reasons for your departure, I was not long in deducing that my actions must have been responsible for it.

A young office worker came and asked me a stupid question. In a loud voice, I announced to him and everyone else that I didn't want to be interrupted for a while.

> If I am bothering you at this point in time, so many years later, it is because I find myself obliged to accept the offer you made to me at our last meeting, when you gave me an account of the circumstances that had led to the release of Isidoro Gómez.

That name again, I thought. Had Morales neither heard nor spoken it for many years, like me? Or had he never really managed to get it out of his head?

On that occasion, you told me if there was ever
any moment when I thought you could help me,
I should not hesitate to call on you. Will you consider it audacious of me to take you up on that offer
now? I ask that question mindful of the enormous
sacrifice I imposed upon you, involuntarily, when
you had to go away in 1976. I doubt whether this
is any consolation, but I swear to you that I spent
many long days seeking a way to liberate you from
such a misfortune.

I wondered about Ricardo Morales's present appearance and tried to imagine the face behind those words of
his. Although I made a mighty effort, I couldn't age him;
in my imagination, he continued to be the tall, fair-haired
boy with the little mustache, the slow gestures, and the
frozen expression whom I'd met almost thirty years before. Did he still dress the same way? His style in clothes
had had nothing in common with the fashions young people his age were wearing at the beginning of the 1970s. I
figured his look hadn't changed, and I noted that his way of
expressing himself in writing sounded old-fashioned, too.

Obviously, I never found a means of extricating
you from your difficulties, even though I was glad
to hear, some years ago, that you had returned to
your position in the same court as before.

He didn't say how he knew that, but I could figure it
out: Morales must have telephoned the court every now
and again, asking about me, until they told him I'd come
back. But why hadn't he wanted to talk to me? Why had
he been satisfied with knowing I'd returned? Why had
he waited until now to call on me? And what was he calling on me to do? I read further.

Needless to say, if you bear me a grudge for the way
I altered your life—again, without any intention of
doing so—I believe you have every right to tear up
these lines and forget them, whether now or when
you have finished reading them. In the next few
days, you will receive two more letters identical
to this one. I beg you not to take this iteration as
obnoxious insistence on my part: I am proceeding in this manner out of fear that my letter may go
astray. The first copy I send you will be dated Monday the twenty-third, and the second Tuesday the
twenty-fourth; they will both be certified as well.
If you receive and read this one, the original, I re-
spectfully ask that you destroy the two copies.

I don't know why—well, actually, I do—the image of
Morales sitting in the little cafe at the entrance to the
Once railroad station came into my mind. The same me-
ticulousness, the identical obstinacy. I felt a little sad.

Sometimes life takes strange paths to resolve our enigmas. Forgive me if I indulge in some clumsy philosophizing here. Perhaps I may have told you already that as a young man, I was a confirmed smoker, until Liliana convinced me that I was doing myself harm and I immediately stopped smoking.

Liliana Emma Colotto de Morales. That name was recorded in my memory, but very dimly. Of course, she'd been a part of my life only fleetingly, during the year following her death. After that, she was fused in my memory with Morales, her husband, and Gómez, her murderer. And now she was back, brought by the man who loved her most.

After her death, as if performing an act of spite, or worse, as if that act of spite could do any possible good, I started smoking again, and as time passed, I smoked more and more. Well, two packs a day have put an end to my good health and my resistance, but paradoxically, they may have solved my final dilemma in advance.

Poor guy, I thought. *On top of everything else, he's going to die of cancer.* Whenever I learn that someone has died or is about to die, I rapidly calculate his age, as if youth and

the injustice of death were directly proportional, and as
if my indignation at early deaths were worth anything.
This time was no exception: by my reckoning, Morales
must have been around fifty-five.

It would be trivial to tell you that the prospect of
death worries me. Neither a lot nor a little, as it
turns out. Perhaps, if you carefully consider my
situation, you may concur with my view that death
will come as a relief. I trust you will not be offended if I offer you my condolences on the passing of your friend, Mr. Sandoval. I read about it on
the obituary page of *La Nación*. You cannot imagine
how his death grieved me. In his case, too, I could
find no way of repaying what he did for me, or for
Liliana and me, which amounts to the same thing.
For reasons that I shall explain farther on (unless
you first decide that this extremely long letter is
an abuse of your patience and stop reading), it is
impossible for me to absent myself from my place
of residence for lengthy periods of time. Therefore
I missed Mr. Sandoval's funeral, but I was able to
get to Chacarita Cemetery some months after his
death and pay him a very modest tribute. At that
time, I should have liked to provide his widow with
some kind of financial assistance, something more
tangible and useful than my respects, but I had

contracted certain large debts that greatly com-
promised my financial situation. Now, however,
things are different. If you are willing to do me this
favor (I should say, if you are willing to add this
favor to the great quantity of favors I intend to ask
for, all disguised as one), I shall ask you to see that
Mrs. Sandoval receives a sum of money that I have
laid aside and which I am honored to offer her as
a demonstration of my gratitude to the memory of
her husband.

He was marvelous, this Morales. I saw Alejandra about
once every leap year, but he expected me to show up at
her house with a wad of dough consigned to her by an
anonymous avenger who felt indebted to her husband,
dead these fourteen years. Did time not pass for the
man? Did he live in an eternal present, where each thin,
transparent day blended into the one before? I gave up,
knowing I'd agree to deliver to Sandoval's widow whatever money Morales proposed to send her.

When I mentioned above my reaction to Mr.
Sandoval's death, I did so in order to erase any
suspicion you may have that I am so insolent as
to consider every death so lightly. That is not at
all the case; I hardly dare to consider my own
that way. And to tell the truth, I cannot say that I

am facing death as if it were something light but
rather as something that heals, something that
brings serenity at last. Upon rereading those last
sentences, I fear I am going off on tangents and
wearying you with my pointless ramblings. I have
given you enough to tolerate, suddenly appearing out of oblivion and requesting a favor to boot,
and now you must put up with digressions. Please
forgive me, and let us return to the matter at hand.
Earlier, I asked you to be so kind, should you not
look upon my request favorably, as to destroy this
letter and the other two letters that will follow it.
Nevertheless, I would appeal to you to contact Dr.
Padilla, a notary public here in Villegas, at some
point during the next few weeks, because I have
been so bold as to bequeath you my worldly goods,
such as they are, in my will. I trust you will not take
this as impertinence. I am not leaving you very
much, except for the property on which I reside,
which I should think would be worth a decent sum
these days, as it includes almost seventy-five acres
of good land, mostly fields.

He surprised me. I'd figured he was living in the
capital or its suburbs, for he'd never struck me as the
rural type. His generosity flattered me, although it also
made me slightly uncomfortable; by that point, without

even thinking of recompense, I'd already decided to
help him.

There is, in addition, an automobile, well maintained but very old.

The white Fiat 1500. Memories never return alone—
they always come in groups. The automobile's image came
to my mind accompanied by a recollection of Báez and me
sitting in the Rafael Castillo train station twenty years before, and my policeman friend telling me about the old
folks in Villa Lugano who'd seen Morales load Gómez,
unconscious but still alive, into the trunk of that car.

Apart from some old furniture I leave to your dis-
posal, there is nothing more. Now, should I be able
to count on your collaboration in putting my final
affairs in order here in Villegas, I would implore you
to make every possible effort to arrive at my house
sometime on Saturday the twenty-eighth. I hope this
request does not seem like yet more presumption
on my part. I might almost say that I make it for your
sake, to forestall even greater inconvenience than the
inconvenience I cannot help causing you already.

I thought I understood. It was dreadful, but very simple.
Morales was going to kill himself, and he was asking me

to come on Saturday so that I wouldn't have to confront
an even worse spectacle on Sunday or Monday. He didn't
say so in the letter, but he'd obviously laid careful plans,
including the detail that I would find it more convenient
to get up there on a weekend than to request a few days off
from the court. Could he possibly know that we were between sessions, and that my workload was therefore relatively light? I wouldn't have been surprised if he'd taken
the trouble to find out about such things.

By this point, you will have guessed—at least in
part—what you will find at my house. I beg you to
forgive me. And I repeat, I will perfectly understand
a negative response. Whatever your decision may
be, I send you my warmest wishes, and I reiterate
my deep gratitude to you for all you did for us.

                                   Ricardo Agustín Morales

I finished reading the letter and put it back in its envelope. Several minutes passed before I reacted. The
secretary asked me what was wrong; I looked funny, she
said. I gave her a few evasive replies. At that point, the
clerk came out of his office. I availed myself of the opportunity to tell him I'd have to leave early to take my car
to the shop for a checkup, because I was going to have to
take a highway trip on Saturday to attend to a personal
matter. He said that wouldn't be a problem.

41

Because I wanted to arrive before noon, I started driving at dawn. Morning seemed to me like the least creepy time of day to enter an empty house or, worse, a house where the remains of a man I'd known and liked awaited me.

The directions Morales had put in a postscript to his letter were simple and specific. I was to go past the exit to the town and continue on past the big YPF service station that would shortly appear on the right-hand side of the road. Four kilometers farther on, I would see three very tall silos on the left, and after going another kilometer, I was to turn off onto a paved local road, also on my left. After two more kilometers, the last, I would see a gate on my right between two tall-grass pastures.

I think it was eleven o'clock when I got out of my car to open the gate. I drove through, stopped, and went back to close it. Then I followed what was essentially a gravel path for two or three kilometers, although perhaps I'm exaggerating the distance. The state of the road compelled me to drive slowly, and the high pastureland on both sides offered no points of reference. If Morales had wanted to preserve his privacy, he'd succeeded. Finally, the path ended in a fairly spacious open area in front of a house. This was a simple, one-story building with tall grilled windows. A raised, bare gallery, with no flowerpots or chairs or anything else, ran around the house's entire perimeter. The Fiat was parked on one side, under the gallery. I didn't stop to examine it in detail, but it looked as impeccable as I remembered it.

I knew from Morales's letter that the property covered some seventy-five acres. To purchase it, I figured, the widower had needed to go into debt up to his ears. I vaguely remembered some allusion in his letter to his indebtedness. Then I remembered the money for Sandoval's widow, and I got the picture. Morales hadn't been able to help her in the period immediately following her husband's death, but now, fifteen years on, he'd evidently been able to settle his obligations. It seemed likely he'd accomplished his financial recovery by making great sacrifices. As an employee at a branch bank, he surely hadn't earned very much money, and that parcel of good land, I suspected, hadn't come cheap. The financial difficulties he'd ventured into in order to purchase the property explained the controlled but obvious deterioration of the building and the road leading to it.

I parked near the house and walked up to the front door, which Morales had left unlocked. As I opened it, a surge of childish hope suddenly welled up in me. "Morales!" I called loudly.

There was no response. I cursed under my breath, because I knew I was about to find him dead. I went farther into the room. Not much furniture, some well-stocked bookshelves, no decorations. Two shotguns hanging on the wall. I didn't get close enough to examine them—I've always felt nervous around firearms—but they looked cleaned, oiled, and ready for use. A carefully placed, thick envelope bearing the name of "Mrs. Sandoval" lay on a ceramic ashtray in the middle of the table. I stepped to the table and picked up the envelope. Since counting the money seemed indecent, I stuffed the envelope into the interior pocket of my jacket. In a hallway off the front room, there were two doors, one leading to the bathroom and the other to the kitchen. So where was the bedroom? I retraced my steps. I'd overlooked a closed door to one side of the bookcase. This one had to be the bedroom door. I opened it with my heart in my throat.

What I saw turned out to be less terrible than I'd imagined. The window shutters were open, and the sunlight came streaming in. Evidently, Morales had figured the bright daylight wouldn't disturb his sleep on that particular morning. There was no blood and no brains splattered against the headboard, which was the scene my fevered imagination had pictured from the moment I read the letter. The widower's body was barely visible, lying supine on the bed with the covers pulled up to his throat.

I'm not going to commit the stupidity of writing that he looked like a man asleep, because I've never understood people who could look at a corpse and make such an observation. As far as I'm concerned, dead people look dead, and Morales was no exception. Besides, his skin had taken on a decidedly bluish tinge. Did that have to do with the method of suicide he'd chosen? I didn't yet know the answer to that question, but I was sure he hadn't been dead long. I appreciated the delicate consideration evident in his attempt to spare me the most shocking signs of his corpse's decay, though I would certainly have been obliged to confront them had more time elapsed between his death and my arrival.

The bedroom was minimally furnished: a double wardrobe, a chest with a closed lid, a bare table, one straight-backed chair, and the single bed, and beside it a simple nightstand covered with various kinds of medications, disposable syringes, and bottles of some medicinal solution. I realized only then how difficult it must have been for that man to deal with his illness alone, with no one to help assuage his suffering.

Because I'd begun by trying to take in the whole scene, or because thus far I'd been too cowardly to look at the body very closely, or because my eyes were more readily caught by the wedding photograph barely visible above the forest of medicine bottles, it took me some time to notice the long white envelope bound with a ribbon and hanging from the night table. On closer inspection, I saw that it was addressed to me. And in big letters, under my name: "PLEASE READ THIS BEFORE YOU CALL THE POLICE."

42

The guy never ceased to surprise me. Not even dead. What could he have to say to me in a second letter? I stepped backward, careful not to touch anything. All I needed was to be involved in a suspicious death. I told myself I had no reason to be worried; I was carrying the letter he'd sent to me at the court, and it ended with what was practically a plea to the authorities to charge no one with his death. I went back to the living room with the new letter in my hand and sat on the only armchair, close to the heater.

Dear Benjamín,

If these pages are in your hands, that must mean you have done me the enormous favor of com-ing to my house; therefore, before I go on, I must express my gratitude. Once again, as I have done on so many other occasions, I thank you. You are no doubt wondering about my reasons for writing you these lines. Let us go slowly, as is only proper when one person is obliged to give another news that could be, in a certain sense, disagreeable to him.

I started to get a funny feeling. Morales might be a stiff, but he was still making things happen.

Among the jumble of bottles and jars and other things on my night table, you will notice a used syringe with its needle in place. I beg you not to touch it, although my warning is probably unnecessary. I presume it will be quite evident at the autopsy that I injected myself with a massive dose of morphine, and that was that. Then again, the medical examiner who performs the autopsy may have a terrible time singling out the drug he's looking for: I've had to dose myself with such a number and variety of medications in these past few months that my liver must look like a pharmacy. Well, that's his problem—I have sufficient concerns of my own.

This was pure Morales: his words and his suffering perfectly dissociated, a hint of irony, and a sincere melancholy that never dwindled into lame self-pity.

But again I digress, and I have yet to ask of you what I must ask of you. Before I do so, there are

two things I want you to know. The first is that I am
seeking to lay this charge on you only because my
remaining strength is not sufficient to allow me to
take care of the matter myself. I have left it undone
to the last not out of neglect but out of principle.
However, I overestimated my stamina. That is to
say, I could have done it myself had I done it two
or three months ago. But doing it then seemed
wrong to me. I thought I should wait until the end;
however, now that the end has come, my body is
unable to make the effort.

Why did he need to be physically strong all of a sudden? He'd recently died, but what was he talking about?

The second thing is that I do not want you to feel
obligated to do anything. If you find it impossible,
so be it. Let the police handle it all. Because, to
tell the truth, the request I have to make of you
springs from a certain vanity, a ridiculous desire
to preserve my good name. You passed by the
town without stopping, but in the next few hours,
you will begin to meet people who may talk to you
about me. I believe I am not mistaken in predicting that they will have placid, perhaps even warm-
hearted memories of my person. Bear in mind that
I have lived out here in the country and worked

in the town for twenty-three years. For reasons that you will soon discern, I insisted on remaining here throughout all that time and refused to be transferred to another branch of the bank. It was difficult, because my bosses frequently insisted on submitting my name for promotion. I was apparently considered an efficient employee, overall. As often as they insisted, I refused, trying not to seem discourteous or ungrateful. I am not going to lie to you: there is no one in town who can say he knows me well. I could not have close friends, nor did I want them. Nevertheless, I believe everyone—to varying degrees, of course—will remember me as a cordial, inoffensive misanthrope. And on this final passage into nothingness (I wish I believed in something that would support me), I would like to think I will be amicably and benevolently remembered by the people I was in contact with out here during these many years.

Where was he going with all that? What was to stop me from showing this letter to the police? Were they so hard on suicides in Villegas? I restrained my habitual impatience as a reader, my tendency to bound ahead, for fear of missing something really important in one of those leaps.

I must ask you, my esteemed friend (please allow
me to call you that, because it expresses the way I
feel), to do me the enormous favor of going out to
the shed. It stands about five hundred meters away
from the house, at the back end of the field. In
case of rain, you will find a pair of boots next to the
kitchen door. Use them, because otherwise your
shoes and trousers will be ruined.

I didn't understand; I didn't see the connection between Morales's request and his death.

Here my instructions end. Forgive me if I go no
more deeply into the matter. Your intelligence
absolves me from explaining further, and your
honesty will, I trust, safeguard me from any ethical
condemnation.

Sincerely yours,
Ricardo Agustín Morales

That was it? I turned the sheet of paper over, looking for a postscript, an explanation, a hint. There wasn't
anything. I left the letter on the chair and walked into
the kitchen. Through the window, I could see rows of
fruit trees and on one side, near the house, a small vegetable garden. I went out the kitchen door and spotted

the boots, which I didn't need on such a splendid day. In order to present in these pages the image of a thorough observer and careful analyzer, I suppose I should say that I was fully engaged in constructing, examining, and discarding hypotheses concerning what Morales had written in his second letter. But it wouldn't be true. What I thought, I thought afterward, when the questions (which I didn't even formulate as I walked among the lemon and orange trees) answered themselves.

43

The vegetable garden had been tended with care. Seen from the back, the house looked to be in worse shape than it had seemed from the front. Maybe its owner had managed his meager finances in such a way as to project the image of a certain standard of living in case some visitor, whether invited or not, should show up. There was neither a clay oven nor a barbecue grill nor a table and chairs outside. It looked to me as though Morales didn't care about living the country life, even though he was out here in the boondocks. Clearly, he'd continued to be a city creature. He hadn't changed.

About fifty meters from the end of the fruit orchard, I could see a dense grove of leafy eucalyptus trees. I'm no good at calculating the age of trees, but I figured Morales had planted them when he got there. Had he said twenty-three years? That meant he'd come to Villegas in 1973, shortly after the amnesty.

The eucalypti seemed to form a thick curtain about two hundred meters long that cut obliquely across the field behind the house and garden. Later, I realized that the trees followed the route of the local paved road I'd

turned off of but hid the road itself from view. Running
from the end of the garden to the eucalyptus grove, a
path was clearly visible, one of those trails worn bare by
frequent comings and goings. Once I stepped into the
eucalyptus curtain, the noonday light dimmed and became moist and shadowy. On the other side of the grove,
I could clearly make out a shed. It appeared to be a building of impressive size, but it was hard for me to estimate
its exact dimensions, because it stood two or three hundred meters beyond the grove, and actually, I wasn't very
sure about the distances, either. I too am a city man, and
I had no urban points of reference on which to base my
guesses with any hope of accuracy. The shed had been
erected on a little hillock, perhaps to avoid flooding, although the entire field looked pretty high and even rose
gently toward the north, that is, on the other side of the
paved road.

I walked toward the corrugated iron building. The
sliding door was closed and locked with three gigantic
padlocks. The keys to the padlocks were hanging on a
hook on the outside of the door. This didn't seem like
a very elaborate security system, putting the keys to the
padlocks where anyone who came along had access to
them. Could Morales have lost his chess player's in-
stincts as he grew older?

The door squealed when I pushed it to one side, and
the sunlight leaped violently into the dark interior. I

looked inside. The closer I got to grasping what I was seeing, the weaker my knees felt, and a sensation of physical revulsion compelled me first to lean against the metal wall and finally to sit on the concrete floor.

The shed was pretty large, about ten meters wide by fifteen deep. Various metal objects stood against the wall: a folding aluminum stepladder, a portable machine that looked to me like a grinder, a few sets of shelves.

Actually, I saw all that later, a while after I collapsed on the floor. At first, as I sat there panting, I spent several minutes unable to take my eyes off the cell, the cell in the center of the shed. The cell was a square construction of thick iron bars extending from the floor to the ceiling, and on the front of the cell was a door with two separate locks but no handles, and down in one corner was another door, this one very little, like one of those used to pass food, utensils, and other small objects into and out of jail cells, and inside the cell in the shed, there was a washbasin and toilet in one corner, a table and chair in another, a bunk against the rear bars, and a body lying on the bunk, lying with its back to me on the bunk in the cell.

At that moment, I suppose, I felt horror, incredulity, apprehension, shock. But over and above everything else, I felt hugely surprised, ferociously surprised, and as I slowly began to grasp the implications of what I was looking at, I was forced to discard, to extirpate and destroy, everything I'd thought about Morales and his story for the past twenty years.

After some time had passed and my legs felt capable of supporting me again, I got to my feet and walked around the square perimeter of the cell. When I reached the bunk, I fought back nausea and squatted down to get a look at the face of the man imprisoned behind those bars.

Isidoro Antonio Gómez's body had the same bluish tint as Morales's. Gómez was a little fatter than I remembered, of course older, with slightly graying hair, but for the rest, he didn't look much different from the way he'd looked twenty-five years before, when I took a statement from him in the clerk's office.

44

I sat on the neatly mown grass of the hillock, not far from the shed.

He'd told me. The last time Morales and I saw each other, he'd told me, he'd said it after I practically suggested he get a pistol and take his revenge into his own hands. How had he answered? "Everything's very complicated," or something like that. No; it was "Things are never simple." That was what he'd said. I thought about Báez. Like me, he wouldn't have imagined that Morales would impose himself on events in this way. Sandoval wouldn't have, either. Who could imagine such a thing? Only Morales. Nobody but Morales.

I stepped back into the shed to look for a shovel. I found one and held it in my hand as I walked around the building again, examining the surroundings. The curtain of eucalypti I'd passed through on the way to the shed was, in reality, a great circle of trees with a perimeter of more than a thousand meters. The shed stood inside the circle, not in the center, but off to one side, probably because that location was least exposed to

prying eyes. I tried to calculate how many trees Morales
had planted in all, but I soon quit. I didn't have the least
idea. But planting them had surely cost him months and
months of labor, performed after he got home from the
bank and on weekends. The construction of the shed had
to have been carried out by professional builders, who
were probably amazed by Morales's insistence on putting it up so far from the house, just as his neighbors no
doubt found it strange that he left his property uncul-
tivated for so many years, and just as the people of the
town, starting with his colleagues at the bank, must have
thought his behavior extremely odd, living in such iso-
lation as he did, and being so disinclined as he was to
receive visitors or participate in any kind of social life.
I remembered the request contained in his last letter.
All of us, I suppose, need at least some form of affection.
Despite his eccentricities, the people who knew Morales
had little by little developed a strange bond with him,
and the widower had wanted his memory to remain un-
sullied. That was why I was walking around his shed and
carrying a shovel.

Scattered here and there on the sizable piece of
land enclosed by the circle of eucalypti were several
little stands or copses of other kinds of trees. One
group included some poplars and two enormous oaks,
which must have been standing there since long before

Morales came. I stopped between them and took a good look around me. It didn't seem possible that I could be under any sort of observation. I planted the shovel and with one foot pressed it down into the earth. The ground wasn't too hard. I started digging.

45

The police came, as well as a few curiosity seekers—very few, because fortunately I'd called to report my discovery during the siesta hour, and between that and the fact that a goodly number of potential gawkers had taken advantage of the perfect weather to go hunting or fishing, the news hadn't spread very widely. I didn't see any dismayed or incredulous faces. The officer who led the proceedings, a chief inspector in the Buenos Aires Provincial Police, knew Morales, and he wasn't the only one. Everyone there had seen him often for years and years, either here and there around town or standing behind the teller's window in the Villegas branch of the Provincial Bank. They'd also seen him getting sicker, and losing weight, and showing up more and more frequently at the clinic and the pharmacy.

"I didn't think it was that serious," said one of the bank employees who had arrived with the policemen.

"Oh, he was very sick, but he preferred not to go around talking about it," his colleague replied softly. There were also two older guys who looked like storekeepers. None of the civilians was very sure what to do, and all gazed at the house as though seeing it for the first time. Evidently, nobody present had ever laid eyes on it before.

As soon as I could, I gave the inspector the letter Morales had sent me at the court. The policeman sat down to read the letter in the same chair I'd sat in to read the other one, the one I'd carefully stowed in the bottom of my suitcase, which was in the trunk of my car. The officer had just about finished his perusal of Morales's missive when the ambulance arrived. One of the other policemen stepped out of the bedroom, carrying a transparent plastic bag that contained the syringe Morales had used to kill himself.

"What shall we do, Chief?"

"Gutiérrez is through with the photos?"

"Sure is."

"Good. The ambulance guys are here, so go ahead and take away the body. No, wait a second." He turned to me. "Sir," he said, "are you—"

"Benjamín Chaparro," I said, introducing myself before he could finish. And since I didn't think it would be a bad idea to produce some sort of safe-conduct, I showed my credentials and added, "Deputy clerk of Examining Magistrate's Court No. 41, Criminal Division, in Buenos Aires."

"Had you and the deceased known each other for a long time, sir?" The inspector's tone had shifted slightly and now expressed more courtesy, more respect, and an inclination to submit. I greatly approved of the change.

"The truth is we had, although we hadn't seen each other for years. Not since he came to live here." I hesitated, unsure whether it would be advisable to say what was on the tip of my tongue, but then I went ahead: "We were friends in Buenos Aires." *No we weren't*, I said to myself. But if we weren't friends, what were we? I didn't have an answer to that one.

"I understand. Would you mind stepping into the bedroom with me? It's so we can have another witness to the removal of the body."

"Lead the way."

They'd taken the covers off him. He was wearing a pair of striped pajamas, cut in an old-fashioned style. It was a useless thought, but the image of Liliana Emma Colotto de Morales flashed into my mind, and I remembered how similar rites had been performed around her corpse, rites in which I'd played an involuntary part. This time, there were fewer of us standing around, and our number included no tight little group of curious onlookers particularly interested in contemplating the deceased.

The policeman had removed the bottles and jars from the night table and set them aside as evidence for examination. On the now bare table, the framed photograph of Morales and his wife, dressed in their

wedding finery, was much more visible. Where had
I seen that picture before? In the cafe on Tucumán
Street, where Morales showed me his photos, in the
proper order, before he destroyed them? No. I'd seen
it in the bedroom of their apartment, a few steps from
Liliana Colotto's corpse, almost thirty years ago. I was
surprised, as I'd often been before, at the iron patience
that objects deploy in order to survive us. I believe
that was the first time I'd ever imagined Morales and
his wife together and alive, drinking coffee in their
kitchen, chatting and smiling at each other; and life
seemed to me unbearably cruel and hostile. It was also
the first and last time that the thought of the young
couple brought tears to my eyes.

We followed the stretcher out of the house to the ambulance in a tiny, spontaneous procession. The ambulance left, and then the cars that Morales's colleagues
and the two older fellows had come in drove off as well.
When they were out of sight, the inspector turned to me
and said, "You're going back to Buenos Aires today, I
suppose?"

"Actually, I think I'm going to stay over until tomorrow, or maybe Monday. I'll be available if you need me,
Inspector."

"Ah, terrific!" The news seemed to make him happy,
because it saved him from asking me to stay over himself. "In any case, there's nothing for you to worry about.

I'll talk to the doctor who does our forensic tests later today. I'll call the judge, too. He's a nice guy, the judge, Urbide by name. I don't know if you know him."

I shook my head.

"Well, it doesn't matter. The case is as clear as can be."

"I suppose it is," I said, confirming his assessment, which I was happy to hear. At that moment, the sound of voices calling to the inspector came from behind the house. I hadn't noticed the pair of cops who'd gone out back and checked the shed.

"Nothing of consequence to report, sir," said one of them, who was wearing the insignia of a subofficer. I suspected he was speaking so formally because he'd learned that the stranger (namely me) was a man with legal expertise. "It's a large shed containing various tools and old furniture."

"All right."

"It's strange, though, Inspector," the second cop chimed in. He was young and black-haired, and he looked as though he'd just graduated from the police academy. "This guy must have been really afraid of being robbed. The door of the shed's loaded with padlocks. But you know what the strangest thing is?"

"No, what?"

"There's a big cage in there where he kept the most valuable tools and stuff. A gasoline-powered lawn mower, a grinding machine, a couple of scythes, some pretty high quality power drills. Looks to me like he was afraid someone would steal them."

"Well, if all the local cops are klutzes like you, he was right. Things don't seem all that safe here," the inspector said, teasing the youngster. He was a novice, but not so new as to fail to recognize that he had to shut up and take the joke.

We walked back to the house. The two policemen hadn't said anything about the washbasin and the toilet they must surely have found against one of the walls, in the corner next to the metal shelves. Inside the cell, I'd covered the supply and drain pipes with earth up to the level of the concrete floor. I relaxed when I saw that the police weren't at all suspicious; they had no idea what had gone on there. That wasn't surprising, because who could have imagined it?

"Vallejos," the inspector called. "I want you to stay on duty out here in case the judge decides to drop by today or tomorrow."

Vallejos looked at his superior with disgust practically written on his face. The inspector seemed to take pity on him. "All right, good enough," he said. "Let's do this: I'll call the judge, and if he gives me the go-ahead, I'll call you on the radio and you can go home. How's that sound?"

"Thanks, Chief. Really, thanks a lot. Seeing that it's Saturday . . . you know?"

"So he had a cage inside the shed to keep his tools in?" asked the inspector, turning to the young officer. There wasn't the slightest trace of alarm in his voice. He spoke of the shed as he might have spoken of anything else, out of a simple urge to keep silence from falling on the company.

"As I told you, sir. With two big fat locks on the door. People do weird things, huh?"

The inspector picked up his hat, which he'd left on the table in the living room. He looked around with the expression of a man who knows he won't be visiting the place he's looking at again. "That's the truth," he said. "People do weird things."

There was no more conversation. They got into their vehicles and drove off; I followed them in my car. It wasn't long before they were able to locate the medical examiner, who did them the favor of performing the autopsy that very night, and the judge gave them the green light to go ahead and close the case as quickly as possible.

Morales's funeral took place on Monday morning. A fine, persistent rain that fell from daybreak to nightfall added an additional touch of melancholy to the proceedings. No ray of sunlight was visible all day long, and that seemed just right to me.

Restitution

Now it's done, Chaparro thinks. Now he's really finished, and he has nothing more to add. Nothing that has to do with Morales or Gómez. Chaparro feels as though the story is definitively abandoning him now. He ponders a question: Are the lives of human beings who have ceased to exist prolonged in the lives of the other people who live on and remember them? However that may be, Chaparro feels that those two men's lives are as good as concluded, because he's sure that nobody except him remembers them.

The last traces of their passage through the world have probably disappeared, or it won't be long before they do. What are Morales's last traces? Some documents with his signature and seal in the archive of the Provincial Bank, Villegas branch. Gómez's tracks must be even more faded: some fingerprint records, maybe, in the elephantine archives of Devoto Prison, along with an order of release dated May 25, 1973. Yet there's something that has survived the two men and still unites them: the signatures they affixed to their judicial depositions, thirty years ago. Morales's signature is on his statements, and Gómez signed his confession. All those documents are collected with many others in a yellowing case folder, masterfully sewn together by the officer of the court Pablo Sandoval during one of his mighty hangovers. The bones of the two also remain: one skeleton lies in Villegas Cemetery and the other in an unmarked grave, in an open field, at the feet of a pair of oaks. But bones don't talk.

This is the end of the story, Chaparro thinks. On the boundary line between those devastated lives and his. He has no wish to say anything in that regard; besides, he's not sure that some parts of his own life haven't found their way, against his express wishes, onto those pages, which are lying there in such a neat stack beside his Remington.

He lowers his eyes to the typescript and feels that the pages are questioning him, because he has to decide what to do with them. Try to get them published? Stick them in a drawer so that someone can find them after his death and face an identical predicament? In the final analysis, for whom has he written those pages?

He must also decide about the Remington. It's his on loan; they didn't give it to him. He has to return it. To the court. It's federal property. Does it make any difference that the said prehistoric artifact isn't worth anything to anyone except a retired deputy clerk who's been banging on it for a year, playing the novelist? No, he still has to give it back, and then they can do whatever they want with it.

He has to carry the typewriter into the clerk's office, greet all the people working there, pull up one of the wooden chairs to the bookshelves in the back, climb up on the chair, and hoist the heavy, ancient Remington onto the topmost shelf. Then, as part of his incurable mania for teaching the people in the office how to do their job, he'll explain that they have to send an official letter to the administrative services, and they'll come and pick up the machine. And then, after his lecture? Then he'll make the rounds again, say his good-byes, and go home.

And what about Irene? Won't she be offended if she learns he was there and didn't drop in to say hello? *Too bad*, Chaparro says to himself, because no, he's not going to drop in on her. He doesn't have the nerve to tell her he adores her, and his former tolerance for the ache of stifled feelings has worn away.

He stands up and places a heavy dictionary on his typescript, lest a stray air current come and shuffle his memories. In the bathroom, he brushes his teeth and tends to his gray hair, perfuming it with lavender lotion and going over it with a little black comb.

Back in his bedroom, he hesitates: tie or open collar? He opts for the latter. He's no longer the deputy clerk, after all. Now that he's a writer—he misses no opportunity for self-mockery—he feels better in informal clothes and without grease in his hair. He looks at his watch. Will he be able to get a seat on an inbound train from Castelar so close to noon? He suspects he won't, and he sure doesn't want to stand up all the way, holding the typewriter. Nevertheless, he walks to the station, and there he finds that God has apparently taken pity on him: it's five after eleven, and the last morning train to the center of town blessedly offers him a wide choice of empty seats. He sits on the right side so that he can amuse himself by watching the automobiles running along Rivadavia Avenue.

All at once, he gives a start. The train's in rapid motion, hurtling along noisily between the lugubrious concrete walls that line the tracks from the Caballito station to Once. What has he been thinking about for the last half-hour? He can't remember. Morales? Gómez? No. They're at rest. Strikingly, now that he's finally got the whole story down on paper, they no longer assail him or disturb him or berate him. *So?* he thinks. He gets off the train in Once station and feels a sudden urge to pass by the little cafe where he met Morales on two occasions back in the mists of time, partly because he's curious to see if the place still exists. But when he steps out onto the sidewalk on Pueyrredón Avenue, he feels, once again, the strange confusion of having forgotten his intention. What was it? The cafe, of course, the little cafe in the station. He can have a look at it on his return trip, so no big deal, but he's troubled by this incipient tendency to go blank, as if he were falling into sudden decrepitude.

He ponders the question as he heads for the number 115 bus stop. The typewriter seems to be getting heavier, even though he keeps changing hands. He doesn't want to enter that cloud of confusion again. As a result, he pays his fare and takes a seat, thinking all the while about nothing so much as what it is exactly that he's thinking about. It works for three or four blocks, but when the bus turns onto Corrientes Avenue, he loses the thread again. Good God, what mental recess has he stumbled into? Not even the lurching curve the bus makes when it leaves the avenue and turns onto Paraná can bring him back to reality. It's almost by chance that he manages to get off just before the driver closes the rear door.

He looks at himself in a storefront window. Benjamín Chaparro, standing on a narrow sidewalk. Tall, thin, gray-haired, sixty years old. In his left hand, he's holding a typewriter from the Stone Age. What remains for him to do in life? Not his novel; he's finished telling the story of those two dead men. Like all difficult decisions, the answer to his question slowly takes shape in his head.

His next step in life is to do what he's been brooding over, without knowing that he was brooding over it, ever since he took the 11:05 train in Castelar, or ever since he borrowed the Remington eleven months previously, or ever since he told a new young intern how to answer the telephone three decades ago.

And therefore he finally goes into motion and climbs the big steps of the Lavalle Street entrance two at a time. He takes the elevator to the fifth floor and walks with long strides along the corridor with the diagonal checkerboard of black and white floor tiles.

He doesn't drop into Clerk's Office No. 19 to say hello. Not because he's afraid the people there will notice how lovesick he is, but because for the first time he knows that today's the day; today, without fail and without procrastination, he must go directly to her office and knock on the door; listen for her voice, telling him to come in; stand before her like a man before the woman he loves; ignore the trivial question she asks as she receives him with a smile; and pay, or collect, the outstanding debt that's the only valid reason he can find to go on living. Because Chaparro needs to answer, once and for all, the question in that woman's eyes.

Ituzaingó, September 2005

Author's Note

In February 1987, I started working as an office employee in the National First Instance Court, Criminal Sentencing Division, Section "Q," in Buenos Aires, the federal capital of Argentina. One morning, my more experienced colleagues related an old anecdote: as a result of the amnesty for political prisoners decreed by the Cámpora government in 1973, and under circumstances that had always remained in the most complete obscurity, an ordinary criminal who was being held in Devoto Prison was released by order of the court. He'd been charged with serious crimes, for which he was certain to receive an extremely long sentence; nevertheless, and without anyone ever knowing the reason why, he'd walked free that very day.

Some time later, I recalled that story and in my imagination added innumerable situations and details to it; although they were invented, they could function as plausible antecedents to and consequences of the unjust release of a convicted murderer.

Apart from that remembered anecdote, the story told in these pages is entirely fictitious, as are all its characters. Actually, at the end of the 1960s, Clerk's Offices Nos. 18 and 19 belonged to a sentencing court, not an examining magistrate's court; moreover, there was no examining magistrate's court in the capital that bore the number 41. As for the bloody Argentina of the 1970s, which occasionally appears as the background of the story narrated here, would that it were equally fictitious, would that it, too, had never existed.

Be that as it may, these lines would be incomplete if I didn't acknowledge, with great affection, the people who worked with me in Sentencing Court "Q," and especially my colleagues in Clerk's Office No. 19: Juan Carlos Travieso, Evangelina Lasala, Jorge Riva, Edy Pichot, and Cristina Lara. I must also declare my profound gratitude to Cristina Lara for her invaluable aid in providing me with a multitude of juridical and procedural details that were necessary to give the story solidity and verisimilitude. If I retain very pleasant memories of that period of my life, I owe them to all my former colleagues at the court.

E. S.

About the Author

EDUARDO SACHERI was born in Buenos Aires in 1967. His first collection of short stories, *Esperándolo a Tito y otros cuentos de fútbol* (Waiting for Tito and other soccer stories) was published in Spain in 2000 under the title *Traidores y otros cuentos* (Traitors and other stories). Three other collections were published between 2001 and 2007, all of which have been best sellers in Argentina. His novel *La pregunta de sus ojos* has been sold into eight countries, and the film adaptation, *The Secret in Their Eyes*, won the Academy Award for Best Foreign Film in 2010.

About the Translator

JOHN CULLEN is the translator of many books from Spanish, French, German, and Italian, including Margaret Mazzantini's *Don't Move*, Yasmina Khadra's Middle East Trilogy (*The Swallows of Kabul*, *The Attack*, *The Sirens of Baghdad*), Christa Wolf's *Medea*, and Manuel de Lope's *The Wrong Blood* (Other Press). He lives in upstate New York.